Lander's Gate

Kevin S. Moul

LIMINAL
FORGE PRESS

To my family
The adventure continues...
Thank You

Chapter 1
Monday,
October 26, 2009 (5:45 p.m.)

D r. Aradice wanted to scream. Another failure.

The patient lying in front of him seemed to mock him. As if to emphasize this point, the man's lips opened to emit a breathy sigh. Whatever his unconscious mind saw, it was apparently pleasurable.

The doctor narrowed his eyes and rocked back and forth on his heels before making a decision. "If that's how you want it, let's try something different."

He pulled a stool beneath him and stared at a row of clipboards that summarized a year of failed experiments.

Aradice ground his teeth, resolute to follow through with his new plan. He walked over to a rolling basket and picked up a set of electrodes.

Standing over the bed, he fixed his gaze on the patient: Lander Gate—mid-thirties, but the tangle of brown hair splayed across the pillow and the unkempt beard speckled with gray suggested someone older. Lander had lost muscle tone during his confinement, and the raised cheekbones of what used to be an angular, handsome face now looked skeletal.

In contrast, Dr. Aradice was a clean-shaven man in his late

forties, with thick, rakish black hair that dusted his shoulders. Even when alone, he stood with a practiced posture. His green eyes were pinpricks of intensity in the bright and sterile room.

Leaning in, the doctor affixed the electrodes in multiple locations around Lander's head, finishing with his temples and just above the forehead. He primed a syringe, inserted it into the IV, and stood back.

Lander's placid smile vanished. His eyes squeezed shut and his face shuddered. Under the sheet, a spasm ran the entire length of his body.

Dr. Aradice spun toward an array of equipment. "With that dose," he mused in a whisper, "and the current from the electrodes, the brain's connections will be receptive. I will break this stalemate."

In front of the ECT controller, he hesitated only a second before he cranked up the dial until the needle on the meter rose into the red zone. He did not even look behind him, knowing the man's body would convulse in a seizure. The bedsprings contracted under Lander's weight as the metal frame banged against the wall and screeched along the floor. The smell of burned flesh permeated the air. After another two seconds, the doctor flipped a black toggle switch on the side of the device. The needle dropped to zero.

He rose and peered toward the bed. The patient's contorted face twisted upward, and his eyes were open and lifeless. The EKG emitted a single tone. Lander's heart had stopped.

"Damn." He kicked at the rolling stool, sending it toppling and sliding to the middle of the room. There was no use in trying to resuscitate.

Dr. Aradice headed to the elevator and toward his office. He cast his thoughts forward to a finger of Irish whiskey from the not-so-secret bottle behind his desk. There was nothing else to be done. After all, he wasn't responsible for putting Lander in this state. That had been an accident.

At his desk, Dr. Aradice slammed down the phone and leaned on his elbows, fingers steepled under his chin, and stared expectantly at the door. The call to the hospital administrator, Monica, had been short and to the point.

"Come. Now!"

He had hired Monica based on her looks so had been surprised at her competence. He nodded to himself. *She can be trusted with this.*

After a few minutes, Monica entered and lingered by the door. She was a tall, slender brunette prone to flicking her head to position her hair over her shoulders. Her deep brown eyes always disarmed him.

"Lander Gate has expired. Please process him as a John Doe. Make up a story. Something to the effect of 'admitted after an overdose.' You can pick the drug."

Lander had a special room that wasn't on the master key. Monica patted her lab coat pocket to make sure she had the "unofficial" key ring.

She took the stairs up one flight to a floor that was predominately lab space. There was only a small ward at one end that handled older patients with dementia and chronic care conditions.

Monica didn't notice the chaos of the hospital room. The empty bed drew her full attention. Dr. Aradice had said the patient had expired, and that she needed to process the body. She must have misunderstood him. *Am I in the wrong room?* There was another room they had sometimes used for this special patient, but it had been converted to an office.

Monica retraced her steps and knocked before entering Dr. Aradice's office. His head was down, and he was focused on his fingers as he poked at the keyboard. She cleared her throat.

He jerked up his head. The look on his face was withering. Monica took a calming breath. "Where did you move—"

"Dammit, woman. How am I supposed to think? Just do it. Shred the file. Process him as a John Doe."

Monica swallowed hard as she stepped away, gently closing the door. It wasn't the first tantrum she'd witnessed, but this one seemed different. She decided not to push back. His personality could be volatile, but she let it slide off her. She still needed his recommendation to get her career jumpstarted.

Lander was now her problem to solve. For the second time in ten minutes, Monica headed up the stairs and stood in the room that was little more than a cell. She recoiled at the stench of stale sweat and antiseptic. On the floor next to the bed, there were droplets of blood where an IV needle lay discarded. Drop by drop, they formed a trail that led out the door.

Monica didn't like the questions that the blood on the floor raised. She retrieved a packet of gauze pads and, after checking the empty hallway, doused the gauze in alcohol, placed the wad under her shoe, and began wiping up the drops with a shuffling gait. If it was Lander, his weak heart pumped a zigzag, Morse-code path of breadcrumbs for her to follow.

There was a puddle of blood inside the elevator that implied he'd stood against the side wall for a few minutes. His room was on the seventh and top floor, and from the accumulated blood, Monica estimated he'd ridden all the way to the basement. She was right. From there, the trail led into a storage closet. Inside, a hospital gown and a torn paper bag littered the floor. The shelves were lined with lost and found items—clothing and personal belongings abandoned by patients.

Two orderlies approached as she pulled the door closed

and locked it. Monica greeted them, forcing a smile. "Have you released any patients this evening?"

"Yes," one of them replied. "Not too long ago. Four men."

At that hour, the patients had most likely had been residents of Ward C, a catch-all for those without insurance and pro bono cases. Monica had a hunch and returned to the elevator.

At the entrance to Ward C, Monica greeted a nurse she'd seen earlier that day, a longtime employee of the Wrimo Hospital and Clinic who was retiring. There had been a gathering that afternoon to celebrate her last shift. "The p.m. shift orderlies said there was a patient release this evening."

The nurse frowned. Monica knew this nurse had difficulty with the hospital's policy about releasing social net patients. At a senior staff meeting, Dr. Aradice had said it was a good thing she was retiring. He'd emphasized that now, more than ever, the economy required a quick turnover of nominally paying patients.

"Yes, three of them, fed, dressed, and released into the wild."

The nurse moved away without looking back. Monica sighed, aware that her life had just become more complicated.

Chapter 2
Monday,
October 26, 2009 (10:45 p.m.)

Lander Gate tried to blink away the darkness, but the asphalt pressing into his face prevented even the smallest of facial movements.

Rolling onto his right side did little to improve his situation.

He could vaguely discern a concrete curb, broken glass, and a sense of being hemmed in by walls. After another moment, a streetlamp revealed the walls were in fact buildings. He lay in an alleyway.

All he found was emptiness when he tried to organize his thoughts. He didn't know how long he'd been lying there. A lingering physical memory—of struggling to walk and being short of breath—was a single, thin thread into the darkness of whatever had come before.

Lander pulled himself to a seated position. The dizziness almost knocked him back to the ground. He closed his eyes to focus on his breath and suppress the nausea that threatened to expel what little he had in his stomach. It was an odd sensation, as he couldn't remember having eaten—ever. The darkness, both in the alley and from his missing memories deepened his sense of isolation.

He opened his eyes and searched for something familiar. He needed a tether, if only to the current moment. This would feel like progress. But, with his mind still adrift, he turned inward to the existential question: *Who am I?* For now, he was willing to forsake his life history to know where he was.

With no spark of insight, his brain demanded that he get up and run, as if his memory were a destination. That was impossible; he was barely strong enough to sit up.

Shifting focus, Lander regarded his ill-fitting clothing. As he flicked away the dried leaves and bits of rock that stuck to his clothes, a medical bracelet caught in the fold of his oversized shirt fell into his lap. Presumably cut from his wrist at some point, it listed a patient name, two dates, and a doctor's name. A hospital logo appeared in a repeating pattern on the thin plastic band.

Was that his name? He didn't recognize it. Was that his birthday? *Who am I?* The question reverberated through his entire being.

He worked to calm his breathing and looked again at the bracelet: *Lander Gate.* Born September 9, 1973. Admitted October 12, 2008, at Wrimo Hospital. The blade that had cut the bracelet had obliterated the doctor's name. *Dr. A* was all that remained visible.

His sense of smell suddenly reengaged, triggering a gag reflex just as he noticed a sodden mass of undetermined bodily fluids a few feet away. It was a foul enough call to action to prompt him to stand.

He didn't need his memory to know that it shouldn't have been so difficult to get up. As he put weight on his left leg, he swooned, arms swinging for balance. A second attempt brought him against the lamppost. He coughed, the shallow breaths providing no relief. The muscles in his legs were soft and atrophied. When he tried to flex them, they were nonresponsive.

With growing determination, he moved away from the streetlight, where a long shadow grew out from his feet. With each step, the hunched silhouette stretched until it vanished, like his memory, in a wash of light from the intersecting road.

A shiver of fear came over him as he contemplated being alone and lost. His first instinct was to ask for help. It was late or early—he wasn't sure which—and the street was empty. Who would help him? He staggered toward the nearest intersection, getting some encouragement from the *walk* sign on the corner. But even that echoed his doubts when it cycled back to *don't walk*.

He thumbed the torn bracelet and looked at it again. *Lander Gate. Wrimo Hospital and Clinic.* It was at least a place to start. In his current condition, he reasoned that his presence on the street must have been a terrible mistake.

At the corner, a police cruiser approached. Lander started to raise an arm to flag it down, but an acute, instinctive fear of authority pushed him back into the shadows until it had passed.

"Idiot," he cursed himself, watching the cruiser disappear down the street. "Now how am I supposed to find this Wrimo Hospital?"

For no reason, he crossed the street and backtracked the way he had just come. A circle wasn't a very helpful search pattern, but partway into his second block, a man approached. He looked to be in his mid-twenties, and he wore an orange shirt emblazoned with the words *Visit Phoenix*. He also wore a tightly woven straw sun hat, which struck Lander as off, considering the time. An overstuffed backpack was slung over his shoulder, and he walked as if his legs were sore. He looked tired. As he got closer, Lander spied a large round button pinned to his shirt that read, *Ask me?*

Lander's first attempt to speak was little more than a

shallow cough. Then, in a scratchy, unused voice, he called out to the man. "Can I ask a question?"

The man startled, then stopped walking, frustration on his face. "I'm off duty." He looked Lander up and down before his face relaxed. "I'm sorry. It's been a long day, but it looks like your day has been worse. What's your question?"

"Can you direct me to the Wrimo Hospital?"

"That's easy. One block down and to the right."

When he pointed, his arm drifted close to Lander's face. This triggered a strange sensation in Lander and an uncomfortable expression on the man, and they both involuntarily stepped back.

"They don't have an emergency room, if that's what you need."

Lander rewrapped the band around his wrist and held up his arm. "I'm a patient. I'm overdue to return from an evening outing."

The man nodded, and taking a wide arc, continued down the street. "Good luck," he called back.

Chapter 3
Tuesday,
October 27, 2009 (12:30 a.m.)

The Wrimo Hospital and Clinic presented as a seven-story modern precast concrete building that filled half of the block. On each floor, the tapered concrete panels drew the eyes upward.

Lander didn't recognize the facade or anything on the street. The building's design, and the prominent backlit Wrimo logo, appeared to him more businesslike than representative of a hospital.

He attempted to enter the front door, but it was locked. The sign read, *No After Hours Access.*

Lander decided it would be best to admit himself in the morning to the regular staff—someone who might recognize him.

In search of cover for the rest of the night, he wandered into the lane along the side of the building.

His instinct led him to see if the garage would be an option, but a gate at the bottom of the ramp locked him out. A fence ran along the rear of the building, enclosing a small surface parking lot and an ambulance bay. Paranoia guiding his actions, Lander stepped wide to avoid the view of a security camera.

Behind a dumpster, he discovered a surprisingly clean area that afforded some shelter.

Lander imagined a hospital Dumpster as a quagmire of medical waste, but he needed to find bedding. The side door to the bin was ajar, and the top was propped open. A lone streetlight shone overhead, revealing overstuffed bags of shredded paper that might double as pillows or a mattress. As he picked through the bags, one split open, cascading the contents over his feet. He scooped up the ribbons paper and dropped them into a space between the wall and a concrete pylon.

Fragments of file folders were mixed in with regular copier paper. Many of the tabs were still intact, listed with names and patient identification numbers. Lander retrieved the fragment of his bracelet and compared his number to those on the folders, noting the similarity. Suddenly his build-a-mattress project switched to research. The folders were all dated over five years before, and all were stamped "closed."

He began sorting through the papers, and his heart rate quickened when he found a scrap with a number that was only five digits away from his own. He tore into another bag, only to be disappointed to find coffee-stained disposable cups, tea bags, and sugar packets.

Undeterred, he moved to the next. Toward the bottom of that bag, he extracted a partially intact wedge of paper. It was twisted into a handle, and strands of paper sprouted from the top like a pom-pom. The shredder had likely jammed against the thick file folder, and the frustrated shredder operator had cast the dossier straight into the garbage. This wasn't remarkable to Lander until he saw his name—or at least the same name typed across the bracelet in his pocket.

Stunned by the discovery, Lander, clutching at the file, welled up with tears and cried. The sensation of being lost in every way possible had become an unbearable weight. At that moment, even the promise of a clue was a lot to handle. Not to mention the growing sense of dread at what the folder might signify.

Lander held his breath and opened the file. Most of the pages were mulched, and the rest were difficult to read in the darkness. Toward the back, the top section of a police report detailed Lander assaulting an officer then being remanded to Wrimo. Even in his confused state, Lander struggled to reconcile the idea that he was capable of violence. But it did explain his reluctance to flag down the police car.

On the medical log, he knew only a few of the medical terms. The prefix *psych* appeared frequently. Lander wondered if they were avoiding the term *crazy*.

Some pages were photocopies of handwritten notes and seemed new. The blend of cursive and printing was at first difficult to identify even as English, but, then again, illegible handwriting was a hallmark of doctors.

Why would a file with recent entries be shredded and tossed away? Even his addled brain knew that whoever had done this shouldn't have been discarding personal medical records. He began to wonder just how official—or voluntary—his discharge had been. His earlier plan to be readmitted dissolved.

Lander spread out the other bags and papers and settled against the wall, resting his head on his arm. Through the narrow space under the dumpster, he caught a flicker of movement as a small animal darted across the lane. But before he could find the energy to worry about critters, exhaustion overtook him, and he slept.

The sounds of a diesel engine revving and a compressor hissing startled Lander awake. A fight-or-flight instinct took over any thoughts of his situation. The dumpsters in the alley were being emptied, and he'd be crushed when the Wrimo container was dropped back into place.

He rolled to the side and used the fence to pull himself up. His movements must have caught the eye of the truck driver because an air horn pealed and an angry driver stuck his head out the window, waving at him to get out of the way. Getting away was fine with Lander, who'd resolved that the Wrimo Hospital may not be the most compassionate place to seek help. There was something very wrong with his situation. For this, he also had no answer.

A half an hour later, Lander collapsed onto a bench at the edge of a community park. Any form of exertion, even the walking he'd just done, sapped his strength. The morning commuters gave him a wide berth and intentionally looked away. A man and a woman in similar dirty, ill-fitting clothes ambled across the park to the sidewalk, asking for spare change. As they passed Lander, the man said, "Let's get some breakfast. This isn't getting us anywhere. It'll be better at lunchtime."

The woman replied, "At least it's not so hot. I hate the summers."

Lander followed the two, aware of his own hunger sapping what little strength he had. They led him to the edge of an older masonry building. A double door opened onto the alley, where a group of about twenty-five other people stood in line. Unlike the businesspeople on the street, this crowd looked at Lander with a different level of interest, more akin to what an eight-year-old might get on his first day at a new school. Lander couldn't remember his school years, but he held back, fearing a class bully might target him.

From out of the shadows, and even down from a fire escape, a steady stream of people converged and joined the line. Unsure as to the etiquette, Lander hung back on the opposite side of the roadway, prepared to fall in when the group passed him.

A woman with a clipboard called out that the kitchen was

open, and the group shuffled in. After perhaps fifty people had entered, the woman made a note on her clipboard and held up her hand to an approaching woman. "Sorry, Jane. That's our quota for today. Stick around. There may be some leftovers."

She was about to turn on her heel when she spotted Lander. Still tired and confused, he thought for the briefest moment that she looked familiar. He recognized a similar reaction in her.

Jane made another plea to be admitted. "All right," the woman said, and she waved Jane in.

It was now just the two of them. "You're new on the street." In a hushed voice, she continued, as if to herself. "You must be very new." She shook her head and motioned him to come forward. "You'll need to be here a bit earlier if you want to get breakfast."

"What time is it?"

"We open at seven thirty. Let me show you around. This seems to be a morning of exceptions."

Like a nervous dog not wanting to be led, Lander rooted himself to the spot, his feet in a wide stance. The only thing missing was a leash. She waved at him, and he followed her toward the door.

She could sense his apprehension and gave him his space. Lander looked into a room that measured about a thousand square feet, populated with boardroom-style tables and a cafeteria serving line at one end. The smell of eggs, ham, and burnt toast wafted toward him. The hum of voices rose and fell in the growing warmth of the room. It was welcoming in its essence of community, but, as a room full of strangers, it was also frightening.

"Don't be shy." With kindness, the woman touched Lander on his shoulder to guide him in. The instant her hand came in contact with him, she screamed as if in pain. At the same moment, a disembodied sense of being engulfed in flames overtook Lander.

The intense heat of the fire made the air shimmer. Immersed in the hallucination, he tried to see through the swirling smoke and flames. The dining tables were gone and he was alone, yet he wasn't. He could feel the women's presence—not beside him but *inside* him. Out of nowhere, a wooden beam materialized before crashing to the ground. With a whiplash twist of his head, Lander avoided the spray of sparks. A chill fell over him as he saw his clothes burn away from his arms. The heat and smoke seized his lungs. As his mind and body separated, he noticed for the first time that it was deathly silent. The total loss of one of his senses was impossible to reconcile with such chaos. He blinked and tried to focus, grasping at a fragment of awareness that this couldn't be real.

Without warning, he was back in the dining room, and the woman was inches from his face. As he stepped away, she fell back against the door frame, her knees buckling.

A large, tattooed man rose from the nearest table and lunged toward them. "Hey, what have you done to her?"

The woman had sagged to the floor and begun rocking back and forth. Lander stood, shaking, swinging his head between the woman and the approaching man. He wanted to help the woman, but for the second time that day, the instinct to flee took over. He moved backward out the door but missed the step, scrambling to keep his balance.

As the man came in line with the woman, she reached and grabbed his shirt. "No, Stop! He didn't do anything. It's me." She raised her voice and called after Lander. "It's not your fault! Be careful."

The police report that purported a proclivity towards violence may not have been wrong.

Chapter 4
Tuesday,
October 27, 2009 (8:15 a.m.)

After the incident at breakfast, Lander, though still hungry, walked as fast as his feeble legs would carry him, navigating a zigzag pattern through downtown Phoenix, resting at bus stops and anywhere he wouldn't be noticed. The scene at the shelter faded, as if the memory were stretching. And, like a picture that has been blown up too large, the details became less defined.

Lander paused in another alley and wondered if he had walked this route before. From the corner of his eye, he noticed a piece of leather partially obscured by a discarded box. When he got closer, he saw a man's wallet lying in the dust. He flipped open the bifold. Inside was a stack of worn twenty-dollar bills and numerous credit cards tucked in rows. His head snapped up, and he surveyed the alleyway, awash in guilt. But he was alone.

He extracted a driver's license and peered at the man's face behind the scratched, laminated surface. Lander recognized the street address on the license: it was the building he was standing beside. And his memory of the front door, which he'd observed just an hour earlier, was unnaturally detailed. He could picture the numbers bolted to the wall; he even remembered that someone had replaced the numeral four. It was an apartment building, likely converted from offices within the last ten years.

A resident had dropped their wallet. Lander turned it over in his hand, fingering the bills and imagining breakfast. But without thinking much about his decision, he closed the wallet and walked to the front of the building. The door had an electronic lock and a list of tenants. Lander matched the name to the license and hit the button on the intercom.

A moment later there was a brief exchange, and a lengthy pause, while the voice verified his story. Then a man with bedraggled hair and a white cotton housecoat peered at him through the glass in the front door. Lander held up the wallet, while the man opened the door just enough to talk through.

"I believe this belongs to you." Lander handed him the wallet before taking two steps back. The risk of replaying the scene from breakfast had shattered his confidence. The newcomer flipped it open and scanned the cards and the bills.

His eyebrows rose, and he smiled at Lander. "Sorry, I assumed you found it after it had been emptied and discarded. I wasn't expecting everything to be there. Where was it?"

"In the lane by the back door. I found it just a few minutes ago."

"I must have dropped it last night. Thanks." He reached into the wallet, extracted forty dollars, and leaned out to hand it to Lander. "I appreciate your honesty."

He had done the right thing, though, as an unhoused person, that wouldn't be a solid strategy for long-term success. At least he now had a little money.

In the next few hours, Lander learned a lot about discrimination. Even though he had some money to spend, the first breakfast diner he stopped at turned him away. The chain coffeehouses sent out the largest of their staff to encourage him to move on. Eventually, a food truck, little more than a converted camper, served him a coffee and a donut and he found a discarded newspaper nearby. He'd gone full circle and was back on the same park bench from that morning.

The newspaper gave him a date: October 27, 2009. He scanned the headlines and frowned. The current stories and scandals meant nothing to him. Even the names of political power brokers, oft repeated in the columns, didn't register in his memory. The president was a distinguished-looking black man. The baseball season was nearing an end, with Philadelphia the favorite to beat the Dodgers in the National League Championship. Despite his memory loss, he had a sense that sports were not his thing. The entertainment pages speculated about the success of the upcoming second installment of a vampire series, the release date announced for a month later. An interview with the author, who lived in Phoenix, filled an entire page. The last item Lander read was an editorial that suggested all states follow Arizona's lead and abolish daylight saving time, which was scheduled to end that weekend.

His inability to relate to the news stories isolated him further. Every time he cast his thoughts to his past, it was like a mental version of being struck in the chest and winded—it left him debilitated and frightened. He felt like his entire being was sitting on the pavement, gasping for air. If only he knew how to reinflate a mind.

Restless, he walked again and found himself in front of the building where he had returned the wallet. A ladder blocked the front steps as a man descended. Lander turned to leave. He wasn't in the mood to be told to move on again.

The circles Lander walked became smaller, and again he arrived back at the same park bench. Lander unconsciously cataloged the faces and attire of the steady flow of people. From across the street, the man he recognized from the ladder headed in his direction, wiping his hands with a rag. A hammer in a tool belt bounced against his thigh.

Lander didn't have the energy to get up, so he waited until the other man stood in front of him.

"Can I sit down?"

"Sure, but don't get too close. I smell bad."

"I'm the superintendent and manager of the building where you returned the wallet. I recognized you from the security camera at the front door. That was a surprising thing you did this morning."

Lander had troubles adjusting to this new tack. After a full day of being shunned, he wasn't programmed to be treated with respect. There was also a strange energy that had begun to eddy between them. He had trouble focusing on what was being said as a competing storybook of images played out in the back of his mind. Thankfully, there was no sign of the conflagration that had consumed the woman at the shelter.

Lander worried about appearing rude and, with some difficulty, refocused on what the man was saying.

"... in Paris a few years ago. Had my wallet and passport stolen by a pickpocket at Montmartre. A huge nuisance, and the loss was more than just the money. Later, I got a call from someone claiming they had found my wallet. They gave it back to me, now empty of cash but with everything else intact. I gave them a reward, but the entire time I was being played."

The man paused to look at Lander. "I'm pretty sure they were the same people who had stolen the wallet in the first place, and I'd just paid them again. You, on the other hand, returned the wallet as you found it. Who does that?"

"Not everyone needs to have a bad day." At that moment, the images in his head coalesced into a blurry silent movie. This prompted Lander, without knowing why, to speak with unusual confidence to a man he'd never met before. "I think you understand. You have a charitable streak in you. I bet you carry pocket change and one-dollar bills so you can give handouts. And it's not about getting the people away from your building. You also support local charities, and not just at Christmas."

The man nodded, and showed no surprise at Lander's assessment. Lander wondered how he knew these details.

The two men talked for a quarter of an hour. The conversation flowed and covered simple topics. Lander, after feigning a cramp in his leg, had risen and moved just beyond the bench. He wanted to see if a little distance would mute the competing storyline that intruded on his thoughts like a song in the back of his head. Although this song, while silent, was accompanied by flashing images like a music video.

When the man rose to depart, he took on a more serious tone. "You did an admirable thing today, and I want to repay the favor. Meet me at five in the alley where you found the wallet."

Lander spent more of his money on a late lunch and didn't drift too far from the park for the rest of the afternoon. At five o'clock, he appeared in the laneway as instructed. The back door opened, and the superintendent exited. He carried two towels and a gallon container of water.

"What's your name?"

"Lander."

"Folks just call me the super. Do you have a place to sleep?"

Lander, still suspicious of anyone, hesitated. "No. This is all very new to me."

The super stepped past him and slipped a key into a lock on a metal plate at ground level. Then he pulled up on a handle, and the hinged door swung open. Lander could see steps descending and the super climbed in, calling behind him as he went. "The light is on a string to the left." With a click, the illumination revealed a short staircase to a room below.

If he was setting a trap, Lander was about to walk right into it. But he suppressed the thought, as he didn't detect any deception in the man, and followed him down.

The room was square, about twenty feet across. The ceiling was low, but not so low that Lander couldn't stand up straight. Two light bulbs illuminated sparse furnishings.

A mille-feuille of mismatched blankets draped across three shipping pallets made up the bed. A few blocks away in a university dorm, and without the dirt and moth-eaten holes, it would have been viewed as a futon.

The super placed the towels on a chair and the water bottle on the end of the bed. "This is the back of the furnace room." He ran his finger along the wall and held it up. "You can still pick up a little residue. It was once the coal storage. It's an old building. This room has no current purpose. If you want, you can stay here for a while. The entry can be locked from both sides. In an emergency, there's a backup entry." He pointed to a small opening at floor level on the interior wall, where shovels had worn gouges into the floor from stoking the furnace. "You'll be able to squeeze through. On the other side, there's a single toilet and a utility sink. The furnace room locks from the outer hallway so you can't get into the rest of the building."

It felt a bit like a cell, but Lander didn't have any other options.

As if on a real estate tour, the super continued his pitch. "You'll appreciate some of its other qualities. During the intense heat of summer, it remains cool. The furnace keeps it warm in winter. It floods from time to time during monsoon season, but it's been a long dry season this year." He waved a hand around the room. "Surprisingly, it's almost never damp."

"Is this where you lure your victims?" Lander kept his voice cheerful, not wanting to show offense at what appeared to be a kind offer.

"You'll be the second tenant. Your predecessor, an older woman, lived here about a year, and then one day last September, she was gone. All of her belongings, everything. She even left the bed made and a flower." He pointed.

Lander noticed for the first time the small bud vase on an upside-down tea crate that doubled as a bedside table. It was empty. "How much is the rent?"

"No strings attached, just a few rules. She helped me by picking up the litter that collects around the building. Once a week, at night, she also cleaned the basement and laundry room. Again, no obligation. We'll take it week by week for a start."

"You said a few rules."

"This has to be our secret. The residents seldom use the back door, and the entry is shielded from the upper windows by the overhang. If you see anyone around, or hear voices, wait and don't use the hatch. No smoking, no visitors, no drugs, no fires or candles, no cooking. And keep it clean, especially the bathroom. If you're out and about, use public facilities. If you are ever seen, I will have to evict you."

The two men stood in silence, the rules hanging in the air. Lander didn't know enough about living on the street to even know if this would work.

"Thanks. I'll give it a try."

Chapter 5
Wednesday,
October 28, 2009 (6:40 a.m.)

W ithout a watch or a clock in the coal chute, Lander didn't know what time it was when he woke the next morning. He felt safe in the cocoon of his little room. But the lack of memories plagued him. All the unanswered questions flashed like sparks in his mind's eye.

It would be easy to do nothing. Physically, he could limit his life to the coal chute and a few back alleys. Mentally, there wasn't much to contemplate, since he possessed only two days' worth of memories. But while there might be comfort in the simplicity of not knowing, he needed to be whole.

Other than the Wrimo wristband and file folder, the woman with the clipboard was Lander's only connection to his past. He couldn't shake the belief that she knew him. And he wondered what she had meant by her warning to be careful.

Not wanting to miss breakfast, he promptly left his new "apartment" and ended up in the designated alley before the line had even formed.

If being homeless with no memory wasn't enough, he also struggled to understand why he became disoriented when he got close to other people. His symptoms were consistent: an overwhelming collision of mental images, twitching muscles, and shortness of breath. Like a pair of magnets that shared the same polarity, he felt pushed away when he got too close to anyone.

And the encounter at the shelter had been a full immersion into the storyboard. What if he found the woman, only for the fiery hallucination to repeat itself? It was only then that he realized what the difference had been. She had reached out and touched him.

He estimated it to be about a quarter after seven, and the lineup was half full. Ten minutes later, the door opened, and a woman with a clipboard stepped into the alley.

Lander's heart raced, and he moved to get her attention. But as he drew closer, he realized this wasn't the same person. This woman was taller than the one from the day before, and she was right-handed.

Getting a hot breakfast was now Lander's only morning goal. He avoided contact with the other diners by strategically being the last person through the door. He ate well and thanked the woman with the clipboard on his way out, but she showed no recognition or even interest.

The rest of the morning he wandered the streets, growing familiar with the landmarks and the faces that populated his bubble.

He was back in the park near lunchtime when a van pulled up and distributed wrapped sandwiches and bottles of water. A church group from the suburbs sponsored the outing. The men's buttoned-up collars and the woman's pastel cardigan sweaters and floral-print dresses looked fairy-like among the earth tones and dirt of their beneficiaries.

In the early evening, Lander fell in with a group in an alley behind a café. The proprietor put out leftover pastry items, sandwiches, and nearly out-of-date-juices. The jostling reminded him of a shark feeding. Lander hovered at the edges, with no interest in joining the scrum.

A scrappy red-haired man in his sixties, only five feet tall, had no such qualms and elbowed his way deep into the throng. He emerged a few minutes later with items clutched in both hands. He stopped and looked at Lander. "I saw you at breakfast. You're new. Take this." He handed Lander a blueberry muffin wrapped in plastic and a green vegetable juice in a small bottle. "The first few days can be tough. I'm Paul." He stood up a little straighter and reached out for a handshake. Thankfully —for Lander feared the physical contact—two croissants and what may have been an Italian sub almost dropped from his grasp. Paul deftly redirected his energy to keep hold of his bounty. Lander thanked him for the kindness as he moved a few steps away.

Paul pointed to the woman standing on the step at the back of the café. "Katherine, the owner of the café, is a good lady. She's tough but fair. Don't sleep, pee, shit, or throw up in this part of the lane." He gestured at the ledge, where only a few food items remained. "They put something out practically every night, though the selection varies. She fired an employee a while back when she overheard him say it was like 'feeding the dogs.'"

Lander thanked Paul again and walked back to his park bench to enjoy his dinner.

Psychologists plot a person's state of being on a pyramid. The bottom and largest section represents the most basic needs: shelter, food, clothes. The next level, a little smaller, stands for personal safety, security, and access to resources. The theory, developed by Abraham Maslow, suggests that before one can move up the pyramid, each of the previous levels needs to be satisfied. The highest layers represent emotional and cognitive needs such as love, belonging, and self-esteem. From Lander's perspective, he had the bottom two sections covered: he had a place to stay, access to food, and the clothes on his back. He even had a nominal friendship with the super, which was a component of the third tier. This was progress, but Lander needed to insert another layer to do with self-knowledge. Who was he? And why did he become confused and distressed in close proximity to others? He was most interested in the second question. On a different tangent, he wondered how he knew an academic theory, but did not know where he learned it.

The perfect evening encouraged Lander to stay outside as a cool breeze replaced the heat of the day. Typical to Arizona, there was no rain in the forecast. He moved through the park and spotted a reposed figure by an ironwood tree. It was Paul, ostensibly sleeping, but Lander suspected he had passed out. It wasn't detective work so much as the empty twenty-six-ounce bottle of whiskey cradled under his arm. He hadn't seen that being handed out behind the café.

Lander decided to test a theory. After calling Paul's name and being satisfied that he was truly unconscious, Lander sat down about five feet away from him. He tried to open his mind to any change in his thoughts or sensations. He looked inward for the strange tableau of images that had obscured his thoughts during earlier encounters. Nothing happened. He shuffled closer and repeated the inquiry.

The next time he moved a little closer, it started: a vague sense, fluttering between unease and calm, drifted into his mind. It wasn't nearly as strong as what he had experienced with the others.

Close enough now to touch him, Lander rested a finger on Paul's wrist as if he were about to take his pulse. As he did, Lander was immersed into a tableau of abstract images. The languid loop of the visualization resembled bubbles in a lava lamp, slowly expanding then slipping free and drifting upward. Even the color palette nodded to a sixties' aesthetic.

A violent spasm interrupted the psychedelic light show. Flashes of faces and buildings intruded into Lander's thoughts. Paul was waking up. Lander let go of his wrist and scrabbled away, suddenly out of breath and fearful. He looked back guiltily at Paul as if caught doing something wrong. But except for a twitch on the left side of his face, Paul remained unresponsive. Apparently, the mind came around before the body, but Lander decided not to be there when he woke.

Chapter 6
Thursday,
October 29, 2009 (7:15 a.m.)

M any local charities and service organizations help people experiencing homelessness. The more established institutions try to keep a schedule but are beholden to the availability of donations and volunteers. A hastily written sign on the door of what was becoming his usual breakfast stop informed him that there would be no breakfast that day. Sorry, it read, with an unhappy face sketched in the corner.

Lander wasn't about to give up; he was becoming more in tune with those around him and looked for clues to another option. Very few of the homeless had cell phones, and as a result, they had developed an informal system of communication. Those with empathy would signal to others that a handout was available. The signal consisted of little more than a gesture passed from one person to the next, something that could be seen from a block away. The recipient would pass on the news to someone else within their view. Smoke signals, if you will.

Lander believed this happened when Jane, the woman who had been a few minutes late for breakfast that first morning, cocked her head from half a block away, encouraging Lander to follow.

A converted community hall had become a makeshift dispensary. The larger room gave Lander the ability to move about freely. Public health staff sat around the perimeter beside tables with hampers. They handed him a plate of scrambled eggs, an oily pinkish sausage link, buttered white toast, and a little packet with knife, fork, salt, and pepper.

After breakfast, Jane followed him out of the dining hall. She got a little closer each time he stopped to catch his breath. At the park, Lander sat on a low concrete wall instead of his usual bench. She made no pretense and came to sit next to him, though she was forced a few feet away to avoid the metal brackets installed to stop skateboarders.

She spoke as soon as she settled. "You're new to the neighborhood. Paul said to be nice to you."

Lander didn't reply, uncomfortable at being in Paul's debt for the food and at Jane's appearance.

"Do you have any money?" She reached up and partially unbuttoned her shirt, letting it gape open. She palmed her breast like an apple. Lander, suddenly shy, snapped his eyes up to hers. Her cheek twitched, and she laughed.

Lander reached into his jacket pocket and pulled out three or four crumpled dollars. He shrugged. "I got nothin'."

"You're right. Not enough for my services, though I will give you a special deal for your first time." Her face twitched again, like a horse expelling a fly.

To add emphasis to her sales pitch, she quickly squeezed in beside him.

It was too quick; he couldn't move away. Lander gagged as a vise tightened on his chest. Her hand, meant to guide him to sample her flesh, gripped him firmly, but didn't move. His surroundings vanished, and nausea rose as a visualization of a room spun around him. A flood of sensations and images took over. He almost passed out in the moment it took the scene to coalesce and settle.

He was in a bright, second-story corner room with rectangular farmhouse windows open to the elements and the vast blue sky. The backlit lace curtains shifted on the breath of a warm afternoon breeze. A bouquet of fresh lavender sat next to a crystal glass of lemonade on a side table. Condensation dripped from the thin glass and pooled on the plain painted tabletop.

Lander felt sure that Jane had emerged with him into the ethereal yet tranquil setting. It was as if they lay propped up in a pristine white bed with a cool cotton top sheet draped over them. The reality—if he could use that word to describe what was happening—there were three of them that inhabited a single point of view: Jane, himself, and the soul of an emaciated woman.

Lander blinked, expecting the illusion to fade. When it didn't, he noticed the nearly imperceptible rise and fall of the woman's chest with her shallow breaths. Perhaps it was the cloudlike shifting of the curtains or the preponderance of white, but it all came together to envelop Lander and Jane in a spiritual and protective embrace.

A group of people crowded around the bed, all ages, and their faces were indistinct. When he tried to focus, Lander blanked out. He surfaced to find Jane shaking and painfully squeezing his arm.

As he struggled to breathe, Lander twisted his arm to break her grip. With faltering steps, he moved to the grass and sank to his knees.

Jane cried. Between her sobs, she sputtered, "That was beautiful. How did you do that? Take me back."

Lander moved away as quickly as he could to seek the quiet and solitude of his coal chute. He sought to understand the origin of what he'd seen. Paul's abstract narrative was nothing like Jane's cinematic tableau; both were unique.

Was he viewing their dreams? Paul, in his drunken stupor, could not articulate a fully formed scene, while Jane, high but lucid, had curated a literal storybook moment. But why that scene? Because there was no doubt the elderly woman had been on her deathbed.

Chapter 7
Friday,
October 30, 2009 (11:30 a.m.)

After his encounter with Jane the previous day, Lander limited his interactions with others on the street. While he ached to experiment, the fear of triggering another violent episode, such as the one with the woman in the mess hall, stopped him. He wondered if, with practice, he could learn to control the collision of images.

Now, late morning, he'd grown tired of inactivity. The less turbulent encounters with Jane and Paul nudged his analytical mind to resume the research. As he walked, Lander contemplated his recent interactions. The mental images weren't literal—it was safe to assume, for instance, that the woman at breakfast had never burned to death. With Jane, the experience had personal resonance, but if that wasn't Jane in the bed, who was it? The storylines gnawed at his consciousness—both had displayed the moment of death and had surfaced from somewhere in the person he touched.

Would the same thing happen with anybody he approached? He had an idea to cast himself in the role of storyteller. While it was a strange choice of vocation for someone with memory loss, he didn't have to compose an original story, only interpret the images that scrolled by in his mind's eye. Like a sports commentator but without the requisite dramatics of calling out when a team scored.

An added benefit of practicing with his strange ability, it might generate some cash. In his few days on the street, Lander had observed several money-making schemes in operation. If the guy at the park sold a custom poem scribbled on a bar coaster, he could do the same by telling a personal story.

The cooler weather brought more people onto the streets. The park presented itself as a suitable venue for his test.

In the center of the park, five benches formed a semi-circle around an incomplete sculpture. On one end, a woman in her mid-fifties with a bichon frise sat reading a paperback novel. On the opposite side, two men studied a chess board. As Lander approached, a thirty-something couple arrived and settled on the middle seats.

The layout allowed Lander to walk behind the people, experimenting with his distance and letting the frequency of what he now thought of as "the connection" ebb and flow. He discovered he wasn't able to differentiate between two individuals who sat close together. Also, the chess players' concentration on their game muted the connection. The resulting images recalled a watermark on thick paper, where only a faint outline defined the edges. They differed from Paul's vivid contribution, but no more readable.

Lander tucked this insight away, confirming that the park, with isolated and relaxed individuals, was a good place to run his tests.

He had difficulty separating the storylines of the young couple, though he detected a powerful presence of conflicting images and raw emotion. Most of what arose was not pleasant, forcing Lander to step back and shake his head. Thankfully, no one noticed. A man with his appearance, standing and shaking his head, could cause his subjects to scatter. He could have been the poster child for mental illness, which was prevalent among those in a state of homelessness.

Relationships were not Lander's expertise, but the discordant rhythms that emanated from the couple suggested there wasn't much future in their relationship. And he worried about the woman. His gut reaction was that the man might be volatile. But he couldn't read their minds, and he also concluded that the visions weren't dreams. So where did the story fragments come from?

Lander decided the single woman with the dog would be his best subject. Focusing on the young couple had tired him, and he paused to catch his breath. He felt like he'd run a marathon. If he followed through on his plan to talk with her, his tattered clothing and wheezy, breathless cough would be a challenging first impression.

When his heart rate and breathing settled, Lander moved closer to her. A series of images played out in his mind's eye. She differed from Jane; her visions were less like a dream and more like a stop-motion puzzle of video clips that needed to be assembled. A story unfolded, and he marveled at the deep unconscious connection that formed between them. He could tell she was also aware of something happening—she looked light-headed.

He sensed her resistance, a firewall of sorts, trying to block his intrusion. On a conscious level, though, she did not appear to know what was happening to her. Lander hesitated. He was violating her privacy and needed permission to continue. It would be awkward, but he had to try.

Lander moved to the front of the benches and attempted to make eye contact. After a passing glance, she looked away with a fabricated distraction, adjusting her dog's collar.

Lander wasn't deterred. He pressed, and the commingling

of his presence caused her to raise her head. After a few seconds, there was acceptance in her eyes and an implicit invitation to proceed.

"May I?" He pointed to a spot further down the bench.

She didn't say yes, but she continued to stare up at him. It wasn't a no.

Lander settled at a respectful distance, but close enough to maintain the connection he had been toying with.

In the next few minutes, she accepted him. He spoke with a measured pace and tone, and the authenticity and authority of his words assuaged the stereotype that she may have formed based on his appearance.

"I want to tell you a story about a twelve-year-old girl. It's in the early nineteen hundreds and she lives with her mother in a derelict building that is about to be demolished. The apartment across the hall has an abandoned upright piano and the young girl is magnetically drawn to it." Lander paused and waited for the woman to look up at him. "You know that feeling, don't you? To walk past a piano and want to tinker with the keys."

The woman nodded. "I've always wanted to take music lessons, but other priorities ..." Lander noticed that her hands, now resting on her lap, had begun to gently spin a wedding ring.

"... I never got around to it."

"The child was in awe of the instrument and even with missing keys and out of tune, she created engaging melodies." In the vision, Lander couldn't hear the music but could sense beauty from the way the girl's body swayed and her feeling of elation. He could see her hands contorting to create complex chords.

Lander cleared his throat as the awareness of the other people on the benches shifted his attention. The domestic spat resumed, and further down the benches the word "checkmate" rose above the sounds of the birds and the hum of traffic. He redirected his focus to the woman. Even her dog looked up at him with curious eyes.

"As fate would have it, a music instructor passed by and heard the sounds from the second-story window. When he tried to investigate, two youths looking for spare change hassled him, scaring him away. Charmed by—and unable to shake—the beautiful melody, he returned the next week, but a wrecking crew had begun the demolition of the building. He eventually found the family and offered to be the girl's mentor. The mother, suspicious of his intentions, said no.'

Eyes downcast, the woman whispered. "That's terrible."

Lander wanted to tell the woman how he interpreted the images from a silent film reel projected in the back of his head. The more he leaned in, the sharper the focus.

"That's where the story ends. The girl went through life without ever again having access to a piano or discovering a talent that lay within her."

Obviously touched by the story, she thanked Lander, asked for his name, and then gave him ten dollars. By setting up the story as an analogy, he hoped she heard it as a call to action.

When she walked away, she held the leash in one hand while the other tapped away at the keys of an invisible piano, nodding to a song that now played inside her head.

Lander, for his part, collapsed with exhaustion, but also satisfaction as he stretched out on the bench she had just vacated.

Chapter 8
Friday,
October 30, 2009 (10:15 p.m.)

That evening, Lander took a chance. Pushed to the limit by his dirty, foul-smelling clothes, he sought out the laundry room. He knew he wouldn't have to venture far into the basement; he could hear from his room the dull rumble of the dryers and the banging of washer lids. He waited until after ten to sneak in.

The super had told him the interior of the building was out of bounds and that the furnace room locked on both sides and couldn't be opened. This wasn't exactly true. They had upgraded the door to code in the last ten years, but the wall was original. And whoever installed it hadn't worried too much about the fit. With a little body weight, the entire frame twisted and the door popped open.

The laundry room was empty. Lint lay like dander across the surfaces and floated in the moist air. While no specific memory arose, the room triggered a feeling in Lander of being embraced. He undressed and loaded a washer before settling into the utility closet. Naked, sitting cross-legged on the floor, he removed an elastic from a deck of playing cards. He had found the cards on a shelf in the furnace room, in a shoebox with a few other items, including a travel clock without a battery, a polished quartz crystal, and a cheap set of earbuds of the sort they give away on planes.

Knowing the origin of the ear buds, and that it was a travel style clock, highlighted the selective nature of his lost memory. He knew that he'd been on a plane but he didn't know where he had flown, or with whom.

The cards had become his favorite possession. The clatter of the shuffle was a physical manifestation of how his brain worked. He studied the caricatures and symbols, especially the impassive assemblage of royalty. The face cards didn't look him in the eye. One of the four kings and two of the jacks, frozen in profile, were looking away—what had caught their attention? Or perhaps they turned their heads away in disdain of those who peered into their world. And why wasn't there a one-eyed queen?

A broken slat in the double louvered doors provided enough light. He laid the cards in front of him to play a memory game—the one where shuffled cards are set out in rows. The goal was to find the matches.

He played the game while he waited and did exceptionally well. He made it more difficult between turns by closing his eyes and counting to ten. Even with the added distraction, he still remembered every card's location.

The gamble he'd taken—that nobody would use the laundry room at that hour—seemed to have paid off. Then the door opened, and a twenty-something couple entered. They were flushed and excited.

The man scanned the room and grinned. "What a shame. We're all alone."

As she reached into a washer to retrieve her clothing, he came up behind her and ground his pelvis into her. He reached under her T-shirt, cupping her breasts. She bucked her hips and giggled, pushing him backward. "Haven't you had enough?"

"Not yet."

"Me neither." As they kissed, she teased him in return. "Help me carry this load. It can dry in the apartment." They were gone a second later.

In the preceding few days, Lander's observations of people had run the gamut of social interaction. From his hiding spot, he'd now become a voyeur, though he didn't like the negative connotation of that word. Observing what normal people did kept Lander grounded.

From the hallway, the closed elevator door muted the couple's voices, and loneliness washed over him. *I don't want to watch all the time.* Because he didn't yet understand, and couldn't control, his effect on others, he required an enormous safety bubble. Touching, embracing, closeness were all out of the question. And his relationships with Jane, Paul, and the piano lady could hardly be defined as friendships.

He looked at the caged clock that hung crooked on the plain white wall. 10:15 p.m. He wondered if the super did an evening inspection.

A prescient thought, as the super walked into the room just as Lander's wash cycle ground to a halt. The machine was preparing for liftoff in the spin cycle. Lander knew his tiny load would attract attention. The spin cycle would race, and the light load would cause the washer to rock back and forth, banging against the adjacent machines. What if the super decided to adjust the feet and level the machine? Lander didn't have to look; he had seen the super's tool kit on the shelf behind him.

Lander and the super had developed a nominal friendship. However, if he found Lander sitting cross-legged and naked in the closet, it would push their understanding too far and mean his eviction.

He needed to be still. The super walked the length of the machines, opening the top-loading washers and peering into the drums. Along the way, he fished out a stray black sock. He stopped in front of Lander's machine, the motor and pulleys now silent. There was only the metronome click of the timer hurrying to its next task. Lander squeezed his eyes closed, willing the super to walk away before the machine kicked into top gear.

As if the click of the next cycle was his cue, the super turned and walked back toward the door. He hesitated before flipping off the lights, looking back at the washer that was gaining speed, then departed. Lander fled with his damp clothes, leaving behind his precious deck of cards.

Chapter 9
Saturday,
October 31, 2009 (1:30 p.m.)

D r. Paul Aradice put down his pen and looked up, aware of that crucial moment when an author connected with a reader at a book signing. He made eye contact, smiled, and returned the book with two hands. Using both hands was significant. It made the book seem more substantial, more important. They would be a fan for life.

Before the next person stepped forward, he checked the length of the line and calculated that the event would be over in twelve to fifteen minutes. He looked up and signaled to the next person, a pretty girl in her late teens. A student, judging by her backpack.

At first, he'd fought his publisher when they suggested dumbing down the book for a broader audience. It required removing some medical jargon and expanding definitions. When they asked him to provide household examples of mental illness, he'd pulled out his contract to see if he could get out of it. His convictions, though, weren't deep enough to prompt him to return the cash advance. So he'd edited his serious medical textbook into something for airport bookstore end-caps.

He'd been wrong to resist. A college had picked it up as a textbook, and armchair therapists everywhere now quoted him.

With a flourish, Dr. Aradice put a dot on the *i* of his last name and returned the book to the student. When a camera flash made him blink, he transferred his smile to the photographer, who clicked off a second shot. They would both be excellent pictures: acclaimed author with admiring reader.

The next fan asked him an intuitive question, and there was a murmur of approval as the doctor answered in a voice loud enough for all to hear.

As another person approached, he held up a finger. "I'll be with you in a moment." Dr. Aradice then turned to his associate, who was standing a few yards away. "Monica, I left my notes on the podium. Would you retrieve them for me?"

Monica nodded and walked back into the vacated amphitheater.

Dr. Aradice nodded to welcome the next in line, a middle-aged woman who asked about a problem "her sister" was having. It was an occupational hazard of writing a medical text, he supposed. Inevitably, some people believed that the price of the book included a free consultation. He was about to cut her off when he spotted Monica coming back into the room with his notes in her hand.

At that moment, a dark-haired man stopped her. Dr. Aradice tensed. The man was Roberto Flores, a reporter whose beat was immigration policy and high-profile quinceañeras. During a recent interview that was supposed to be about the book, he'd probed the doctor on the treatment of lab animals and then segued into a case history in which a teenage girl under the doctor's care had committed suicide. At that point, Dr. Aradice had stopped the interview and refused to talk to the reporter further.

Dr. Aradice turned back to the woman with the personal

question. "I'm sorry, Ms....?" The prompt was an attempt to personalize the interaction by using her name.

"Wilson."

"Ms. Wilson. These situations are seldom isolated. It would be inappropriate for me to comment without making a more detailed inquiry. The Wrimo Hospital has a drop-in clinic. Please encourage your sister to come and see us." He handed over the signed book to dismiss her, then beckoned for the next person in line as Monica came up behind him.

"What did the reporter want?" he asked her.

"He said you owe him the rest of his interview."

Fifteen minutes later, a firm handshake from the host marked the official end of his responsibility. It had been a successful event. Fifty people had come out to see him—an impressive number for a Saturday daytime signing.

This was just the beginning. The book had been out only ninety days and was gaining momentum; a second printing was already ordered. He'd done two local talk shows, and the publisher had landed him an appearance on a network daytime show.

Monica drove him back to the Wrimo Hospital, the seat of his neuropsychology practice where he was also the managing director. An exaggerated glance at his watch was more for show than to check the time. She would know from this gesture that he wanted to review his schedule. He often treated her like a personal assistant. Monica, to her credit, didn't complain about that or for working on a Saturday.

"You'll be a few minutes late for your 2:00 p.m. You have three patient appointments, back-to-back. The second appointment is a first timer. A pro bono case from the children's hospital."

She paused for any questions, but the doctor sat looking impassively out the side window. A quiet "uh-huh" confirmed he was listening, but his attention was on the people that populated the sidewalks. With Lander dead, where would he find another test patient?

Monica, unaware of the doctor's preoccupation, droned on. "An interview for a print magazine, voice only, but they want their own picture of you."

In a bored voice, Dr. Aradice completed the agenda. "And I've got rounds with the resident students at the hospital at five."

Suddenly, Dr. Aradice sat upright, placing a hand against the glass, his heart racing. A white male, with the same height, build, and basic features of his deceased patient Lander Gate, was just turning to open the door of an office building.

How is that possible?

Chapter 10
Saturday,
October 31, 2009 (1:50 p.m.)

"Stop the car!"

Monica flinched at the doctor's sudden outburst. She lifted her foot off the accelerator and punched on the brake so they both rocked forward as the car screeched to a stop. A peal of a horn from behind them preceded an over-revved engine, and a car shot by.

"I can't stop here. What's going on?"

"I just saw Lander."

"Where?"

Dr. Aradice pointed, and Monica let out a gasp at the similarity in the man who stood, angled away from them, at the building's entrance.

When another car honked, the man turned in their direction. Not Lander, but close enough to unsettle the doctor and drain all the color from Monica's face. Dr. Aradice slumped in his seat, muttering, "It's not possible."

Thankfully, he didn't see the panic splayed across Monica's face. She knew it was possible. It could have been Lander. A stone's weight of fear settled in her gut when she anticipated how the doctor would react to that news.

Then, as she twisted her head to check for pedestrians, she saw another doppelgänger. But this time there was no doubt. It was Lander. From the sidewalk, he was focused on the car and Dr. Aradice. And the fear in his eyes was unmistakable. It lasted only two heartbeats, and before the doctor looked up, Lander moved beneath an archway and disappeared.

Monica navigated the vehicle back into the traffic, and they drove in silence until she parked at Wrimo. But she remained in her seat and stared straight ahead, afraid to move. Dr. Aradice noticed and turned to look at her, his hand resting on the door handle.

"It could have been Lander," she said meekly.

"What do you mean?"

Monica swallowed hard. "That night, you told me that Lander had died." She paused before lifting her eyes to meet his. "But his body wasn't there to be processed."

"And you didn't think to tell me about this?"

"I tried. You wouldn't talk to me, so I looked into it on my own. They discharged him with some Ward C patients. It seemed to resolve the problem. I left the file for shredding as you asked."

The doctor stared at her, his small eyes pinpricks of anger. "And again, you didn't think I needed to be told this?"

A memory arose of the zigzag trail of blood she had followed. "After being unconscious for so long, he could barely walk. And imagine his state of his mind. I would have been surprised if he lasted the night." She stopped speaking, but her thoughts continued. *But I was wrong. He's alive, though he didn't look very happy when he saw you.*

Dr. Aradice fingered a key ring as he marched with Monica to the room where Lander had been treated. Until now, he had no reason to consider that his patient had survived.

"There's one way we will know for sure."

As the door opened, Dr. Aradice tuned into the sounds coming from the darkness—the low-frequency hum of medical equipment and fans. But buried in the electronic rhythm was a pattern that showed life. His hunch was correct. Lander's implant was still transmitting. His heart was still beating.

This was a problem. And there was only one solution: find Lander and silence him.

He flipped on the light, upended the rolling stool, and sat in front of the monitors. The printer had jammed on the last sheet of paper. A mass of red and black ink had congealed where the print head had repeatedly overwritten the jagged lines of the graph.

As if seeking a subtitle in a foreign language movie, his eyes settled on a small green monochrome monitor, where a tiny Pong-like cursor was spastically jumping to differing heights, pulsing out the mantra that Lander lived. A new question blistered in the doctor's brain. Why hasn't he reported me?

The doctor spun on the stool and faced Monica, who stood in the doorway. "Tell me exactly what happened."

Monica recounted the trail of blood drops that led to the closet and the mismatch between the numbers given by the orderlies and the nurse in Ward C. An unknown person had been discharged from the rear exit.

For the first time since they had returned, the doctor spoke with confidence, as if a plan were forming. "But nobody saw him. We have to be sure. The range on that transmitter is limited. He could still be in the building."

For the next hour, Dr. Aradice walked through Wrimo. The staff, accustomed to his moods, scattered upon his approach. He searched the wards, slammed through the metal clipboards, peered into rooms, and made his first-ever visit to the security office. This stop was a waste of time. "How far back do you keep the recordings?" he asked.

The security guard, who in his five years at the facility had never once spoken to Dr. Aradice, stammered a reply. "We don't have recordings. The equipment is too old." He pointed a quavering finger at a shelf stacked with VCR machines. The layers of dust on the faceplates didn't mask the blinking blue LED lights.

Monica returned to her office, dug into the computer, and confirmed that only three patients had "voluntarily" checked out of Ward C the night Lander went missing. She deepened her research to see if there was any trace of Lander anywhere else in their system. She hadn't got far when Dr. Aradice passed her desk. "My office. Now."

A few steps into his office, the doctor turned on her. She sidestepped to avoid colliding with him.

"This is major fuck-up. He's not here."

"I already told you that."

Dr. Aradice stiffened and slammed his palms down on a small conference table. It shook, which seemed to infuriate him all the more. He flipped it sideways, sending it skidding across the floor. One leg broke off as the table bounced off the radiator that ran along the bottom of the window.

"We need to find him."

Monica took a step backward.

"Don't move."

She stopped, rocking slightly between steps.

"I don't have time to deal with your stupidity. Get me

everything you can on that transmitter, check the hospitals, the police, and our own admissions desk. See if there is any trace of him."

Dr. Aradice turned and walked to the window, kicking the severed table leg toward the carnage as he passed.

Monica used that as her cue to leave.

Dr. Aradice paused his search to attend several appointments. For his media interview, he had to suppress his anxiety and appear relaxed and approachable. He wasn't confident about the photo they took. When he returned to his office, someone had removed the shattered table. All that remained was an adjustable metal foot from the broken table leg.

Monica's research on Lander's implant and transmitter was on his desk. It concluded that Lander had to be somewhere in the downtown core. While the range of the system was about five miles, the battery life of the device was in question. The doctor didn't know whether the recorded signal drops were a function of the implant's distance or a sign that the power source was failing.

There was no telling what Lander might remember. Was he aware of what had happened to him? Dr. Aradice had never imagined his clinical trials would last so long, almost a year. Lander had been resilient and survived many invasive therapies. If he died, no consequence, he had already been declared deceased. The reverse, Lander waking up, would have been a new problem, but his research was too important to stop based on a lack of a plan for that outcome.

Even if Lander recalled everything, he wouldn't be able to prove his confinement or the experimentation. Then again, the implants were traceable, and Wrimo had in fact reported

Lander as having died. That falsehood alone would be a major problem.

Why hadn't Lander already exposed him? And where would he go?

Dr. Aradice leaned across the desk and palmed a golf-ball sized brass Buddha that seemed to wander around the tabletop. It didn't have magical qualities beyond a magnetic attraction. Over time, after being handled by many nervous hands, a patina had formed on the brushed brass surface. Most of his visitors picked it up, as if rubbing its belly might bring them luck. It wasn't even that kind of Buddha. The figurine had been a secret Santa gift at one of their holiday parties from a nurse who had the misfortune of drawing his name. "It represents awakening, the core of your research," she had told him.

The nurse hadn't been wrong. The essence of his investigations was to discover a doorway into the unconscious, in particular for those in a coma. To circumvent the mechanism that closes off the body from the waking world would be a revolution in the treatment of brain trauma.

That research was now in jeopardy. Ethics. If he couldn't find Lander, all could be lost.

Monica emailed him to say she had checked local hospitals to no avail; there had been no police inquiries and no calls from the admissions desk. Lander might as well have died if not for the pulses on the monitor.

A few minutes later, the phone rang. It was Monica. "Lander's mother just came by to see you. I told her you weren't available. Most important, she was agitated, but said nothing about having seen Lander."

The doctor clenched his teeth to subdue the caustic words he was about to unleash on his de facto assistant. The enormity of the situation depleted his energy. It couldn't just be a coincidence that Lander's mother shows up within a week of her son's escape. But if she had seen Lander, she would have been more vocal. Then a more terrifying thought arose—Lander could have been with her.

A new tactic was required, and his thoughts turned to reversing his behavior to secure Monica as an ally. He couldn't fix this on his own.

He relaxed his jaw and softened his voice. "When you have a moment, can you come to my office?" He leaned back in his chair. Lander's mother, Rosalyn, could be an opportunity. At some point, Lander would contact her.

But why hasn't he already?

Chapter 11
Saturday,
October 31, 2009 (12:30 p.m.)

As he walked the streets, Lander's exhaustion translated to bouts of loitering inside doorways, where the recess created a natural shadow. It was like looking out from under a hoodie. Doorways, though, were problematic if they were busy. Lander needed to keep a safe distance from people to maintain his strength.

Passengers in cars provided Lander with continuous entertainment. Most drivers were consumed with their handheld phones. He watched people having animated conversations or singing along to the radio. The hands-free technology covered for the crazy people who talked to themselves.

Most people looked away when they saw him. He hadn't adopted the drive-by solicitation model, but they didn't know that, and no doubt thought eye contact would only encourage him to approach and ask for spare change.

A school bus waiting at a light provided a case study in sociology. The rows of school-aged faces pressed up against the glass resembled an elevated art exhibit. Each window framed a child's face, distorted into a caricature of distaste for what they saw. It was a public service message to his young audience. *Stay in school, study hard, or you might end up like me!*

It was Halloween, too, which added a surrealistic bent to the scene as people in costumes paraded by. A vampire wearing a sequined vest greeted a man and a woman in golf attire as if it was nothing unusual.

It was early afternoon when Lander stopped in front of a converted warehouse. The tall arched entryway had at one time accommodated railroad cars. Now it opened into a courtyard that was home to a café, a designer furniture store, and a real estate office.

A small brown sedan idled at the light, and the passenger sat absently nodding, as if agreeing with something the driver was saying. Then suddenly, the man jerked and took on a wide-eyed look of horror. He had seen something alarming off to Lander's right. But his face, now visible in profile, consumed Lander with dread. Lander didn't recognize the man, but a visceral hatred overwhelmed him.

Feeling a sense of immediate danger, Lander pushed back from the wall and retreated through the archway, just as the panicked man pointed to the building next door. But the woman driving directed her attention at Lander with an unmistakable look of recognition. *Who are they?*

Lander pushed up against the wall and waited a moment before peering back into the street. The car was gone, but not the disquiet.

Turning to orient himself, he discovered he had emerged into a café, where patrons in the partially filled courtyard stared at him.

Unlike the corporate chains sprinkled throughout the downtown core, the Coffee Train was an independent café. Tucked into the back corner of a restored warehouse, the acid-washed cement floors and open beams were unrefined. A sparse grouping of patio tables filled what had once been an elevated loading dock.

At street level, customers entered through a wrought-iron gate, and partially buried railroad tracks poked through the uneven asphalt, parallel smudges of rust that disappeared under a cinderblock wall. An artist had begun painting a mural from the bottom of that wall. The charcoal markings outlined an old-fashioned red caboose. So far they'd completed the black hitch, the handrail, a part of the rear door, and the big yellow light.

The onlookers' curiosity had waned. But Lander felt out of place, conspicuous, among the casual yet well-dressed patrons. He tucked in his shirt, tied his boots, and used his fingers to flatten his unruly hair. He removed his tattered gray overcoat, rolled it into a ball, and pushed it under his arm.

Katherine, the woman who put on the back-alley buffet a few nights before, approached. She was solidly built, but one would never refer to her as being overweight. Her movements had the grace of someone comfortable in their frame. Narrow but inquisitive eyes looked out over angular cheekbones. She had a skinny person's face, and Lander wondered if that observation was judgmental and unkind.

Paul had said, "Katherine is tough but fair."

As she stopped in front of him, her stern countenance was replaced by a generous smile. "You're new." She looked him up and down. "I have some rules."

"I've heard. Don't sleep, pee, or throw up in your alley, and your name is Katherine. Is that with a C or a K?"

This elicited a chuckle.

"Spelled with a 'K', and those are excellent rules, though that's a different list." She held up her hands and began counting down with her fingers. "No begging, no shopping carts, only one duffle bag or two smaller shopping bags. If you smell, you stay outside. The bathrooms are off-limits unless you buy something, and if I catch you leaving a mess, you're out for a month." She hadn't used up all ten fingers, so she dropped her hands. "We have a regular rotation of police here—at least those officers who prefer croissants and muffins to donuts—so this is not a good place if you're high or drunk."

Lander nodded and introduced himself before following her up the ramp to the counter. There was an awkward moment of silence as, once again, he was struck by the arbitrary nature of his memories—how some remained vivid while others had vanished completely. He had no sense if he had a favorite beverage.

"Can you suggest something? I have ten dollars." He paused. "I've been unwell and haven't been out much. This is all new to me."

Katherine didn't seem to find this unusual and busied herself for a couple of minutes before handing him an oversized mug and a plastic-wrapped piece of banana bread. "It's a cappuccino, no sweetener, whole milk. The perfect place to start your discovery." A smiley face had been sketched in the foam.

Lander sipped at his coffee. Getting his money's worth was more about passing time than the beverage. The condo parents and work-at-homes drifted in and out, many stopping to sit. He preferred to observe the patrons from a table where he could eavesdrop on their conversations. He inserted the ear buds he'd found in the furnace room, though he had nothing to plug them into. It enhanced the illusion that he wasn't eavesdropping.

He had seen many of the patrons during his walks. Some lived in his building; most came from the rows of new town-homes that circled the neighborhood. A few were artists who lived in converted lofts in buildings like the one that housed the Coffee Train.

He cataloged their wardrobes and routines, and reflected on their mannerisms to determine their moods. He was reluctant to draw attention to himself but eager to continue his training. At first, he limited his investigation to watching the nearest table. Despite his uncertainty about what might happen, he ventured twice among the patrons to experiment with his special skill. Just like in the park, the strength of the connection fluctuated based on proximity. He smiled as he learned more than his test subjects even knew about themselves.

Chapter 12
Sunday,
November 1, 2009 (6:30 a.m.)

The next morning, he woke comforted by the familiarity of his surroundings. Also, he felt more human, having used the furnace room bathroom to clean up the night before.

His sense of time had improved, but without a battery for the clock he'd found, or windows in his coal chute, he didn't know for sure. The same applied to the day of the week. A Saturday newspaper from the building's recycling bin the night before informed him that today was a Sunday. At least he wouldn't have to adjust to the start of daylight saving time, unlike most everyone else in North America.

Lander emerged into the alley to find it was still dark. A tint of blue in the sky between the buildings to the east suggested it was near dawn. He preferred the cover of darkness. The incident with the brown car had put an end to his carefree wanderings. He didn't know why, but his eyes darted in all directions for fear of seeing that man again.

He found himself back at the Coffee Train when it opened at seven and enjoyed a leisurely morning spending his last few dollars. Katherine arrived at around seven thirty and began supporting her staff. The line persisted until nine thirty.

As Lander contemplated leaving, Katherine sat down across from him. "I hear you're quite a storyteller. My neighbor, Alice, described meeting a man in the park. There can't be that many people named Lander. It must have been you. Alice bought a piano. Just in case you're on commission."

Lander smiled and nodded, feeling pleased with himself. "No. I'm not sure what it is I'm selling."

The two talked, and Katherine's proximity triggered a mosaic of images. Just like with Jane, a specific story surfaced, and Lander found himself back in the role of storyteller. Time fell away as a story emerged. When the telling wound down, his breathing became shallow, and he hunched over. He thought he might pass out. Katherine, concerned, suggested they take a break. She had also become distracted, as business had increased and they needed her back at the counter.

Her muted thank-you and her lingering smile confused Lander. He believed his story had caused her anguish, but they didn't have time to talk further. The café had filled up and Lander, sensitive to occupying a table without buying anything more, departed.

He stayed out of sight for the rest of the day and then headed home. In front of his building, the super was picking up trash with a long-handled set of trash tongs.

"I'm sorry; I guess that's supposed to be my job."

He acknowledged Lander with a smile. "This type of paperwork I can deal with. The real garbage is the inbox on my desk." He gestured to the window up and to his right.

An idea formed, born from his acuity to spot patterns and a near perfect memory. "If you trust me, I've got a head for numbers and organization. I could use something to do."

The two men stood close enough that Lander detected the other's presence, but he let the images stay on the periphery. Once again, the super seemed to relax when Lander was near.

"I was joking about the invoices, but what the hell. I hate office work. Follow me."

He led Lander into a first-floor room next to the front door. A studio apartment had been converted into an office with a desk, two large filing cabinets, and a seating area by the window where new tenants could sign their leases. A security monitor, divided into four sections, showed the front door, back door, and what might have been the roof. The last view gave Lander a jolt. It featured the hallway outside the laundry room.

The super showed Lander how to categorize each expense or payment with a complicated series of account numbers, or GLs, as he thought they were called. Lander scanned the reference list and, in about fifteen minutes, had the piles sorted and was completing the forms the building's owner required, tagging each document with a log line.

"This is easy." Lander showed off by increasing his speed as they worked through the pile.

The super shook his head in amazement. "That would have taken me all morning. Here's the deal. It's twenty different ways of wrong to even have you in here, but I can't pass up on your skills with this. You've got to be discreet and only come in here after hours. The basement stairs are across the hall. We'll work out a system so I know when you want to be here."

The super looked on while Lander finished the task . "You're amazing. Now, if you could get the tenant in 304 to stop playing his music so loud, I'd let you sleep in here."

Lander spent most of the afternoon asleep, then ended up in the park, pitching his storytelling routine with limited success. There were too few solitary people to focus on. He needed a way to pluck a candidate from a crowd.

Around midnight, Lander rested in the shelter of a bus stop. A man in his early forties approached; he had been drinking but did not seem intoxicated. Relaxed and in a pleasant frame of mind, he hummed a tune under this breath.

When he pulled out a wallet and extracted a bus pass, it slipped and skittered across the bench toward Lander. As he reached out, Lander grasped his wrist. A low moan escaped the man's throat, and he teared up. Immense grief washed over them both.

They were transported to a small churchyard high on a bluff overlooking the ocean. A squat ancient building, little more than a tumble of stones, sat to one side. Weathered grave markers, both wood and carved stone, leaned haphazardly. Four parishioners in seventeenth-century dress stood apart from each other with heads downcast as another man appeared to mime a graveside ceremony. A chill wind, heavy with ocean salt, slapped at their faces.

Lander's vocal cords strained with an involuntary scream. The sound of his voice bridged the two realities. In the merged experience of the vision, they stepped around the priest before turning toward the lych-gate. Lander became an unwitting passenger in their flight, disoriented by the shared point of view. He tried to extract himself, wanting only to be back at an ordinary bus stop on an ordinary Phoenix street.

Gravel slid beneath the man's feet as his speed increased. Lander refocused, blinking against the expanse of brightness that rushed up at them. They careened toward a cliff face where sea birds circled in a frenzy of flapping wings, as if goading the man to go faster. Lander's disembodied conscious-ness could not steer the man to a different course or slow him by stumbling. He couldn't even close his own eyes as they went over the edge.

His stomach lurched as weightlessness consumed them both. They were now falling, and a rocky shoreline rushed up toward them. Lander willed himself to release the man's wrist.

The instant his hand came free, Lander fell to his knees in front of the bench at the bus stop. He was convulsing, his lungs desperate for air. The man was crouched just a few feet away, half on the sidewalk, half on the road, swaying back and forth as he stared across the street.

Drawn to the sound of a diesel engine approaching, Lander lifted his head, but his view was blocked when the man leaped to his feet and bolted into the path of the speeding truck.

A screech of tires preceded a sickening, bone-crushing impact. Lander fell sideways to the ground, and from this viewpoint he saw the man's mutilated body, inert and twisted like a wrung-out towel, the head arched at an impossible angle, the neck broken. He was dead.

A truck door opened, and footsteps approached. He had to get out of there. Still gasping for breath, he dragged himself crab-like into the shadow of a doorway, where he hid until it was safe to sneak away.

Lander couldn't shake his complicity in the man's death. What he'd done, forcing his power on the other man, was dangerous and irresponsible.

Now more than ever, he feared contact with people.

The stories that played out in his mind, he knew, were best explained as scenes from a person's past life, in particular the moment of death. Jane's story was of passing in a peaceful farmhouse. The woman at the shelter had, at some point, burned to death, and this likely wasn't Paul's first incarnation as an alcoholic.

He analyzed the physical quality of what happened. When he got within a foot of another person, a pinprick of pain in his gut signaled a descent into the shared experience. Translucent images would then scroll through Lander's mind, and a story manifested as a flickering slideshow.

But this was not meant to be a spectator sport. With even a

fingertip on bare skin, the sensation was immediate. Both Lander and the target were consumed by a surreal, virtual reality that engulfed all the senses except for one—sound. Lander tried to dismiss the memory of skin melting away by fire. And during his encounter with the unhappy couple in the park, he had brushed away an unpleasant image, but now, in sickening detail, he relived a knife edge cutting into flesh.

There was a benefit to being unhoused: people naturally gave him a wide berth. Comfort zones—those imaginary circle defining everyone's personal space—expanded in the presence of the unpleasant. The raiment of a homeless person and the geography of a sidewalk provided exponential growth to this protected sphere. Lander was also realistic. Avoidance, even within his own social circle, was also the safest route. Some members of his adopted street community were prone to violence, and the preponderance of mental illness created unpredictable and often volatile situations.

How was he going to live with this?

Chapter 13
Monday,
November 2, 2009 (8:55 a.m.)

On Monday morning, Lander abandoned the line for breakfast when he saw Jane pacing and looking around. It wasn't a stretch to imagine that she was looking for him.

An hour and a half later, all it took was the discovery of an abandoned boxed lunch on the steps of a building's rear entrance to distract him. He had just opened a bag of chips and was contemplating the pickle when Jane gripped his shoulder.

"Take me to my happy place," she breathed into his ear.

It was a stark reminder that for most people, a simple touch might be unremarkable, but for Lander, the results were devastating.

The effect of her touch was instantaneous and, unfortunately, predictable. Jane, like the others, collapsed the instant her fingers grazed his skin. With no choice but to let her fall against him, she dropped with only a slight bump onto the step. He slipped a protective hand behind her head as she slumped into the doorway.

Lander knew now that fainting wasn't the only complication when Jane—or anyone—got too close to him. In most situations, he unwittingly caused the other intense pain. Jane's

69

response differed from the others in that she wanted to be near him so he could transport her into a blissful state. This gave Lander hope he wasn't a monster.

The prolonged connection with Jane in the farmhouse threatened to consume him. Lander closed his eyes and counted to three to bring himself back to the present. His next breath, less ragged, reminded him his skill was improving, but it still drained him and he needed to get away.

He eyed the boxed lunch, which only a moment ago had been his lucky find. It had fallen underfoot and was now mashed into the asphalt of the laneway.

Taking care not to break their link, Lander slid his hand from Jane's arm to her shoulder. If she were to awaken, she would be angry at him for not staying with her. He looked at her for the first time. She must have had a rough few days. A two-day-old bruise, now a yellow smear across her cheekbone, could have been from a fall or the back of someone's hand. Her clothes, already mismatched scraps from donation bins, were filthy and torn. The serenity of her smile was incongruent with her battered appearance.

After a few minutes, Jane had either fallen asleep or passed out, and Lander moved away. A few steps were all he managed before a sharp pain pierced his left temple. He leaned over and dry heaved until his eyes wept. He lifted one hand to his chest as if a self-directed heart massage might increase his circulation. With the other hand, reached out like a punter on a river, poling himself slowly along the wall. When he tried to take a deeper breath, his lungs clenched, throwing him into a fit of shallow coughs.

Behind him, Jane stirred. He forced himself to keep moving.

He stopped just before emerging onto the street. Someone familiar was approaching. He'd seen the man more than once the previous week, and always at the same time. A glance at a clock through a bank window confirmed that something about his schedule had changed. Was he late?

Lander, though still weak from his encounter with Jane, had an idea. He had to act quickly and cleared his throat to gain the man's attention.

"You can think of it as being in two times at the same place," he said.

The man was in his late twenties, and he wore a light summer sport coat and pleated linen pants. He stopped to identify the source of the voice. Lander waited. enjoying the man's confusion and using the time to plan his next move. He was getting better at reading people, which resulted in bigger handouts. His mouth moistened as he imagined the melted cheese on a warm croissant that might be in his immediate future.

Lander stepped out from the shadow of the alley and squinted in the sudden brightness, his grizzled face puckering as his eyes adjusted. In a nervous tic, he pinched and pulled on his gray-speckled beard with his thumb and index finger. The gesture pulled open his jaw like a ventriloquist's dummy to reveal a wide, yellow-toothed smile.

The man grew cautious and shifted the shoulder strap of his computer case closer to his body, sidestepping toward the curb and away from Lander, who now leaned against the masonry of the building's corner. "Pardon, what'd you say?"

"I imagine you're wishing you'd pretended not to hear me." Not expecting a response, Lander continued. "I thought I was being clever—instead of two places at the same time, two times at . . . I guess they didn't warn you when you checked in at your hotel."

The man pressed his palms against his linen pants, wiping away the sweat. Lander didn't want to scare him and had underestimated how uncomfortable he would become.

Although they'd never spoken, he had seen the man on two previous mornings, which had created a false sense of familiarity.

The two men eyed each other, suspended in the street noise on an empty sidewalk.

"I'm Lander. Anyway, it's funny. Your hotel installed new high-tech radios. But they forgot to turn off the automatic program that resets the clocks from daylight saving time. All the guests woke up yesterday to a blue display telling them it was an hour earlier than it actually was." The man, to his credit, was at least trying to follow the logic.

"Everywhere else in the country, except Arizona and Hawaii, daylight saving time ended yesterday at 1:00 a.m. The clock in your room doesn't know it's in Arizona. We don't change, and you don't wear a watch. I'm guessing you haven't looked at your phone."

Like a puppet, the man glanced at his empty wrist and then dug into his pocket for his phone. As he angled the screen away from the morning sun, the young man frowned. Any second now, he would figure it out.

"Shit. I went home for the weekend and got in late last night and didn't notice."

"I bet if you complain, you'll get a fruit basket or something."

The man pursed his lips. "How did you know I would be late?"

Lander smiled; he enjoyed being one step ahead. "This is becoming my corner. Last week, you would pass this spot about eight fifteen. When you weren't rushing this morning—at nine fifteen—I figured you had the wrong time. Now, Mr. Peller, don't you think you'd better be going? You're late!"

The man stiffened. "Look, dude, this isn't cool. You know my routine. You know my name. Are you stalking me?"

Lander displayed his palms in a calming gesture. "No. I'm just an observer. In my line of work, I have lots of time to watch the world go by. Just like you, I have my routines. I didn't know your name until just now." Lander shifted his focus to the man's computer case while raising his eyebrows. Tracing his gaze, Andrew Peller also looked down. His name was on the laminated business card attached to the handle.

"Andrew, Andrew Peller. Thanks for straightening me out."

"One more thing," Lander began. "It may exceed eighty degrees later today, but here in Phoenix, we stop wearing linen after Labor Day."

Andrew laughed and walked away. "I'll be seeing you, or you'll be seeing me first." He walked forward, but his steps faltered before stopping. Without turning, he dug into his pockets. Lander stepped up behind him, but not too close. Building on their rapport, he decided to push this timid young man one step further. If he could get close enough, Lander was confident there would be an anthology of past life stories to sift through. He needed to choose an experience relevant to his present life, but one traumatic enough to capture his attention.

Andrew turned and reached out, placing a few crumpled bills in Lander's palm. "Go have a nice breakfast."

"Thank you." On these last words, but before Andrew withdrew his arm, he let their hands touch. Lander pushed past the sensation in his gut, anticipating what Andrew might experience. First, his wrist would tingle and his mind would become foggy. It was then Lander's job to filter the pain, emotional or physical, so as to not overwhelm him. He had to be in control to prevent an unpredictable reaction, like the chilling experience of the night before.

The story he chose, now consuming both of them, focused on a broken right arm and shattered collarbone. Lander allowed a modicum of the pain to seep into his subject. Andrew grimaced, and his briefcase slid off his shoulder and bumped onto the ground. He massaged his neck above his right collarbone.

"Looks like that shoulder's bothering you."

Andrew shook his head and hesitated before responding. Lander counted on him seeing past his bedraggled appearance and confiding in him.

"It often aches, but it's never this painful."

"That doesn't surprise me," Lander whispered.

A look of uncertainty flashed across Andrew's face. "I gotta run," he stuttered, twisting to grab his case with his left hand as he departed.

A risky but successful test. Lander watched Andrew walk away before glancing down the alley. The deep shadows prevented him from seeing if Jane was still asleep. Exhausted from two interactions in a brief time span, he walked slowly in the same direction as Andrew.

He was buoyed that his sleight of hand had worked. As with the woman in the park, he'd been able to read a specific memory. But it seemed a minor victory in the face of the over-whelming flood of questions that reminded him how little he understood his condition.

These encounters were as close as he ever got to people; brief interactions that left him empty. While he couldn't remember, Lander sensed that he'd been a loner all his life. He wanted that to change.

He paused at the midpoint of each block to catch his breath and let his heart rate settle. Although he was only thirty-six, he felt ancient. To avoid getting close to anyone, Lander needed to navigate the world like he was in an Atari video game where people were land mines. Thankfully, the side-walks en route to the Coffee Train were nearly deserted.

Lander was depleted and needed the isolation to regain his strength.

At the Coffee Train, he hovered just inside the doorway. The pungent aroma of coffee and bakery ovens made his emptiness more acute.

Katherine looked up. "Good morning, Lander. The usual?"

"No, today I'm going to splurge. A chai latte and one of those." He pointed at a loaded breakfast burrito steaming on a plate for another customer. "And please put the latte in a mug. I hate paper cups."

A block away, on the eighteenth floor, Andrew Peller entered the boardroom late. Thankfully, the door was silent , but there was no stopping the bright hallway light from washing across his associates and disturbing the presentation. A few of his colleagues looked up, indignant, but his boss said nothing.

Andrew settled in the shadows at the back. The charts and graphs blurred together as a voice droned from a speakerphone in the middle of the conference table. The news wasn't good. Their vice president threatened reorganization if the division's performance didn't improve. Andrew, a Canadian who lived in Vancouver, handled the western states and provinces.

Andrew ran his hand up and down his arm, squeezing the shoulder, trying to pinpoint where the pain had come from and wondering why it had gone away. There had been the briefest moment, out on the street with that strange man, when he'd experienced a flash of memory of his arm in a sling. The phantom sensation, of a twisted knot pressing against the opposite collarbone, lingered. Andrew had never hurt his arm and couldn't remember ever wearing a sling.

The man, Lander, seemed harmless enough, but an act of

kindness often disabled his common sense, making him gullible. Was he being set up? Was his hotel room being robbed right now? He slid his hand into the front pocket of his briefcase and rested his fingers on his dog-eared Canadian passport and hotel room key card. Maybe it was just a one-shot deal to get money for breakfast. He had given him twenty dollars. Either way, Lander had done something to him, and his curiosity was now piqued.

Andrew's musings were interrupted. "Andrew! Speak up, damn it! What's your update for the west coast?"

Chapter 14
Monday,
November 2, 2009 (9:35 a.m.)

L ander didn't want his back exposed when he was sitting, so he drifted to a table at the end of a row, where a railing and a wall prevented him from accidentally getting too close to anyone. Plus, there was less risk of another ambush from Jane. Lander sat, watching the customers come and go. He interlocked his fingers and pulled the oversized ceramic bowl into his palms, enjoying the lingering warmth of his latte.

He reached into a pocket for his deck of cards but came up empty. Frustrated, he remembered leaving them in the laundry room.

A woman who looked like a grad student approached the entry ramp. When he'd seen her the other day, she'd had old library books stuffed in her bag. This intrigued him. He tried to get a look at her computer screen, but the split-screen blocks of text were too small. He wondered what she was studying.

Today, she carried her computer, a water bottle, and a stack —at least half a ream—of old yellow typewriter paper in a shallow box without a lid. As she passed Lander's table, a whip of wind captured the top sheets, flipping them out of the box. She fumbled, almost dropping the water bottle, as the sheets cascaded onto the railing, some falling onto Lander's table, others at his feet and onto the ramp. He smiled at her and began picking up the pages, but his hand brushed against hers when they both reached under the table for the same piece. That was all that was needed. His mind filled with images of confinement and suffocation. They were trapped in the cabin of a small boat as it filled with water. Lander cursed himself for not being more careful.

A muffled scream caught in the woman's throat. Gasping for breath, she dropped to her to her knees, one hand clutching her chest and the other struggling to prevent the remaining stack of paper from falling to the floor. Lander stepped back just as another patron rushed over and began helping her. By then, Katherine had appeared at the top of the ramp and was looking suspiciously at him. The helpful patron escorted the young woman inside and Lander saw others fussing over her as the barista gathered up the remaining pages. "I'm fine," she kept repeating. "I'm new to the area and must be dehydrated."

Back in his seat, Lander caught glimpses of her each time the big sliding door rolled back across the steel track. When she made a trip to the restroom, Lander slipped through the door and over to her table. He put a sheet that had been missed, the title page, on top of the stack. When she returned, she noticed and looked around. Although he caught only a brief glimpse of her as the door rolled shut, Lander imagined that she'd smiled at him.

The paper had borne the title "Methodology for Post-Clinical Observation and Treatment of Mental Illness," a PhD presentation from September 1954. It seemed to Lander an unusual thing to be studying in its original manuscript form. Even more interesting, the author's name, Dr. Warner Lampkin, sounded somehow familiar.

That flash of recognition intrigued him. Lander didn't have

any memories prior to waking in the alley, but this was coming out of the darkness of *his* mind, not someone else's.

Now that they had a connection, he wanted more time to study her. But to stay, he needed to buy something else. Lander used a side door to avoid walking past her table. At the counter, he stood back and waited for the line to dissipate, hoping that Katherine had forgotten about the incident on the entry ramp. She looked up, and with surprising kindness in her eyes, said, "Thanks for helping Cassandra when she fell."

Lander responded with two shallow nods and a close-lipped smile, wanting to change the topic but awash with a sense of excitement at discovering the woman's name.

"I have three dollars I can spend." He looked at the crumpled bills in his hand. "I need to save some money for laundry." This would appeal to her compassion. "I would like to remain in your fine establishment a little longer. What would you suggest?"

"Why do you come here? I'm more expensive than anyone else in the area."

Lander wasn't sure if she expected an answer. "I don't know what normal is supposed to feel like, but sitting here, drinking from ceramic mugs, I just have a sense that something good might happen."

"You've been coming in every day now," she said as she scanned the serving area. Two people stood ready to order, and her staff was busy plating up breakfast items and steaming lattes. "You seem like a good sort. You're not strung out on drugs; nothing has gone missing when you're around. I don't know your story, even though you seem to know mine... Probably better that way. Stay there."

As he waited, Lander moved closer to the counter, where a dried flower arrangement included stalks of lavender. A flashback from Jane's repeating dream gave him an idea. A surreptitious glance confirmed that neither the staff nor Katherine was watching. So he pulled three of the sprigs from the tied bundle, rolled them in a paper napkin, and stuffed them into his pocket.

Katherine returned with a steaming cup of coffee and a chocolate croissant. The pastry had been warmed, and the chocolate oozed, puddling on the edge of the plate.

"Don't expect me to make a habit out of this," she said playfully, waving off his money. "Get back to your table and leave me alone."

The fresh-baked croissant smelled heavenly, and, with a jaunty bounce, he turned on his heel to go back outside. As he did, he collided with Cassandra. The croissant slid forward off the plate, and the chocolate-tipped end mashed up against her right breast. She wore a pale gray satin shirt, tucked in and pulled tight, and the top two buttons were undone. Lander froze, unable not to stare at the chocolate smudge.

At that distance, someone hypersensitive might have detected her heat, or the pheromones, but Lander shared something altogether different. His eyes filled with tears, and the weightlessness of vertigo corrupted his ability to respond. A sexually charged memory—not one of his own—engulfed him.

Chapter 15
Monday,
November 2, 2009, (9:45 a.m.)

I t all transpired in seconds. Lander clamped his mouth shut and fell back a step. He frantically shuffled the images that careened through his mind to keep any single memory from coalescing. He was trying to avoid the suffocation sequence, but he wanted to bookmark the memory where Cassandra was steeped in trust and passion. It seemed important.

If they had known each other, it might have been comedic. Instead, he stood awaiting her certain fury at his clumsiness. When she didn't say anything, he felt more ridiculous with every second. He held up the errant croissant, now back in the middle of the plate, as if to serve her or create a matching stain on the other side. "I'm, I'm... really sorry," Lander stammered.

Up close, her hazel eyes sparkled, and the tip of her tongue darted across bleached white teeth. Lander guessed she was in her thirties. She kept her body trim, and her skin was smooth. A red cloth-covered elastic pulled her thick, cinnamon-brown hair back into a short ponytail.

She looked up from the damage to her shirt. "It's okay. Pretty funny, actually."

As she made light of the situation, Lander reflected sadly

on the loneliness that permeated his life. Over the last week, except for his test cases, he had dealt with his curse by avoiding people. It was exhausting to spend every living moment in fear of getting too near to someone.

Katherine interrupted his reverie. "Lander, what have you done? Shit! Leave her alone. Get out of here." She made a dismissive gesture with her hand before turning back to the woman. "I'm sorry," she said. "Let me find a cloth for you."

"It's no problem. It was an accident; he was very sweet about it. I will take you up on the cloth, though." The two women walked away toward the restroom.

Lander returned to the patio and shifted his chair so he could watch for Cassandra through the large picture window. She returned to her table wearing a black cardigan. A few minutes later, the sliding door opened and Cassandra approached.

"She shouldn't have yelled at you." Stopping in front of him, she lowered her briefcase onto the chair and slid the manuscript box to the center of the table. "Do you mind if I sit?" Lander leaned back. She wasn't going to wait for his answer.

"I've seen you before; thanks for helping me pick up the papers." She paused as if evaluating Lander, before an imperceptible nod confirmed that she'd made a decision. "Can we agree to be straight with each other? I'm a very direct person. Katherine likes you. I also want to. But be warned: I don't have much of a filter once I decide to speak to someone."

"You don't normally talk to people?"

"No. Acquaintances would describe me as quiet. They misinterpret it as being shy. Do you come here a lot, or just the days I am here?"

"Depends on my economic circumstances, which can change hourly."

"Fair enough. I should have thought of that. Would you agree we both like people-watching? Cappuccino voyeurs." Her friendly intonation informed him this was a rhetorical question. "It's unusual, the two of us meeting this way, but no more bizarre than when I collapsed. That wasn't dehydration."

She paused, and Lander worried he was supposed to speak. "I'm Sandra." She twisted her mouth as if tasting something bitter. "Actually, it's Cassandra, but I thought I'd make a clean start in this new town." Lander tensed in fear of the requisite introductory handshake. Thankfully, her hands were occupied with removing her computer from its case.

"What difference is a name going to make?"

"I think it matters a lot. Don't you agree? *Sandra* suggests a simpler, more easygoing person. Consider when Richard becomes Rick, Stephen Steve, or Ed becomes Bud. Strike that last one. That's old-school, and I never understood it. Lander. What kind of name is that?"

"How do you know my name?"

"Katherine said it." She finished unpacking her briefcase and opened the computer.

Lander looked down, embarrassed that her questions were getting personal. "I don't know—maybe I was born on the day of a moon landing."

"That's easy enough to check," she said, pointing at the computer that had just flashed on. She took a moment, looking around with the power cord in her hand and then, resigned to working on battery, she coiled the cord around her wrist before stuffing it back into the case.

"I'm sorry about your shirt."

"Don't be. It'll wash out." With that, she undid the tie on her sweater and opened it as if to show no harm done. The blouse, still wet, clung to her breast, the nipple imprint visible with a halo through the damp translucent material.

83

Lander dropped his head, and Cassandra snapped the sweater closed.

"I'm sorry. That wasn't very discreet." She retied the sweater and leaned back, the bistro chair creaking with the shift in her weight. "I'm no prude, and I don't have issues with my body, at least not from the neck down. I'm like one of those picture games for kids, a triptych of cards where you can swap out the head, body, and feet with different people or animals." She mimed with her hands, placing three cards on the table, and pointed her finger where the head should be. "But always horse-face. I've a good figure and my hands and feet are nice. I guess I only drew one bad card." She stopped and redirected her attention to her computer, where she typed a login sequence.

At that moment, Katherine approached with a multi-layered latte in a tall glass mug and a bran muffin on a small plate. "I see you two made up." In a partial whisper loud enough for Cassandra to hear, she leaned toward Lander with a warning. "You behave."

Steam rose when Cassandra used a knife to break open the heated muffin. She opened a foil-wrapped piece of butter and the warm knife melted into it.

Lander studied the butter as it transformed. "Butter face," he whispered.

Cassandra looked at him, eyebrows raised.

"It's another phrase, similar to horse face. Everything about her is hot *but her face*. Butter face."

Cassandra's gaze dropped. Lander cursed under his breath and wished he hadn't said it. *Stupid.* In a conventional sense, Cassandra wouldn't be judged as being pretty. Some people would fixate on the sharp bridge of her nose or protruding brow. Lander's appreciation went deeper, intrigued by her eyes and how she carries herself.

She broke off a piece of muffin and placed it on her tongue. Her mouth went wide as she blew across the heated morsel. She slid the plate toward him, but he didn't take the offer; they then sat in awkward silence. It was both refreshing and scary for him. He didn't want the personal questions to resume and reveal his amnesia. A deflection to a different topic was in order.

"Are you studying mental illness?"

She stopped typing and looked up at him. "No, not really. I have a two-year contract to study how patients with mental illness are treated. Not the treatments, but what happens after they're discharged. Precious few get better, though some can manage their situation. She tapped her finger on the loose-leaf manuscript. "This is a good example. I stumbled on a Dr. Lampkin essay on this exact topic in a journal from the late 1960s. He had great ideas but wasn't taken seriously. He'd been treated for mental illness himself and, against huge odds, got out of the system, attended medical school, and received both his MD and a PhD. I tracked down his granddaughter, who lives in Rochester, and she let me go through a box of his notes. His doctoral thesis is where it all began. Unfortunately, most of his work has been lost. The daughter said he'd also published a book, but no one in the family had a copy. I haven't been able to find it either."

Lander had a mental flash of Dr. Lampkin's name on the spine of a book. Though it was a poorly defined memory, he wanted to be helpful. "I have an excellent memory for names, and I've seen that book somewhere. I'll try to remember where."

A clink of mugs drew both of their attention to a nearby table where Katherine was clearing dishes. "She acts as if she doesn't care for you much, but behind the facade, I have a hunch she likes you."

"Katherine is a good person, but doesn't really know me—she knows my kind."

"And what kind is that? The recent down-and-out who cling to their past lives by sitting in a café drinking overpriced coffee?"

Lander hesitated; her use of the phrase "past lives" disarmed him. If only she knew that seeing everyone else's past lives didn't compensate for losing his own memory. "Something like that, I guess." Lander picked up his own cup and inhaled the lingering vapors. He'd always liked the aroma more than the taste. "Is your research connected to the Wrimo Hospital?" He hoped the question came out flat, as if he were making casual conversation. "I've heard they treat mental illness."

"I don't know much about it. Five years ago, they spent big money on a renovation. I haven't come across any papers from their team for my research. Only one doctor is high-profile—he's now a bestselling author. They have a base of wealthy patients, but they must take welfare cases because they show up on a lot of government funding rolls. Why do you ask?"

It was time for another deflection. "No reason. It's the only connection between this neighborhood and your topic. I thought you might work there."

"No. I'm a contract researcher. I'm working for a medical think tank in Washington. My foundation has a partner that intends to lobby government to make changes. My job is to summarize all the ideas out there." She pinched off another piece of the muffin and idly placed it in her mouth.

"We were going to check on the moon landing dates to see if that's the origin of your name." She tapped on the keyboard and from the side angle, Lander could see the NASA logo come up on the screen. She looked up and studied his face. Lander wanted to look away, but he held her gaze. She then shook her head. "I don't mean to be rude, but I can't figure out how old you are. The first landing was in July 1969 and the program ended in 1974." Cassandra considered him for a moment. "You could fall in that range. I'd peg you as early forties."

"I guess that puts things in perspective. A little on the high side—I'm thirty-six." He only knew this because of the hospital wristband.

Cassandra counted off on her fingers, stopping at nine. "Nine months prior to Apollo 17, the last of the missions." She leaned in, her finger tracing along the screen. "It was the only night launch. Perhaps the night you were conceived?"

She twisted in her chair and rested her palms on the tops of her thighs. A loose strand of hair fell forward, blocking her right eye. She peered out from under her thick brow and then tucked the wayward hair behind her ear as their eyes locked. Lander didn't want to appear intimidated; he wanted her to break the stare. In seconds, he failed when he shifted his focus to a now-empty mug.

"Are you shy or embarrassed?" she asked, once again not expecting him to answer. "I think you're uncomfortable in social situations. A lack of practice. Don't worry, I won't ask for all of your secrets. Just one."

A flashback of a different interrogation consumed Lander. For a brief second, he was at a small table in a clinically white room. Instead of Cassandra, it was the man he'd seen in the car, wearing a dark suit and lab coat, sitting across from him in a relaxed pose, leaning back, legs outstretched. He was chewing on the end of a pen and nodding, though Lander had no sense he had said anything. Lander probed the dissolving vision, grasping at the fleeting memory, wanting more.

Cassandra leaned forward. "You okay? It was like you were suddenly gone."

"I have memory issues, but just then, I remembered something." Like his memory of Lampkin's book, these images had been from *his* past, and not a past life. This was both exciting and unsettling. Up to that moment, he'd had no memories. Regaining his composure, he looked back at Cassandra. "You said you only wanted to discuss *one* of my secrets. Which one?"

"Why did I suffocate when you touched me?"

Chapter 16
Monday,
November 2, 2009 (9:55 a.m.)

Cassandra looked straight at him with an air of expectation before she repeated the question. "Why did I suffocate when you touched me?"

Lander adjusted his feet, drawing his knees up to increase his distance from Cassandra's painted toenails. She rested her elbows on the table and steepled her fingers. Every second he hesitated made him appear guiltier.

"Why do you think I had anything to do with you collapsing?"

"Not sure. It all happened so fast. In my panic, I looked to you for help, and you weren't surprised that something was happening. You were caught up in it as well." Cassandra leaned forward, her intensity growing. "Tell me what you saw." Cassandra stopped, and took a breath to calm herself. "I'm sorry. I'm not being very sensitive, but I need to know more."

Lander wanted to flee. His leg bounced. He fidgeted, and shifted erratically as he looked around. She wanted too much, too fast. His voice wavered when he finally spoke. "I don't know anything about why this happens. I've already said enough and need to go."

As Lander made to stand up, Cassandra reached to stop him. Desperate to avoid contact, he jerked away and stumbled. The chair fell backward onto the concrete and bounced with a jarring steel clang. From across the patio, Katherine looked up.

Lander fumbled to upright the toppled chair. "I'm sorry. I can't talk about it." He dodged Katherine, shuffling along the railing to the ramp and wishing he could jump down and sprint for the exit. He reached up and grabbed at his heart, a useless response when his breathing became labored. At the bottom, he heard Cassandra call out again, but he didn't stop. At the street entrance, a diesel truck pulling away from the corner drowned out her voice.

———

Cassandra's frustrated gaze lingered on the archway through which Lander had just departed. She'd pushed too hard.

Katharine approached her table. "Perhaps I was wrong, warning you against Lander. It seems he was the one who needed to get away."

"I asked some personal questions," Cassandra said, tracing her finger across the track pad on her computer to keep it from going into standby mode.

"I don't make a habit of getting involved in my customers' affairs. But there's something unique about Lander. Nobody belongs on the street, of course, but he *really* doesn't. And he isn't some social worker's lab rat."

Cassandra sat up straight. "Is that what you think I am? I may have an agenda, but I will not take advantage of his situation. I feel a connection with him. You sense it, too. I'm betting you also want to know more." Cassandra forced herself to take a sip from her latte before saying something she might regret. "I may not be as patient as you are, or as skilled socially. And

I'm unsure what I can offer him in return, but I don't use people. In fact, the reverse—being used—is rather my specialty."

Cassandra slumped back into the chair, the fight leaking out of her. "It's like he's out of sync. This is not his place, and it's not his time either. Do you get that feeling with him?" Cassandra didn't give Katherine the space to respond. "I have this sense I've known him before, and that he has something important to tell me."

Katherine, nodding in agreement, lowered herself into the chair Lander had abandoned. She smoothed out her apron, tracing the embroidery of the café's logo: a stylized train, like a coffee can, emerging from a tunnel. "Have you ever heard the expression 'old soul'? Sometimes he seems ancient. One of my customers says he's a wonderful storyteller. It provides him with a few dollars. But don't be fooled by the strength of his voice. He is physically a wreck. I suspect heart or lung disease —he is easily winded by any exertion."

"I live across from the park, and I've seen him as well. Uncanny how he makes a story so personal. Has he told you any?"

"Just the other day. It was like he could sense exactly what was on my mind," Katherine replied. She paused.

Cassandra took this as her cue. "Please, go on."

"It was on the anniversary of my mother's death. Lander had no way of knowing about that. He told me a story set around the turn of the century, about a farmer's wife. I quickly realized that he was telling a story steeped in the lore of my family. The woman in the story, my great-grandmother, had a premonition that her mother was in trouble. She rode for an hour to the next village, then farther up into the mountains, to the homestead where she had grown up. Her mother had been thrown from her horse. Internally bleeding, she was dying."

Katherine paused for a moment and glanced around, like she was nervous to be overheard.

"Despite her injuries and her isolation, the mother remained calm, confident she wouldn't die alone. When her daughter found her, she pleaded with her not to judge her father harshly in death. The girl's father, who had died mysteriously the year before, had been a scoundrel, and her mother had hidden his lies from her and everyone in the community. With her dying breath, she told her daughter where they had hidden money and urged her to leave. 'Get away, do something good, never come back.'" When Katherine swallowed hard to moisten her throat, Cassandra gently slid her latte across the table. Katherine took a shallow sip before continuing.

"The money became the family's second great mystery. By the standards of the day, it was a huge amount. More than a typical homestead family could have accumulated in five lifetimes. The daughter and her husband wondered where it had come from but didn't ask too many questions. A week after the mother's funeral, they told the neighbors they were heading east to make a fresh start. But they went west, changed their name, and started a new life. Even today, there is a prosperous shelter and community program in New Mexico that bears our adopted family name."

Katherine looked down. Her voice cracked a little. "Another generation later, my mother continued the legacy, the third in our family to run the foundation. My sister took over after my mother died."

"How did Lander know your family's story?"

"I don't understand it either. It started out as just a story, but he added such vibrant details. His version filled in holes and revealed answers to questions, information I may have forgotten or perhaps never knew. Through his words, I relived the experience of my great-grandmother watching her mother die. But after he told the story, Lander realized he had upset me." Katherine looked up, and Cassandra met her gaze, opening the door to a new level of trust between them.

"As soon as I was old enough, I left home. I wanted nothing to do with the family charity. I betrayed my forbears by not continuing on the path of compassion. Lander assured me—as if he could look into the minds of my ancestors—that they would have approved. There are many paths to help people, he said, and I had made the right decision." She shook her head as if trying to shake the memory free. "I was thirsty when the story ended. We both seemed exhausted. "Afterward, he became pensive. When I pressed him for what he was thinking, all he would say was that he didn't understand."

Katherine rotated the handle of their shared mug, and Cassandra pulled it toward her.

"Eventually, he told me it was rare to be connected in this way to my family. I didn't understand what that meant. What way? Why wouldn't I be connected? After that, he wouldn't elaborate."

Both women sat for a moment in silence before Cassandra spoke. "How does he know things? Before today, I was curious about him. But now I want to gain his trust. I think he can help me understand things. It may be crazy, but he might have explained why I'm so terrified of swimming."

Chapter 17
Monday,
November 2, 2009 (2:05 p.m.)

Frustration from his morning meeting with Cassandra still churned inside Lander, making him restless. The dustiness of his small room irritated his throat. The closeness of the grimy brick walls, once comforting, was now oppressive.

What had started out as a nice breakfast had resulted in an encounter that had brought him closer to a person than he could remember. He could only remember back a week, but this interaction had been different. It wasn't a one-sided act of storytelling. His normal audience was understandably selfish. In a strange way, this also applied to the super. They were being entertained. It was about them. They didn't inquire about Lander. With Cassandra, there had been a genuine conversation. The tiniest building block of a relationship.

To shake off his mood, Lander pushed himself through the hatchway to the basement and headed to the super's office. His pretend office job would be a welcome distraction. He didn't know why, but the system made sense to him. The fifty-odd expense categories and their associated numbers were easy to memorize. He would then complete the forms and put the information into a computer, then compile a mental catalog of existing vendors versus new ones. These, of course, required more forms.

Lander was halfway through the most current pile of receipts when the super wandered in.

"Here are a few new ones. Don't forget it's month end. I need to mail October by tomorrow."

"It's already finished." Lander pointed at the wire mesh out-basket on the filing cabinet by the door.

"Thanks." The super paused for a moment; Lander watched him shift his stance and avoid eye contact. Confrontation wasn't the man's strong point. He would spend an hour fixing a broken pump with a safety pin, a rubber band, and a magnet, but if he had to talk to a tenant about delinquent rent or being too noisy, he became stressed. "Look, Lander, it's fabulous that you handle all this for me, but you can't be in here during the day. I could get in trouble. Worse, you might lose your room. Same applies if any of the tenants find you in here."

Lander sighed; it was his day to be pushed around. "Whatever. I'll see you later."

"Hey, don't be like that. I want to keep helping you. I really do."

Lander shuffled back down the corridor, ignoring the super's voice as it trailed off and letting himself out the back door into the alleyway.

A radio playing in a shop window celebrated the unusually warm weather: ninety-five degrees for a November day. Lander didn't know where he'd grown up—but he hoped it was somewhere else. The weather in Phoenix wasn't in keeping with the natural order of things. One hundred days above one hundred, that same radio voice had said of the previous summer.

Lander walked to the end of the block before he noticed he hadn't stopped to catch his breath. Perhaps he was getting stronger. He inhaled, relishing the benefit of his expanding lungs. Maybe it was the proper breakfast and a nap. Unfortunately, the problem with eating was that it made him want to eat again. On Mondays, the Catholic church served a light dinner. It wasn't for two hours, so Lander distracted himself by learning more about Cassandra.

At least now he had a first name. Her building was a long city block south of the Coffee Train, and Lander walked past it multiple times every day. The first time he'd seen Cassandra was a week ago, when she had been coming out of it. It was a steel and glass structure of indeterminate height. The entry, set back from the corner, opened into a small lobby with a security desk and a seating area.

For a newer building, it had an old-style reader board that listed only last names and first initials. As he scanned the register, a security guard glowered at him. Lander recognized him. He typically worked the overnight shift. After a couple of minutes, when Lander hadn't left, he rose and approached the vestibule. Lander doubted he would be very helpful. Then he saw a clue. Each name was typed on a label. But each morning, the eastern exposure caught the directory, and the newer labels were much darker. Lander returned to the top of the list and began a rapid scan. The names flitted past. The handle clicked as the door opened. Then he found a new name. Boyes, T. No good, he thought.

"Hey," the security guard bellowed. "Move on. Nothing on that list that matters to you."

There was a second name, Morada, S. The S made him pause. Cassandra had said she now went by the name Sandra. Buzzer thirty-one.

"I'm going. I have what I need." He stopped. "Actually, I do have a question. What's the buzzer number for the building manager?"

"You've got no business here."

"I don't think that's for you to judge. I have some information on the vandalism in the parking lot."

"What vandalism in the parking lot?"

Lander had him now. He looked him in the eye before continuing. "Oh, that's not good. You've just switched to days, haven't you? Maybe it happened on your watch." The man shifted his weight, expecting Lander to continue. "When you do your rounds, check out the cars along the north wall. A little dust, and it doesn't take a rocket scientist to know who doesn't use their car very often. Could be a while before an owner reports a theft."

"You stay right there. I'm calling the police."

"Go ahead. They'll thank me and ask why I didn't phone the tips number. Everyone will then question how thorough you are. Perhaps if you spent a little less time whacking off to those porn magazines..."

This last gambit was pure speculation, but what else would a twenty-something man be doing to pass the hours? The man's denial went limp, confirming Lander's conjecture. The vandalism story was a spark of an idea that had only just occurred to him. He rapidly pieced the facts together. Three men, whom Paul, at one of their breakfasts together, had described as the Dunk Tank Drunks, had been fooling around the night before in the park, reading and tearing up expensive-car manuals. They laughed about the wimpy features: heated seats, ten separate cup holders, and ergonomic steering wheels. They also drank real alcohol, not jug wine, and one had a pricey music player.

This was Lander's beat. He knew Cassandra's building, and now remembered seeing one of their jackets hanging from a pipe behind the building and two steel bars missing from the exhaust vent for the underground parking. It was a basic guess it led to the interior north side of the garage. These clowns wouldn't venture too far from their escape route; therefore, the cars on that side would be their target. Lander had a talent for finding patterns and making connections.

"Look, I'm only trying to help. A friend of mine just moved into the building and I don't want to see anything happen to her car. Have you met Sandra?"

"You're full of shit. Sandra, would have nothing to do with the likes of you. And if I find even a scratch on any of our cars, I've got you on camera, and the police will be on to you."

"Don't bother. It would take a smaller and fitter man to climb down that ventilation shaft. I can't even stand up without losing my breath." Lander turned to walk away. "Call the police. If you ever want my help again, don't tell them about me. If they want proof, have them start at Riker's Pawn on Camelback. That's where these boys cash out." Lander stopped and faced the guard from the outer edge of the entry. "On second thought, I bet they'll be back tonight—try to catch them in the act."

Lander shuffled away, feeling clever—twelfth floor. While the buzzer numbers didn't represent apartment numbers, there might be a pattern, such as the odd numbers for the south side. He'd memorized the names listed before and after Cassandra. The recycling bins in the alleys were jammed with recently issued phone books that nobody wanted anymore. Because Cassandra had just moved in, she wouldn't be listed, but the other residents would be. Through a process of elimination, he would solve the puzzle and soon know her unit number. He was unsure what he hoped to do with this information but enjoyed the challenge.

An hour later, Cassandra emerged from the elevator and stopped at the sight of the two police officers talking with Ray, the security guard. When he saw her, he excused himself and came over.

"Hello, Ms. Sandra. A friend of yours came by. At least that's who he said he was. He helped us, though."

"My friend?"

"Yeah, middle-aged guy, street folk. At least he dresses that way. Sure doesn't speak like it, though."

Cassandra nodded. It had to be Lander. She remembered that the first time she'd seen him was out front of her building. He knew where she lived. "How did he help?"

"Some of his kind..."

"Careful. Don't denigrate them all. You would do well to know him."

"Sorry, ma'am." Picking his words carefully, Ray continued. "He knows who's been breaking into our garage. He showed us how they've been getting in and gave the police a clue to how to find them."

"Has someone has broken into my car?"

"No. Only the ones on the north side. Everyone by the main gate or near the camera is fine."

"Why was he here? Just to tell you about the thieves?"

"No." Looking down, Ray became increasingly uncomfortable. "I guess he was calling on you. At least until I interrupted him."

Puzzled by his use of the word interrupted, she finished the conversation. "Thanks, Ray. Good luck with the investigation."

Without a destination, Cassandra left the building. She thought to walk over to the market to collect items for dinner. She also hoped that she might bump into Lander. An additional worry now occupied her thoughts. If the group that was stealing from the cars somehow found out he had snitched on them, he could be in danger. She'd seen enough cop shows to know sources don't stay secret long. Why would he do that? Was he trying to curry favor with her security guard? Why was he poking around her apartment building? Could he be dangerous? It wouldn't be the first time she had been a poor judge of character, she thought with exasperation. She really didn't want to move cities again. It was her go-to response to escape a toxic relationship.

As she approached a small boutique hotel, a man dressed as if for a garden party spoke to a middle-aged woman on the sidewalk. His jacket and pants were linen—unusual attire for this time of year and especially among the after-work crowd. He seemed to be asking for directions. She laughed to herself; I guess some guys are different. She hoped he wouldn't ask her. Being a newcomer to the neighborhood, she doubted she could help. As she passed, she overheard part of his inquiry.

"He seems older than he is, a white guy, scraggly beard, about forty, a street person. This morning, he wore a long gray coat..."

She almost stopped and stared—shocked that someone else had an interest in Lander. That man gets around and attracts attention. This thought unsettled her. She dismissed her concerns from just minutes earlier and acknowledged how possessive she'd become in a day. He was to be her personal project.

Chapter 18
Monday,
November 2, 2009 (5:10 p.m.)

The mission dining room served an early dinner and Lander was one of the first through the door. It was larger than his usual breakfast location, and he could tell by the scuffed hardwood floor and the painted lines that it served as a gym during the day. The room quickly filled up around him.

As he drained the last of the chicken broth from his bowl, he peered over the plastic rim across the room. The Dunk Tank Drunks he had ratted out were clustered at a table in the corner. One of them, proud of his new watch, kept looking at it, pointing to it, and fiddling with the metal ring and pushing buttons. Lander knew better than to look in their direction for more than a few seconds. In a few hours, they would be caught. If they suspected him when things went wrong, the word would be out. A beating would likely kill him.

A wave of diners emerged from the buffet line; one pointed to the table with empty seats at the back where Lander sat alone. By the time they reached it, he had gathered up his tray and departed.

Out on the street, fed and a little sleepy, Lander pulled his coat around him. At five thirty, dusk was fading. The evenings cooled off into the sixties, still a manageable temperature. He didn't want to go back to his coal room and so began a random trek through the streets. The theater crowd might arrive soon— if the theatres were not dark as they often were on Monday nights. He rounded a corner and saw that the ornate Orpheum Theater marquee was turned off, but the glow of lights from two nearby sports arenas confirmed it was at least a game or a concert night. A small gathering in the theater plaza caught his attention.

He came up alongside a curved brick planter and stepped up on the bench seat. Just beyond, a street magician juggled four items while pretending not to look. The audience cheered when the man took a final bow. Many stepped forward to pitch coins or drop bills into the old felt hat. No rabbit tonight, Lander thought.

Before the crowd dispersed, Lander shuffled along to where the bench swept in behind those in the back row. A single streetlight pinpointed where Lander had stopped.

In a loud, uncharacteristic voice reminiscent of a carnival barker, Lander turned some heads. "You've seen great skill here tonight; you've been duped by legerdemain and dazzled by gravity-defying objects. Now it's time to peer inside yourselves. Turn around. Join me, and I will tell you secrets about yourself that even you don't know."

They weren't buying his pitch. "A tough crowd, I see. A group of doubting Thomases—then allow me to demonstrate. I need a volunteer."

A few people paused. If he wanted to keep the others, he needed their attention, and fast. Lander diverted his gaze for a brief second to scan for any sign of a police officer. He didn't have a permit to perform and risked getting sucked into the system. In the end, they would release him with a warning, but it might take a couple of days.

A young man in his late teens stood with a mixed crowd; they were probably on a group date. This was Lander's best bet. Any guy trying to impress a girl would have to rise to the challenge. "You, in the red shirt. May I show my awesome skill?"

The man laughed, and the girl beside him poked him in the ribs before he held up his hands in mock surrender. "Okay, what's your gig?"

Lander, still elevated on the bench, beckoned him forward and then, with a raised palm signaled for him to stop about a foot away. This both added to the dramatic effect and isolated a single mind that Lander could access without distraction.

"May I have everyone's attention, and some quiet to assist with my concentration?" Lander leaned forward to address his volunteer at eye level. "I will not touch you, but I need one of your friends to come closer and be ready to catch you. Once in a while, it's just too much."

Including a little danger seemed a productive ploy to increase the engagement of the audience. Now he just needed to get close enough, scan the fanned images, and pluck a story to weave into the teenager's current life.

Lander took a deep breath before continuing. "Now tell me, sir, what's your first name? Or, if you prefer, a nickname."

"Nick."

"I didn't mean for you to be so literal, Mr. Nick Name."

"No, it's really Nick."

"Aha. My power is already in play." A few people chuckled at this attempt at humor. Lander winced internally. "Pleased to meet you, Nick. Let's begin."

This was a much larger audience than the park benches. Newly promoted to the busker's stage, he needed to add more theatrical elements. He began by using his hands like an orchestra conductor and then reached into the pocket of his jacket to extract an object into the palm of his hand.

"I want you to follow this." Lander made a slow arc with his arm. He held between his thumb and index finger the grape-sized crystal he had found in the furnace room. The circles slowly became smaller and Lander leaned in. "Remember, I won't touch him, but when I reach the smallest of the concentric circles, he will feel the power of the hypnotism. Watch him carefully." He pointed at Nick's friend, who now stood closer. "Be ready."

In those last words, Lander made the connection. He knew enough to avoid a touch, but he felt confident enough to use distance as a valve to manipulate the flood of images. The flashes began and resembled an imaginary deck of cards; he pushed them around in his mind, looking for just the right one. He wondered if the crystal had any effect. Then he spotted a suitable memory.

"Nick. Are you okay?"

"Yes, I'm fine." His slow response was not convincing, and the crowd grew quieter. They were opening to the possibility that something might actually be happening.

"Now, Nick, a painful memory has risen to the surface. Would you rather I look for a happy memory?"

"No, I'm fine. Give it to me straight."

Lander raised an eyebrow in a caricature of surprise. "Have you ever wondered why you're so afraid of dogs?"

Nick took an immediate step back. *Damn*, Lander thought. The distance broke the connection. *What if I can't reorganize the cards?* It shook his confidence. Could he still concoct a convincing story?

With a slight stammer, his complexion paling, Nick looked up at Lander. "How do you know that?" The crowd was attentive now. Even the magician had stopped packing up his tools to listen.

In a soothing voice, Lander continued. "Nick, step forward. Let me look deeper, and tell you why you have this fear." Nick turned around to face his girlfriend. She shrugged her shoulders, then nodded with encouragement.

Lander repeated the sequence and thankfully had no problem isolating the memory of the dog. He read the audience correctly, playing to their vicarious need to watch someone else in pain. He was flush with the power he had over them, and it was dangerous to him. As a person who had spent the last week in the shadows, it had been a day of wanting more. Hungry for closeness, he longed to connect with people, but something about this felt wrong.

Lander decided to play the story in a more literal manner instead of using his typical analogy. He didn't have the time to consider the consequence of revealing the source of his stories. Not that anyone would believe he had that power. "I would estimate you're about seventeen now. This is from your previous life. I can see you at perhaps seven years old. You love to explore. You have a dog-like desire to escape—your bedroom, your backyard. In fact, you have been begging your parents to buy you a dog. You live in a wet climate. It's the fall; there are golden and yellow leaves strewn across uncut grass. There is a loose board on the wide planked fence that runs along the side of the yard. Two apple trees flank a vegetable garden. You have new neighbors." Lander stopped, looked up, but was careful not to change the distance between himself and Nick. The crowd was wrapped tightly around his words.

It was as if he were reading a story for the first time and exhilarating in the telling, in being so specific. But the tactic had the potential to backfire if he asked too much of his audience. The universal appeal of "let me tell you a story" had been successful. Now he had to keep it going. Could they see he didn't know what would happen next?

"The neighbors have a dog. At least you've heard barking and the rattle of a chain. You push the board on the fence so it swings out. Their backyard is the same as yours, except the leaves have been raked and someone mowed the lawn before the end of the season. A gnarled dog toy is on the cement slab that runs along the back of the house. At the side, they have installed a doggy door into the garage." Lander was telling the story as it unfolded in his vision, in real time, but he had a growing, alarming premonition that it didn't have a happy ending.

"At the edge of the door, you can see the wood is scored from being rubbed against a chain." Lander paused like one peering around a corner. He needed to see what happened next. The imagery assailed him; the violence of it made him sway and buckle over. His voice faltered as his weakened heart raced.

"I'm sorry, folks... I do this to entertain... Make people laugh. But this is a terrible memory. I must stop. Nick, all you need to know is the dog attacked you, and you died. I'm sorry, but maybe this will help you work beyond your fear—and be assured that in many of your other past lives, you loved dogs." This last part Lander fabricated to lighten the mood.

The somber ending to the story broke the spell with the audience. They shifted restlessly and quietly dispersed. In whispers, they commented on how strange the performance had been. They had connected with the energy, but with their shallow perception of the world, they would dismiss his performance as a parlor trick. To believe in Lander would spoil their evening.

Lander didn't even try to collect tips. He didn't own a hat. Instead, he lowered himself to the bench and tried to find calm. The characteristic ache and shortness of breath unsettled him.

He stared down at his ragged running shoes. One of the shoelaces had broken; the knot connecting the two strands pushed up against the eyelet, causing the canvas to bulge, breaking the symmetry. He was vaguely aware of the envelope of sound around him, from the overhead hum of halogen street-lamps to the footsteps that shuffled across the bricks. They had built the plaza with donations; each brick had a name engraved on it. He read the names, one by one, slowing his thoughts. But a question hovered above the recitation. How many of these people carried with them a horrible death?

Lander cursed his clumsy busking effort. He had to figure out how to access stories other than dying, like he did with the piano protege. And when in doubt about the ending, fast-forward to prevent this from happening again.

Lost in his thoughts, he was slow to notice that a person now stood just on the edge of his periphery. Tan loafers, the scuffed toes curled up slightly. Lander guessed it was Nick, wanting more. He wasn't prepared to finish the narrative.

This story was even more terrible because it didn't end with the dog dragging the boy into the garage. The attack was horrific, the teeth tearing away at the boy's throat, the mixture of fluids as frothy saliva floated in the puddles of bright, oxygenated blood.

There were flashes of the owner finding the body, standing over the boy in the last moments of his life but doing nothing. With the life extinguished, the memory went dark, the curtain fell, and the show was over. Lander had a strong sense that the story didn't end there. There was something very wrong in the way the man looked down upon the boy. His reaction revealed mild irritation, as if he had come home and found the dog had chewed a favorite pair of slippers. The slippers could be thrown out. But what happened to the boy?

By repeating the sequence of events, he increased his likelihood of memorizing them. He felt there was still something more to do.

The person in the brown loafers shifted from one foot to the other. He wasn't going away, so Lander looked up to face Nick's inquisition.

It wasn't Nick. Andrew Peller, arms crossed, was staring down at him. Lander smirked. Andrew had at last removed his white linen jacket.

Andrew walked for an hour, wondering just how many places a homeless person could hide. It was prime time for hustling pocket change. The thought made him pause. With the proliferation of credit, debit, and automatically reloading retail cards, Andrew imagined how much harder it had to be to beg for cash. He knew from personal experience that he seldom carried coins anymore. Even tipping at his hotel was a challenge. It required a special effort to keep his pocket stocked with singles. In Canada, his pocket always jingled with loonies and toonies.

In Phoenix, the downtown core exhaled, and the streets became deserted after business hours. Whoever heard of a Starbucks closing at five o'clock? He drifted toward the newer area where apartment and condominium developers had tried to reverse the trend and revitalize the area. He joined the flow of people heading toward an arena basketball game.

Beneath the blank marquee of a theater, an audience of about twenty people surrounded a magician. As he scanned the crowd, he spotted Lander walking along a concrete bench that traced a semi-circle around the perimeter of the plaza. Andrew slipped into the back of the crowd as the applause for the magician signaled the end of his show. He would have preferred a more isolated location for his next encounter. Andrew tried to see over the heads, concerned he might lose Lander to an exit on the opposite side.

To his surprise, a moment later, Lander was calling for attention. Some in the crowd looked at their watches or cell phones; others appeared uncertain about what a shabbily dressed man might do to entertain them.

Lander's demeanor had changed since their meeting that morning. Andrew recognized him now as an actor establishing his character with a commanding voice, and he nodded in approval as the audience grew.

Lander's boast about his ability to see into people didn't sit well with Andrew. Perhaps what had happened to him that morning was nothing more than a parlor trick. But Andrew's interest piqued when he saw something happen to the man who had stepped forward. While Andrew was a spectator now, he had stood in Nick shoes. And, like the crowd, Andrew also wanted more.

Chapter 19
Monday,
November 2, 2009 (7:25 p.m.)

L ander wasn't surprised to find Andrew, though he hadn't expected him so soon. He was too exhausted to handle another mental incursion. If Andrew came any closer, he would have to move.

Andrew spoke first. "I guess it was a privilege getting a private session this morning. You're quite a showman."

"Sometimes it doesn't work out so well."

"You said I had a story. I could have written that off as some sort of ploy, but your little performance a few minutes ago has either sucked me in further or given me a glimpse of a very unusual talent."

Lander leaned into his hands and pushed himself to standing. "It's late, and show business is tiring work." Andrew fell into step beside him. His proximity triggered the connection, and Lander stepped away as they walked. He set a slow pace as he navigated them back to Andrew's hotel.

"It's not part of my act, but I sense you want to learn more. Before I help you, I need something from you. Tonight's story was disturbing. I don't believe it's over, and I wonder if we can somehow help." Lander deliberately used the word *we*. He sensed Andrew was a good person, and while he had poked fun at his wardrobe and his routines, he didn't want any harm to come to the man. Lander guessed that Andrew's association with a homeless man, in particular one with strange psychic abilities, might isolate him from his friends and colleagues.

"What do you have in mind?"

"Go get your computer and sign in to your hotel's Internet. I need you to look for an old news story. You'll have to sneak me into the lobby. My kind aren't welcome."

"There's a side entrance with a staircase to the second-floor restaurant. It'll be quiet on a Monday night. We'll go in that way."

At the top of the stairs, they waited for the hostess podium to be vacant before Andrew pulled Lander purposefully through the restaurant to an isolated table. He parked Lander and suggested ordering them both a coffee. Lander declined and asked for an herbal tea, rooibos with honey, if they had it.

Andrew stopped to place their order with a server before leaving to get his laptop. After he departed, Lander scanned the uninspiring room. There was no apparent theme, just gaudy carpet with geometric shapes in bright colors. A row of banquettes along one wall were covered with bland wood paneling and topped with dusty silk plants and plastic cacti.

The room was empty except for two people seated a short distance to Lander's right. At that table, the man leaned heavily on his elbows; his back arched over the table as he spoke in earnest to the woman across from him. He was trying to enter her space, and she was being circumspect, leaning back in her chair. Lander guessed the man had a personal agenda, but it didn't require his special abilities to see it wasn't going well.

Lander considered helping her, but she didn't need it. She already knew her date wanted into her pants. Whatever he was selling, she wasn't buying.

Observing the unfolding social cliché, Lander's curiosity rekindled his energy. He wondered if he walked by, would he learn more—peer into either of their pasts and look for something influencing their current lives?

The server delivering the beverages stalled his plan to get up. Lander shrank into himself, now avoiding eye contact and the challenges of proximity. He was aware of being out of place. Observing a giant stain on his coat, he shifted the panel and splayed his hand to cover it. *Why was he still wearing his jacket?* The alternative, his faded and torn flannel shirt with missing buttons, was worse.

His tea arrived in a stainless pot with a loosely hinged lid. The paper tag from the tea bag was stuck to the side. The server added a teacup and a saucer, then a mug of steaming coffee for Andrew. Lander wanted to ask for a mug. He preferred something more substantial to hold, but he was too distracted by the young girl's proximity. A silver tray with sugar packets, honey, and cream completed the delivery before she slid away.

Lander looked at the broad sheets of glass that formed the exterior wall and framed the urban landscape. It was unusual for him to be on the inside looking out. Streetlights reflected pinpoints of light on the tinted windows. The top edge of a row of flagpoles just visible, the nylon flags hanging limp. He tried reasoning his ability as genetic evolution. Scientists suggested that humans used only a third of their brainpower. If the world was replete with psychic specialists, there would be nowhere to hide. A new era of honesty would create an entirely different social structure. Imagine if certain people could see the past, and others the present; it would leave the fortune tellers to set the trail.

While his internal monologue played out, Lander poured

the tea into the cup, aware of the steam curling up over his fingers.

The girl at the nearby table stood, obviously trying to disengage from her suitor. For his part, the man awoke to the impossibility of his situation. His shoulders slumped and his focus switched to twirling the plastic straw against the fragments of ice that lay in the bottom of his glass. His head jerked up when she spoke sharply, upset he had tuned her out.

Andrew returned, pulling Lander's attention away from the drama. He was balancing a silver notebook computer on his upturned palm, the lid flipped open, the startup sequence engaged. He offered it to Lander, who held up a hand to stop him. "You'll need to do it. I haven't much experience with computers."

"What are we searching for?"

"Did you hear the story I told? A young boy attacked by a neighbor's dog. It didn't end there. The dog dragged the boy through a doggie door into a garage. The owner found him before he was dead, but did nothing."

"Shit, that's terrible." Andrew paused for a moment. "You're thinking he didn't report it?"

"Exactly. I'm just not sure what we can do about it. Based on Nick's age—and my gut—this is recent, a more modern imprint; it might be seventeen years ago. Use your machine to check if there is a registry of missing kids. Let's start with the assumption that it's the early 1990s. It seemed like the west coast: Oregon, Washington, perhaps Canada. I can't describe the boy." Lander paused, his mind faltering. He had never put into words, for anyone, how his skill worked. He felt conflicted even talking about it.

"The visualizations are from the person's perspective. If the boy had looked in a mirror, I'd have more." Lander scrunched up his eyes in a mock effort at remembering. "Sometimes they have a 'last seen wearing' section. He wore a sports jersey, blue and green, with a bird's beak..."

"That's easy—Seattle Seahawks." With only a few keystrokes, the screen filled with a mosaic of football images featuring the Seattle team logo in the banner. "Now let's see what we can find out about missing children." Andrew leaned back, pulled the computer into his lap, and punched away on the keyboard. After a few minutes, he sat up and slid the device sideways so they both could view the screen. "Who knew there were so many kids?" When the screen stopped scrolling, Andrew rested his finger on the glass. "Unfortunately, none of the listings go back sixteen years. This will require old-fashioned research." He cleared the screen and snapped the lid shut. "I agree. This story is important. Let me think more on it. But now, let's talk about me."

Lander knew he'd have to play along, though he felt Andrew had given up too quickly on the computer search. It frustrated him to have the knowledge from the vision but to be unsure what to do about it. Maybe he could sneak into the library.

Andrew looked at him, expectant. Lander sighed, knowing he had promised. "I'll give it to you straight, no theatrics. Put your hands on the table, palms down, and don't move them." Lander's hands hovered just above Andrew's, and the show began. Andrew's eyes widened as the connection strengthened. Lander shuffled through the deck of images. Most were disjointed and offered little of interest. He wanted a memory imprint linked to Andrew's shoulder. Then he found it.

"You remember the pain this morning? When you touched my hand, you created a link with my visions. I was seeing into your past life. It was during a war; you were in the trenches and you had just been shot. A bullet lodged in your shoulder. It became infected, and you lost your arm."

Lander looked up to see Andrew's reaction. A frown crossed his face as his gaze locked on an imaginary spot on the tile floor.

"The trick for me," Lander continued, "is to find out what aspect of a past life manifests in your life today. Earlier, for Nick, it was easy: his fear of dogs. I would expect that you may favor your left arm, harbor anti-war sentiments—or sometimes the opposite occurs."

"A friend of mine broke his arm in eighth-grade PE class. From then on, I've worried about hurting myself. And when I sleep, that side of my body often goes numb. I have irrational fears about the blood flow stopping and losing the arm."

"You were brave in the war. There was confidence and teamwork. You held your post until the medics took you. Not that it matters, but you weren't on the Allied side. The gun you were using was a Luger. I can't hear anything in the visions, so I couldn't tell if you were speaking German." *Or thinking in a language other than English*, Lander mused.

Andrew pressed on his temples. "That doesn't make sense. My grandparents were Scottish and Welsh."

"It's not that unusual. I've only seen one instance where a person's past life is within the same family."

"Do you realize how crazy this is? Twenty-four hours ago, I didn't know you. Now I'm sitting here listening to a wild story of my past life and believing every word you say." He hadn't touched the coffee and pushed the mug to the center of the table. "I need something stronger." Andrew signaled the server with a raised finger.

Lander picked up his teacup. "It's a little late to become a skeptic. Believe what you want. I'm not asking for anything. In fact, my world has been upside down since I met you this morning." He took a sip of his tea as the server sidled up to the table. Looking bored, she spun a pen on the top of her hand. It was an adept balancing move. Turning to Lander, Andrew asked, "Do you want anything different?"

"No, the tea is fine."

"Single malt scotch, neat."

"Any preferences?"

"Glenlivet 12, please."

The server walked away, and Andrew picked up from where they left off. "Why? How has your life changed?"

"Forget it. I just want to go home. The fact that I'm having this conversation with you tells me I'm losing it. Combined with my big-tent performance in the plaza, I feel like a nutcase. What's making it hard is that you and this girl I met this morning are treating me like I'm normal. That's probably the weirdest thing of it all."

Lander pushed his teacup and saucer toward the middle of the table, signaling he was about to stand. "Stop treating what I do as being so special. What I say is like a newspaper horoscope, a bunch of vague references open to multiple interpretations. Everyone wants it to be written just for them."

"Listen to you. You talk like a college professor. Yet you're on the street. You see things that can't be explained, yet you deny that it's anything special. I don't believe you're a fake. Show me I'm right. Tell me something about the server."

Now on his feet, Lander began edging toward the entrance. "You're right. I'm not a fraud, but I shouldn't be shouting at the top of my lungs about being different. You want me to tell you something about the server? I'll show you."

Lander picked up the small glass jar of honey he had used for his tea; an art glass votive from which he dumped the expired tea light; and finally his empty teacup, which he wiped out with the napkin. When the server was a few feet from the table, he lobbed them at her in quick succession. Without missing a beat, she lowered the hand holding the beverage tray and plucked the three items out of the air with the other, snapping them down beside the rocks glass with Andrew's drink. She had to adjust for the different shapes and sizes—the votive in particular weighed much more than the others. The scotch on the tray splashed around but didn't spill. Only after she'd placed the third item did her eyes widen at what she'd done.

From the entryway, Lander called back, "She can also juggle them. She spent an entire lifetime in the circus, and now she's afraid of heights. Remember what I said: sometimes the effect is the opposite."

Andrew looked up at the girl, assuming she was aware of the strange conversation she'd walked into. "Well. Aren't you going to try?"

The girl hesitated for only a moment before placing her tray on the edge of the table and picking up the three objects. Andrew could see her fingers exploring their outer dimensions, her hand bobbing as if recording their weight.

"Don't think about it. Just do it."

She flipped her wrist to launch the first item and continued until the three objects began a rotation in a perfect arc. After three cycles, she laughed, and her concentration broke. She palmed the teacup and the honey, but the heavy glass votive, at the top of the arc, came crashing down. It impacted against Andrew's temple before it shattered on the floor.

The girl shrieked. Andrew flinched. Then, disoriented, he dropped his head into his hands, tearing up at the sharp pain. He reached up and felt an ooze of blood. His forehead ached. He grabbed a folded cocktail napkin to use as a compress.

Andrew looked around, trying to find a distraction as the girl prattled on, exhausting every possible apology. The man he'd seen sitting with a young woman was now by himself and looking in their direction. He first glanced at Andrew, but lingered on the server with an uninhibited leer, especially when she bent over to pick up the larger shards of the votive.

Andrew leaned toward her. "Could I get a clean towel and some ice?"

As she moved away, the bartender came out from the service area with a broom and dustpan. He slowed his approach as a stern-looking man in a dark suit appeared in the main entrance with a first aid kit.

"Good evening. I'm with hotel security and trained in first aid. I understand there has been an accident."

"Yes, accident is exactly the word." The server came up beside him and handed him a towel and a bag of ice. "Thanks." Andrew tried to catch her eye with a smile. He wanted her to know everything was okay. "As I said, it was an accident. Your server came up behind me to replace the candle. I suddenly leaned back and stretched, bumping into her so the glass holder fell. Entirely my fault."

"Perhaps I should look at the cut before you put the ice back on it."

The guard used a penlight as he wiped the cut with an antiseptic cloth. He applied a sterile strip to close the laceration. "May I suggest, sir, that we have the hotel car take you to the emergency clinic?"

As the guard shuttled him out of the lounge, Andrew located the server, who was standing at the bar, tossing a matchbook up and down and smiling. She nodded at him, and he hoped they would see each other again. Andrew wanted to know how she felt about this dramatic revelation of her skill.

As the hotel's black sedan drove him to the hospital, it stopped at a light, and police activity outside diverted Andrew's attention. He counted four police cars in an alley behind an apartment building. Three men were being led to a waiting van. The squad car lights flicked against the walls, and a splash of red pulsed across Andrew's hand where he held the ice pack.

As if triggered by the darkness and flickering light, the phantom pain from the morning coursed again through his shoulder. He blinked as the interior of the car dissolved. When his awareness returned, he sat in a medic's tent, a rough gauze dressing on his shoulder dark with seeping blood. The altered state only lasted a couple of seconds, but the vivid déjà vu scared him.

Lander lay back on the makeshift futon in his dusty bunker. He couldn't remember a day when he had interacted so closely with one person, let alone three. Then, on his walk home, he saw the police cars behind Cassandra's building. His story to the security guard had produced results. *That's different—a real-life story in real time.* This was his last thought before he fell asleep.

Chapter 20
Tuesday,
November 3, 2009 (6:05 a.m.)

L ander woke to the windup travel clock he'd procured from the shoebox. It was six o'clock. He'd learned of a different breakfast option at the Arizona mission: simpler fare, but served earlier. This was to be his first stop for free tea and donuts. A successful street person developed routines and schedules, he'd discovered.

The mission was around the corner from a hospital. As Lander approached, it stunned him to see Andrew standing at the taxi stand. He hadn't changed since the night before, and his unkempt appearance suggested that he had slept in his clothes. Lander came up from behind him.

"Either you're taking grooming lessons from me or you've had a shitty night."

Andrew turned in surprise, giving Lander a first glimpse at the stitches that ran across his temple.

"Both, I guess," Andrew replied, as he gingerly pressed two of his fingers against the wound.

"I didn't see a history of barroom brawls in your past. Where did you go after I left?"

"Nowhere. The waitress—the one you empowered to defy

gravity—did really well launching the juggler's objects. Next time, check she has the ability to stop juggling. Three stitches and overnight observation for a possible concussion, and here I am, soon to be late for my meeting—again!"

Lander laughed and shook his head. "Follow me. I'm going for a free coffee. The way you look, you'll fit right in."

"No thanks. I need to clean up and get to work." A taxi pulled up, and Andrew opened the rear door. "This afternoon, I'm flying to Seattle, but I'll be back in a few days. I might make a few inquiries about your story. The one about the dog."

The smile dropped from Lander's face. "That's not a good idea." But knew his voice lacked conviction. He was interested in what Andrew might discover. "Don't let anything lead back to me. It would reflect poorly on you."

Andrew looked at Lander for a moment before nodding in agreement. "See you later."

Lander watched the taxi pull away. The circumstances in which he found himself were both confusing and comforting. Andrew spoke to him like an equal, like they had a shared goal. In the week since he'd awoken on the street, Lander had accepted the discrimination against homeless people. He assumed everyone would look down on him, judge him, and dismiss him. But the depth of his conversations with Andrew and Cassandra confirmed he was an educated man. His reservoir of knowledge on a variety of topics was extensive. His memory of where he'd accumulated these teachings, though, was completely absent.

When he arrived, the mission dining area was busy. The coffee had run out, but hot water and tea bags were plentiful. And although the donuts were picked over, another box suddenly appeared and Lander snagged a plain glazed.

Conversation around the room was about the arrest of the Dunk Tank Drunks. The group's name came from an incident that preceded Lander's arrival. As the story went, a carnival had been set up on a large parking lot. They had snuck in after hours and were fooling around with the dunk tank, taking turns submerging each other. The police arrived just as one of their group went under. Unfortunately, in all the commotion, no one noticed he didn't resurface. In his drunken stupor, he had passed out and drowned in the shallow canvas tank. It was tragic accident that earned their troupe a permanent name.

This time, the police caught them in the garage. Tax dollars would house, feed, and ultimately train them to be better thieves until they were released again. For the sake of a few trinkets and insurance deductibles, Lander wasn't sure he had done anyone a favor.

Speculation about where they might have hidden cash or valuables would launch a treasure hunt among the locals. One man boasted that he had already broken into their room at a halfway house but found nothing of value. The trio carried pawn shop tickets, so the police would recover some items.

Lander had his own idea of where the treasure might be. He had instinctively cataloged what he knew of the men's movements. The two most probable locations were the park near the sculpture garden and the alley behind the mini mart where they bought their booze. He would test his theory when it was dark and he was less noticeable.

Relaxing with his tea, Lander monitored the surrounding conversations. He was listening for references to how they'd been caught. If even one person suggested someone had ratted them out, word would spread like a bush fire and a witch hunt would begin. But most of the chatter centered on how they went back too soon to the same location. This line of reasoning was just fine with Lander.

In his usual fashion, Lander sat alone. He was about to

leave when his chair was bumped from behind and a gravelly voice called out, "I got you."

Jane leaned in too close. Lander swallowed hard to hold back his gag reflex as the aroma of rotting teeth and garlic grabbed at his throat.

"You're not taking off this time."

Jane's montage revealed itself and, just like in the alley, Lander mentally shuffled through the pictures for her favorite: the death of the elderly woman in the beautiful country bedroom.

Jane leaned against him and lowered onto the chair beside him, taking his hand into her calloused palm. Her oily, congealed hair slapped the table as her head dropped. Lander wanted to move away, but instead, he settled back in his chair, extracting his hand and moving it to her forearm. This was as good a place as any; the dining room was nearly empty, and it was air-conditioned. He listened to the change in her breathing. As the pace steadied, he could feel her tension dissipate. It wasn't too much to ask that he give her a few moments of peace.

He wondered if she might be asleep—and what would happen if he let the memory play out to its logical conclusion. He had never done that. The pain and disorientation of most death experiences were impossible to maintain—he always broke the connection. Jane's was different, tranquil and calming.

If the touch lingered enough, where would it lead? Jane's life was tragic and unhappy. It might be within his power to fulfill her greatest wish and give her the option of a peaceful death.

Would that make him a murderer? She might get a better circumstance in her next life. But Lander couldn't reconcile his role in such a decision. It wasn't for him to decide when she was finished with this life. At any moment, a chance happening could bless her, just as he'd experienced the day before by meeting Cassandra and Andrew. Her situation might improve. Life was precious. He wasn't choosing for her but simply giving her an option. The drug dealer hands the junkie a needle and feels no guilt because he doesn't engage the plunger. *Am I any different?*

Lander closed his eyes, joining the familiar experience of being in the bedroom of an old farmhouse. As always, a lavender tincture infused the room. A clipped bundle of the fragrant stalks, tied with a pink ribbon, rested on the bedside table. The lace curtains wafted in on a farm-scented breeze. Above the bed, a mobile of origami birds twisted as the air curved through the room. The woman's breath lifted in long, inaudible sighs. Jane's breathing synchronized with that of the woman. The two incarnations magically joined in transcendence, forming a bridge between a death and a rebirth. Lander was in awe of the power of his gift. He cradled a life. He conjured a smile from deep within him—a response to the waves of appreciation that Jane sent him.

Lander remembered the lavender from the Coffee Train. He extracted it from his pocket and placed it in Jane's hand, closing her fingers around it. She squeezed the fragrant bundle, and her head jerked as the tactile sensation connected with a scent; then the worlds merged even more tightly. It encouraged both manifestations of Jane to face the threshold of their deaths with grace and poise. Then, as if on cue, the dying woman in the farmhouse reached out for the lavender on the side table. Before she could grasp it, a draft from the window caused it to slip across the painted surface and drift to the floor. The dried flowers crumbled on impact; the scent grew stronger for just a second before dissipating into the currents of air.

Jane's hand became limp in Lander's and, despite the silence of his visions, he imagined hearing, "Thank you."

Lander gently released her hand and looked up from the table. The crowd had thinned, and no one was paying any attention to him or the woman who now lay silent beside him.

A volunteer appeared in the doorway with a bucket of sanitizer and a handful of folded rags. Fewer than a dozen people remained. Once the food ran out, the room naturally emptied. But a woman on the far side of the room was hunched forward, asleep, her head cradled in her arms. *She might need coaxing.* The volunteer wiped down the rows of boarding school–style tables. The other patrons took this as their cue to leave. Only the sleeping woman remained.

The volunteer tapped her on the shoulder. No response. She cupped the woman's shoulder and shook a little harder, poised to jump backward when she startled awake. Nothing happened. She grew bolder and reached for the woman's outstretched hand. At the sensation of cool flesh, the volunteer's years of nursing experience came into effect. She twisted the arm and placed her fingers on the underside of the wrist to confirm the absence of a pulse. As she released the hand, something slipped from between Jane's fingers and landed softly at her feet. The volunteer stepped back, her foot crunching lightly on the stalks. As she bent to retrieve them, she inhaled the fragrant tincture of lavender.

Chapter 21
Tuesday,
November 3, 2009 (10:12 a.m.)

L ander sat on his usual bench in the park, conflicted about what he'd done. His initial euphoria was now a rising tide of despair. Had he taken her life, or was it her time? Serendipity, a convergence of fates, karma—whatever you wanted to call it—seemed to have come together at that exact moment. Perhaps she would have died either way.

He couldn't understand the source of his power, and without his memories, he didn't know if he had been born with it or if it was the result of some intervention. Each incursion into someone's past forged a connection, and a little piece of that person became lodged within him. Lander also sensed that it wasn't a one-way exchange. He left behind a tether. What if the people he channeled pulled on the cord to summon him?

This last thought amused him, but with a sinister undertone. It wasn't an unreasonable hypothesis that, like Jane, they all might be drawn to him at their moment of death. He imagined zombie-like creatures swaying back and forth on stiff legs as they came up the street in search of him.

Instead of waiting until evening where the darkness would hamper his search, Lander headed to the park to test his theory that the Dunk Tank Drunks might have hidden their stash there. Behind the benches, a thick granite block wall bisected the plaza. It was about seven feet tall and five feet wide, sloped, and it appeared to be flat on top. The trio had been known to climb it and swagger up and down as though on a catwalk at a fashion show. Lander understood, from overhearing city workers, that the original design was meant to accommodate a sculpture at one end but, following a controversy about the religious aspect of the piece, the issue now sat with the courts. Nobody was in much of a hurry to resolve it. Before stopping the project, the city installed the mounting brackets and power for the lights.

Lander reasoned that with its electrical infrastructure, a control panel or utility box could be used as a hiding place. On the park side, a few feet from the ground, he found a hinged steel plate. It was locked and dusty and clearly hadn't been touched since the last rainstorm.

He assumed the Dunk Tank Drunks had relied on a tree or something else to help them climb to the top of the base. Lander circled the wall one more time before he made his discovery. At the far end, in the shadow of a giant ironwood tree, another steel cover traced the entire height of the plinth. Unlike the first steel plate, this one bore scratches and wear marks. After a first tug, Lander concluded that it, too, was locked. On closer examination, though, the exposed hinge revealed an interior latch, and traces of metal in the mortar suggested that a protective plate had once covered the hinge but had been pried away. With deft fingers, Lander slid the pin out of the hinge and a small section of the panel lifted away, exposing a release mechanism for the door and access to the ladder.

Lander complimented the boys on the ingenuity they'd shown in breaking through the locked barrier. This also explained how, even at various levels of intoxication, they climbed up and down. Lander considered his options. Was he strong enough to climb the ladder? There were only eight rungs, he reasoned, as he summoned the will to try. He stepped onto the first bar and reached up to pull himself straight. He tentatively lifted his foot to the next rung and pulled his weight up with his arms. "One at a time," he murmured to himself.

He hesitated and nearly slipped when his foot was only half-engaged on the third rung. Now only a couple of feet off the ground, he felt ridiculous. His chest hurt, and his breathing was shallow. He closed his eyes. He might as well have been twenty stories up, clinging to the side of an office tower.

He was descending in defeat when a voice pulled him from his irrational fear.

"What the hell are you doing?"

He didn't have to look. The voice belonged to Cassandra, and relief washed over him.

"Let me help you."

"Stop!" Lander hollered, without turning his head. He heard her step onto the crushed rock below him. "Don't touch me! Remember what happened at the café?"

"You think I'll collapse again?"

"Yes. I'll explain everything, but we need to take this slowly. You can come up behind me and reach out, but no closer than six or eight inches."

"Are you kidding? Stop the games. Turn it off and let me help you."

"Just humor me. Play along with my delusion."

Lander heard her take another step, and she was in range. He needed to find another memory, one he could use to block her from drowning. He gritted his teeth in frustration. It wasn't like there was a training manual to show him how to handle these situations. He slowed his thoughts and tried to flip a mental image as he would a playing card in the memory game. He pulled forth an experience that was dark and angry, but not crippling. It seemed visceral enough to mask the first one.

"Count from five. If you think you're strong enough, grab me by the waist and lift me down. Count now."

"Five, four, three…" As she reached the count of one, she put her arms around him. He let go of the upper rung and fell backward. She caught him, breaking his fall, but then screamed in his ear and pushed him away. Lander stumbled to his knees, bringing his arms up in time to prevent his head from crashing into the base of the wall.

"You bastard!" She was about to kick him, but at the last moment she redirected the momentum of her foot and spun on her heel in the gravel. "What the fuck just happened? I wanted to kill you. I was so angry."

Lander twisted around and sat with his back to the ladder. Cassandra's hair had escaped her ponytail and hung down in front of her face. In a comical gesture, she puffed out a breath and the wispy strands rose and fell. He had to laugh. He was elated. She'd touched him, and despite the rush of images, he could feel where she had made contact. It was sweet and sinful at the same time.

As Lander tucked in his legs and twisted around to get up, Cassandra reached out with a helpful hand. Lander stared wide-eyed at her and shook his head. She retracted her hand as if it was about to be burnt.

"I'm so confused. Why do I lose my mind when I'm with you?"

Lander suppressed his laughter. "All in good time. Why are you here?"

"I saw you enter the park and wanted to see you again."

A warmth surged through him at her comment. He turned away, wondering if it had shown on his face.

"I need you to climb up there." He pointed up the ladder."

"Why?" she asked, pronouncing the word really slowly.

"A group of thugs—we called them the Dunk Tank Drunks —were arrested for breaking into the cars in your building. They spend a lot of time hanging out on top of this wall. It's my theory that, since they live in a public rooming house, they probably have money or valuables stashed somewhere. It wouldn't have been secure in their dorm."

Lander turned back to face her. "It's solving the puzzle that's important. I don't really care about what's hidden."

Cassandra put her hands on her hips, considering Lander's request. She looked again at the ladder, shrugged, and started climbing. About halfway up, she called over her shoulder, "Any idea what I'm looking for?"

"No. It's your garden-variety secret hiding place. Look for a loose brick or an access panel that might be open, or a sign that reads, 'Drugs Hidden Here' with a big red X." He laughed feebly. Anything was possible. "And keep low. I'm guessing that climbing around up there is not encouraged."

Unconcerned by his warning, she continued upward. Lander backed away and to the side so he could track Cassandra as she walked the length of the plinth.

He wanted to call up to her but preferred not to draw attention. There were people scattered throughout the park, but no one seemed to notice. She reached the end and looked down, then shrugged. Nothing yet. Then something caught her eye, and she hurried out of sight. Unable to see, Lander returned to the foot of the ladder to wait.

Cassandra reappeared about five minutes later. She had a cloth laundry bag in her hand, which she lowered by the draw-string. Lander took it and looked back up as she started down the ladder. He admired her figure as she descended.

"Stop staring at my ass."

"Sorry, I lead a *sheltered* life." He paused to see if she got the joke. When he didn't get a reaction, he continued, "The last time I was propositioned for sex, when the woman touched me... well, you know what can happen." Cassandra was now standing across from him.

"That sucks."

"That was her intention, but it would have required contact." In stark contrast to his joke, Jane appeared in his thoughts and he was awash in guilt. It was a chilling reminder of how their brief relationship had ended.

Cassandra grimaced and playfully made to slap him, but she stopped short, aware that Lander's mood had changed. She reached forward and took the bag. "What do you think is in here?"

"I don't know, but I don't think we should open it here. Where did you find it?"

"There was a drainage pipe. The debris spread across it looked too precise. Below it, this bag hung from the grate."

Cassandra tucked the bag under her arm and the two walked back across the park. "I saw you from my apartment," she said, gesturing towards her building.

"Sorry for coming on so strong yesterday. I know how it feels when someone wants something and then forgets it involves two people. In my case, men assume that because I'm not attractive, it would be a privilege to fuck them. They never think to ask what I want." Lander kept his eyes forward, unsure how to react when she spoke so graphically. They stopped at the corner and waited for the light.

Lander scanned her building. Since he now knew which side her apartment was on, he tried to pinpoint which window was hers. He was about to ask her what floor when Cassandra changed the subject.

"You're a strange and enigmatic person. Out of sync. I can

help you with that. It may look like I'm only in it for me, but I promise you that's not the case."

As they crossed the street, Lander looked up and caught sight of their reflection in the large window of a bank. Lander walked with a stooping gait and his ill-fitting jacket looked dirty, even in the forgiving reflection of the window. Cassandra walked with poise, her head up and shoulders back, her jacket cinched neatly with a knotted belt.

"What are you looking at?" Cassandra had noticed his attention on the window.

Their pace slowed as Lander pointed at the glass. "The reflection of the two of us. Did you ever watch Sesame Street? One of these things is not like the other."

"Your appearance and current situation don't matter. This surprises me as well. I'm not a compassionate person, especially where men are involved. I never give money to the homeless." At the crosswalk, the light changed to green, and they stepped onto the road without pausing. "I think we are good for each other."

Lander sensed that this was where he was supposed to say something, but he kept walking. At the next laneway, he pointed to a staircase. "There's a patio; the restaurant is closed, so it'll be deserted and private."

The bistro tables were cast haphazardly around the deck. They pulled two together and extracted a chair each from a stack in the corner. Cassandra lowered the bag, and its contents shifted as it puddled on the metal tabletop. Lander slid it toward him and untied the drawstring.

He stretched the opening wider and peered inside the bag. Cassandra looked up at him, expecting a reaction. "Predictable," he muttered. The first item he extracted was a dog-eared porn magazine.

"They buy them for the articles," Cassandra commented, then smiled weakly.

Lander reached in and scooped more items onto the table: an unopened box of condoms, a folding corkscrew, and eight partially full prescription pill bottles. Cassandra picked through the collection, sorting the medications by their basic purpose: sleeping pills, antidepressants, anti-inflammatory, hyperactivity medications, and Viagra. She placed that bottle beside the condoms and the magazines. "Everything in its place," she said.

Lander twisted the orange plastic containers to view the labels. "They're all from a Dr. Aradice." He shivered as he spoke the name but didn't know why. "Each one has a different patient's name on it; this one was filled last Friday." He held up one bottle and Cassandra nodded in confirmation.

The next handful from the bag yielded a pair of brand-new gloves with the tags still on them, a collection of colored ball-point pens, and a family-size box of strawberry-flavored lip balm. Given the nature of the items, shoplifting could be added to their list of crimes.

But the last two items were significant to Lander: a thick prescription pad and a ring of keys with a metal disk, both branded with the words *Wrimo Hospital*.

Chapter 22
Tuesday,
November 3, 2009 (11:45 a.m.)

L ander fingered the key ring, stopping to notice the writing scratched on the back of the metal disk. In the shadowed light of the patio, he couldn't make it out.

Cassandra picked up the prescription pad and thumbed through the blank pages. She pointed at the hospital's logo. "You asked me about Wrimo the other day. Why so interested?"

Lander sighed. "More questions?"

"That's not fair. This time, it isn't about me. I'm asking because somehow, Wrimo is connected to you. This isn't a coincidence. Especially given your reaction when you I showed you these labels." She held up one of the prescription bottles and Lander flinched, moving to the back of his chair. "Did you work there?"

She stopped, her eyes suddenly wide: he sensed her mind racing ahead. "No, you were a patient there... and it's linked to your abilities? But if they knew what you were capable of, they never would have let you out... unless you didn't show them." Cassandra tilted her head, and her lips moved as if pre-playing different scenarios to herself. "Please tell me more about what's going on."

Lander gave in. He was tired of being alone and trusted Cassandra. He explained how he had woken up on the street with amnesia, how he found the Wrimo medical bracelet and the shredded file folder. How, whenever he got close to someone, he saw images.

She interrupted his story. "Do you think the Dr. A. on the bracelet is the Dr. Aradice on these prescription bottles? He's the head of the facility and a minor celebrity as an author."

"That's a good question. I don't know. But before we go any further, and need you to honestly answer two questions." With just the index finger raised, he said, "First, can you accept I have an unusual ability, a so-called 'magic' skill? And, second, do you believe in past lives—reincarnation?" He gave up on the gestures and dropped his hand onto his lap. "I'm convinced the vignettes represent a person's past lives. A violent death in a past life usually becomes the dominant story in my visions. When you first touched my hand, we were both dropped into a scene where you were drowning. I'd guess that you don't enjoy swimming in this life. Are you claustrophobic?"

Cassandra nodded.

"I didn't have time to see the entire story, but you were trapped in a small boat as it sank. Those images manifest themselves in this life as suffocation. I didn't mean to scare you. But it made me curious to know your story. I hoped to see you again." Lander paused a moment to let his words sink in. "I felt like I had hurt you, and I wanted to apologize, but more importantly, I hoped I could somehow help you."

"Then earlier, on the ladder, why did I hate you so much?"

"I had to shuffle the memories, look for something powerful but not debilitating. I found one where you were angry. Based on the clothing you were wearing, it was a long time ago, 1800s, in a gas-lit area. Unfortunately, I don't hear any sounds or voices in the visions. But you have a history of being mad at men." He attempted a wry smile, but she wasn't looking at him. She stared at an imaginary spot on the floor.

"It was so real. I wanted to kick the shit out of you. If you touched me now, would you be able to choose the memory?"

"This is still new to me. I'm not very good at it." Lander thought again about Jane and shuddered. If he held on to Cassandra long enough, would she suffocate?

To lighten the mood, Lander made her laugh when by recounting his attempt at street busking. He did not tell her about playing god with Jane. Instead he used the examples of Nick and Alice to illustrate two different outcomes.

Cassandra was being careful not to push too much. She poked at the items on the table. "What do we do with all this junk?"

"Throw out everything but the keys." Lander scooped it all back into the bag, then had a change of mind. He retrieved the pill bottles and poured them down the floor drain at the edge of the patio. "It may not be the best for the environment but..."

When he sat down, Cassandra was twirling the keys on her finger. "And what do you plan to do with these?"

"Break into Wrimo and see what I can find out about my past."

"Why not just ask them?"

"There's something wrong with how I was treated. I can't be specific, but I'm at risk going there."

Her curious smile faded, and she looked away. The silence separated them, and Lander fidgeted. After less than a minute that felt like five, she leaned forward. "I can help you, and in a less risky manner. My research at the foundation I work for opens a lot of doors for me. Institutions don't want to appear like they have anything to hide. But in my experience, the more open the door, the more reason to look behind it."

Lander nodded. With legitimate access, she could poke around, maybe ask questions. His secret was out in public, and partnering with Cassandra would be beneficial. Then he changed his mind. "No. We can't do anything that might connect us."

He once again reflected on how much his life had transformed in just thirty-six hours. They had a connection, and he wanted to be around her. He looked over at her; she had pulled out her BlackBerry phone and was thumbing away on some messages.

Lander let his hand drift forward on the table while sliding his feet closer to create a stronger bond. The telltale signs clouded his mind. In this third visit to Cassandra's library of past lives, he found it easier to steer clear of the drowning and the infidelity scenes. The other moments coalesced as a pastel impressionist artwork. Like Monet's water lilies, he thought, but with fewer colors in the paint box. They were steeped in feelings of relative comfort, or perhaps it was just the lack of major suffering that had marked her previous lives. He wanted to find something that could help her.

Cassandra had different plans and abruptly stuffed her phone back into her purse. "I need to get going. I'm supposed to be working." Their connection broke as she stood up and headed toward the stairs. Lander followed a short distance behind, unhappy that the real world had encroached on their moment together.

They walked up the alley and stopped at the main street, where Cassandra's apartment was visible about half a block to the left.

"I was about to ask for your number, but I guess you don't have a phone."

"No. I'm pretty much a word-of-mouth kind of guy."

"Please don't take this the wrong way, but if I bought you some new clothes, would you wear them?"

"That's a generous offer. While I'm not attached to this look, or this lifestyle, my status gives me the advantage of anonymity while I figure things out." Lander allowed himself a moment to imagine the change. He approved of what he saw. "I don't know. I'm already an outcast on the street. Clean new clothes will not help me fit in."

"That's not our goal. We have some errands to run, and I need you to fit into my circles without drawing attention to yourself. Meet me back here at five. We're going shopping."

Lander leaned against the wall and watched her until she turned into her building. Her gait was sprightly, and she seemed happy. Lander smiled to himself. He was enjoying this way too much.

Before he could try his own variation on skipping up the block, someone seized him and pulled him deeper into the alley. A hand grappled at Lander's jacket, bunching up the fabric. The material strained as the assailant leaned into Lander's weight and added enough purchase to throw him sideways. Lander's foot scraped the roadway then slid in some oil, and his ankle twisted under him. Unable to stay upright, he sagged, his arms flailing as the man wrenched them backward, leaving his face exposed as one final push sent him sprawling to the ground. Rinds of skin grated against the pebbly asphalt. Lander was only vaguely aware of the sound of a bone snapping in his nose, but pain consumed him. Warm blood clogged his sinuses and bubbled over his lips in a turbid stream. In shock and out of focus, he couldn't concentrate on latching on to the man. He was disarmed.

Rolling onto his side, Lander tried to push himself away. Two pairs of scuffed black cowboy boots approached. He looked up to find a stranger standing over him while another man remained a few steps back, peering up and down the alley.

"You fucked us up good, snitching on my boys." A swift kick followed, and Lander curled into a fetal position. Winded, he choked for air, the pain in his gut overwhelming even with his throbbing nose. The man shifted his foot and flicked his boot against the side of his head.

"Street trash." The second man stepped forward and spat on Lander, his spittle landing short and floating on the growing puddle of blood.

"Search him," the first man ordered.

The second man yanked off Lander's jacket and searched the pockets. He drew out the key ring and regarded it for a moment before throwing it in Lander's face.

Lander was close to losing consciousness. He desperately needed to focus on the man who was rifling through his clothing. Lander's hatred increased as the images coalesced. He looked for the man's darkest and most painful memory. Then he had it. It was ancient, but it didn't matter. He snapped out a hand, grabbing his assailant by the ankle.

Even through the coarse leather of the boot, a connection forged, and Lander's entire focus burned a disabling imprint into the man's consciousness. Flashes of light converted to a physical memory of a time when their situations were reversed. Now, the man was the victim; he trembled and screamed, his voice shattering the silence of the alleyway. He spastically tried to pull his leg away as Lander revealed to him with crushing realism the experience of being attacked and torn apart by a wild animal.

The volume of the outburst stunned the first man. "Shut up, you idiot. Are you trying to get us caught?" The second man fell to his knees. At the end of the alley, some passers-by stopped, nervously looking into the passageway. The first man pulled hard on his associate to break Lander's grip. He dragged his partner to his feet, and the two retreated down the alley. "We're not done with you," they shouted, before vanishing around a corner.

Lander rolled onto his back and tried to breathe. Blood from his broken nose drained into the back of his throat, choking him further. A small crowd gathered around him as he pushed himself into a sitting position, but they dispersed at the sound of a police siren and a rapid pulse of red and blue lights.

Lander slumped to the ground, unconscious.

Chapter 23
Tuesday,
November 3, 2009 (4:15 p.m.)

He woke on a gurney in a side hallway at Mercy Hospital. He didn't have to look at the thin plastic band on his wrist to know his name would be listed as the equivalent of *John Doe.*

The ceiling was a linear constellation of acoustical tiles decorated with sprays of what looked like dark, northern beach sand. Lander focused his eyes and counted the panels to confirm that his cognitive faculties were intact. The tiles, composed of two distinct patterns, formed a crisscross design on the T-bar ceiling, but the pattern had a flaw: one panel was in the wrong place. *I know how that feels,* he thought, satisfied that he had passed this simple mental test.

Thankfully, it appeared as if he had no effect on people while unconscious or asleep or he wouldn't have gotten this far. This proved to have been convenient allowing for his to be retrieved from the alley and receive first aid.

His challenge now was to find out if he could he leave—and to avoid any direct contact until then. Just taking his pulse would be a traumatic experience for a caregiver.

Lander didn't think they would keep him for very long.

Other than wrapping him with gauze and giving him a couple of aspirin, they would only wait for him to wake up and leave. While government subsidies covered the basic cost of the visit, most procedures required insurance. The faster they could be done with him, the smaller the loss they would incur.

The buzz of fluorescent lights and the hum of industrial ventilation unsettled him. Had he been medicated? He closed his eyes, and the whiteness pushed against his eyelids. The growing sensory input overwhelmed him: the click of heels on linoleum, the squeak of rubber wheels, an electrically charged voice that bellowed over a PA system—all ignited flashes of memory, an association with another hospital at another time. These glimpses teased his hunger to know more about his past.

With other people, each past life resembled a different playing card, and his level of control over the deck improved with each interaction. He could discard, draw, or drop to build his hand. But Lander's own memories were beyond his control. The cards were thrust at him, flipped out of the deck, ejected into his face. Like a game of fifty-two pickup, but with a twist: he couldn't reach the cards.

The memories that now assailed him included physical discomfort, and in them his limbs were often constricted in a stiff canvas straitjacket. The flashbacks transported him to a pie-shaped room with a single shrouded window. A montage of many days seeped into his awareness; he knew he had stared at that window for hours. The gray metal pull-down shade allowed in a ribbon of light on three sides. Sunlight? It was unsettling. It seemed on some days the building faced east, and the light gradually grew brighter; on other days he faced west, and the light shone with a brief intensity before falling into darkness. Had someone tried to confuse him? Finally, he'd used a zipper pull to etch a symbol onto the back of the bed frame, and he realized that when he was sedated, they moved him between identical rooms whose furniture mirrored each other, but which were located on opposite sides of the building.

Why these memories and nothing else?

The pat, pat, pat of approaching rubber soles caused Lander to refocus on his present situation and lift his head. A woman in a pale pink hospital coat walked up to the end of the gurney. She opened Lander's chart and drew a pen out of her jacket pocket with her left hand. To his surprise, he recognized her. It was the women who volunteered at the morning shelter. And he was certain he'd seen her somewhere else. Her brown hair, streaked with gray, was pulled into a bun, and Lander guessed her to be in her early fifties. She had a round, soft face and smiled without showing her teeth. Her thin lips and eyes were unadorned.

She tucked the clipboard under her arm and stood, eyebrows raised.

"You're awake. Good. Can you tell me your name?"

"Lander. Lander Gate."

She nodded, as if confirming something she already knew.

"I know you. You volunteer where I get breakfast, and I've met you somewhere else, too."

"Yes, there and at one other shelter.

"We need to talk. Where do you know me from?"

"Let's not discuss that right now." After a pause, she let out a sigh tinged with disappointment, then assumed a professional tone. "Do you remember what happened?"

Lander suppressed his agitation and prepared to answer her questions. "Until the moment I got kicked in the head. I was beaten up by two guys with expensive boots."

"The police said they'd come back if you wished to make a statement."

"I didn't recognize my attackers. They weren't regulars in the neighborhood."

The woman moved to the side of the gurney and looked down at Lander after making a notation in the file. "I'll have a doctor look this over, but your head scan showed no serious damage. Remarkably, your nose wasn't broken, but it suffered extensive soft-tissue damage. We put three stitches at the base, above your lip. The tissue around your ribs is also bruised." The nurse paused to see if Lander had any questions.

"What time is it?" he asked, remembering Cassandra and their meeting.

"Half past four. You will be in pain for at least a week. The local anesthetic in your nose will wear off soon." For the first time, Lander acknowledged a tingling sensation near his nose. He'd been breathing through his mouth and tried to switch. His nasal passageways were restricted, as if he had a stubborn cold.

"Now that you're awake, I'll flush out your nose." She adjusted the gurney to prop him up.

As she began the procedure, Lander fought to focus his mind—a difficult feat because of the pain of his injuries and the assault of images that resulted from the nurse's touch. But he had to shuffle away any visceral or disconcerting narrative. He acted skittish and nervous to limit the time she tended to him. Thankfully, the nurse was a good woman and had been a caregiver through many of her past lives. If anything, his power drew on her deep well of compassion, resulting in her being more thorough than usual.

Despite the condition of his nose, Lander tried to identify the subtle fragrance surrounding her. His eyes dropped to the gaping pocket of her nurse's coat and a crushed bundle of lavender sprigs tied with a pink ribbon. Had she been at the mission that morning? He wanted to ask her if she was the one who'd found Jane.

After clearing the dried blood and mucus, she replaced the

dressing and wrapped a tensor bandage around his black-and-blue ribs.

"You'll feel better if you can sit up." She pointed at a wheelchair a few feet away that he hadn't noticed before.

The intensity of the pain when he tried to step down from the gurney caused him to stumble, but the nurse was surprisingly strong and got him into the wheelchair. Even more surprising, Lander had blocked his influence in the confusion of that moment.

As she finished, she looked up furtively. At first, Lander thought she was reacting to something he had done, but he realized it was a response to the two voices approaching from around the corner. She wheeled him in the opposite direction.

"I wasn't supposed to medicate you and should have already released you. It's not my place to say anything, but the attending doctor isn't thorough. You may have had complications from the head trauma."

She moved Lander to the end of a quiet corridor. A second-story window looked out over a side street, where a motorcycle accelerated as it passed. The vibrations shook dusty cobwebs on the window frame. Lander winced as he involuntarily scrunched up his nose, imagining with horror the pain he would experience if he sneezed. With a deflating sigh, he relaxed as the urge dissolved.

On one side of the hall, the treatment rooms were busy with a parade of broken limbs, wheezy lungs, and a man familiar to Lander who was bemoaning a phantom pain to get a supply of painkillers. When he mentioned a particular drug, Lander remembered it as one of the pill bottles in the drunks' cache. The man was desperate to find an alternative source.

Lander was about to turn his attention back to the window when a nearby voice triggered another flashback. He surreptitiously looked around and saw the two men the nurse had dodged earlier—presumably doctors—walking toward him. A dark-haired man faced away from his view while addressing the second man, who walked a pace behind. His words had a lilt, a faint British, or maybe Canadian, accent. The cadence of the words, the tone, and articulation were familiar. Caught up in the vision, he could not decipher the words themselves, but they transported him back to the pie-shaped room at Wrimo.

In the memory, a man with that voice was talking. Lander struggled to focus beyond his fear and loathing. The restraints secured him to the rigid steel frame of a hospital bed. They positioned him with his back to the covered window. The doctor stood motionless, arms down, cupping his hands palm to palm. Only his left thumb moved back and forth with syncopation across the knuckle of his right thumb. Lander stared at the hands. He had once seen a logo with two helping hands, but helping wasn't this man's intent. In the vision, Lander looked up and was startled. It was the man from the car outside the Coffee Train—the one who had scared him so much.

Lander blinked out of the vision. His knuckles ached from gripping the wheelchair. He gagged from the combination of holding his breath and the pain in his ribs. He tried to slow his breathing, but the involuntary spasms made it difficult. Through the strain, he heard the men stop their conversation. He feared they were looking at him. *The person behind that voice knows me; what if he recognizes me?* It wasn't the first time he wondered if he was thrown out of Wrimo—or if he'd escaped.

Another wet cough shook him. A painful spasm in his ribs threatened to knock him out.

A woman's voice rose above his exhalations. "Don't worry, doctor, I'll assist him." He felt the nurse's hand push him back into the chair while she placed a plastic mask over his mouth and nose. Lander was as grateful for the mask that covered his face as he was for the oxygen.

In a calming tone, she encouraged him. "Count your breaths. Make each one a little longer than the previous." It was a powerful combination, and Lander relaxed.

When his breathing was restored, the nurse scolded him. "What did you do to get yourself all riled up?" Changing to a whisper, she went on, "Not a good idea, especially in front of those two."

"Why? Who are they?"

"The attending—the one I don't like—is a neuroscience specialist and our head of psychiatry. I have a history with him and don't approve of his methods. Now, shh."

The nurse wheeled him around and, as they rolled down the corridor, Lander looked sideways to see the two men settling into chairs in an office. Lander confirmed that the man with the accent was linked to his stay at Wrimo. His black wavy hair was marginally too long compared to his more conservative peers, but it was likely popular with the ladies. He was trying to hide his age. Lander also knew he had a dark secret, and it somehow connected the two of them.

The nurse parked the wheelchair in a curtained area near the front desk and eased him over to a bed before adjusting the side rails. Lander flinched as they clicked into place. She reached under the wheelchair and extracted a paper bag, which she opened to show him a bundle of folded clothing. "These are from donations; your others were torn. I hope they fit okay. Everything that was in your pockets is also there. I packed it myself." Her hand trembled as she placed it on the bed beside him and turned away.

At the open curtain, she turned back. "I'm sorry, there's nothing more I can do for you. If you'd like, I'll call for a social worker. Perhaps they can help you with resources outside the hospital. It will be at least an hour's wait." This suggestion she gave with little enthusiasm. It was a hospital script that he believed was not her own recommendation.

Lander glanced at a wall clock. It was after five; he'd missed his appointment with Cassandra.

"No social worker. I should get changed and move on, but I have questions." The nurse considered this for a moment before lowering the bed so that Lander's feet were on the floor.

"Not here. Not now."

After she departed, Lander dressed, the pain in his ribs slowing the progress. A male voice drifted through the curtain.

"Carol, the John Doe in Curtain Three,—you said you got a name?"

"Yes: Gate, first name Lander." A tapping of keys coincided with Carol's voice coming closer. "Has he been here before? No. Wait. There's an alert." More keystrokes followed, and Lander got to his feet, grabbing the lowered bedrail to steady himself. "That's interesting. The alert is linked to Wrimo, but it says there's no patient file."

Lander peered around the back side of the curtain. A long hallway led further into the building. He guessed he could only reach the main entrance through the electronic doors next to the admission desk. How was he going to get out?

"The alert requires Psych to be notified, specifically Dr. Aradice. You're in luck." With unmistakable sarcasm, he said, "The sunny doctor is here. I saw him a few minutes ago." There was the sound of a phone being picked up, and a punch of buttons preceded the crackly male voice on the PA system requesting Dr. Aradice to come to ER Administration.

"I'll make sure he's dressed." Carol came around the counter and stopped in front of the closed curtain. "Mr. Gate, may I come in?"

Lander hovered just inside the curtain, closer than she

could have known. He shuffled through her memories, encouraged that he was getting faster at organizing the album of images. The woman in the image was protecting an injured soldier. It was a bit cliché, but exactly what he needed.

She pulled the curtain back, and Lander took hold of her hand before gently pulling her inside, channeling the memory. He managed an impressive level of control over his talent. He drew his other finger to his lips for her to be silent. She looked confused, but nodded with a growing understanding. They both twisted their heads, looking for some form of escape.

Beyond the curtain, the clerk said, "Dr. Aradice, there's a message here for you."

Carol raised her arms and, without touching him, gestured for him to step backward and up. Without understanding her plan, he let her reposition him up on a stool snug with the curtain. She stepped forward and whipped the curtain back. The tiny metal wheels screeched along the aluminum track. Her plan was simple. The curtain gathered right where Lander now stood, and the footstool lifted him out of view. From the desk, all they could see was the curtain, the stool's chrome legs, and an empty room.

"He's gone," Carol called out.

"What?" screeched Dr. Aradice. "Where?"

"We were about to release him. I left him here to change about ten minutes ago."

"What sort of shit admission system do you have where you enter a patient's information after he's gone?"

The admission clerk reacted; the affront to his skills only added to his visible dislike of the doctor. Without hesitation, he played along with Nurse Carol's fabricated story. "He came in as a John Doe. Our system's been down for the last hour. This was the first chance I had to match his file. Take it up with your friend the director—these computers crash all the time."

"Idiots. Find him!" Dr. Aradice stormed away, his lab coat splaying out behind him.

Everyone in the area—patients, nurses, visitors—had all stopped to watch the altercation. But after a moment of silence, the hum of activity resumed, and nobody seemed compelled to think about the incident again. An elderly woman sitting to one side could see Lander hiding up against the curtain. She smiled, pleased to be in on the practical joke.

Carol turned to her coworker and mouthed the words, "Thanks." The clerk held up a finger for her to wait. He picked up a pole with a hook on it, the kind that was used to open upper windows. He reached up and tucked it behind a ceiling-mounted camera. With a quick tug, the power cable fell loose and the red light went out.

"Oops. Strange how that keeps coming unplugged. Now get him out of here. Tell him to stay to the right on the sidewalk of the ambulance bay, and to keep up against the wall."

Lander stepped forward. "I heard. Thanks to you both."

Chapter 24
Tuesday,
November 3, 2009 (4:30 p.m.)

Throughout the afternoon, Cassandra worked diligently on her research. She often glanced out her window toward the cluster of benches where she knew Lander practiced his storytelling. He was such a strange man, and his unusual abilities made him either a talented con artist or psychic phenom. Cassandra dismissed the first possibility. His ability had brought her to her knees. In the time since their first encounter, he'd awakened trace memories that explained many things. She vividly remembered her panic and revulsion when her parents had forced her to swim when she was a child. She disliked being in small spaces. During sex, she hated being underneath and smothered. She was not a hugger.

Cassandra wasn't the type to wrestle with philosophical or spiritual issues. She dwelled in an objective and fact-based world. The scientist inside her poked at her conscience, asking for more information. She could dismiss the big questions, at least for now. For the sake of her curiosity about Lander, she would play along with the concept of rebirth. His apparent magical ability, on the other hand, was best left in the "pending decision" file in her brain.

Earlier that day on the deserted patio, she'd feigned an interest in her BlackBerry while Lander had not-so-discreetly moved closer. She understood that proximity made a difference, and she realized he was trying to read her. For her part, she'd sensed something intoxicating as forgotten memories coalesced, both in her mind and with an electrifying physicality.

The cold blue light of her phone broke the spell. An email from her boss. The immediate demands of her mundane life flooded in, and she needed time with her thoughts.

As five o'clock approached, she formed a basic plan. She showered and dressed, taking extra care with her hair. It felt like getting ready for a date—and it was an irrational act since she was meeting a man who hadn't bathed in a week.

Lander was her Pygmalion project, the goal, to help him. No one belonged on the street, but she knew instinctively that Lander's situation was more complicated. She wanted to uncover the truth. The possibility of helping him and the prospect of an exciting adventure equally motivated her. If she could just quell the fear that rose and fell in her gut.

Away from the mirror, Cassandra dressed. She pinched her skirt between her thumb and index finger; her thumb bumped along the cotton weave, while her index finger slid effortlessly across the silken polyester lining. She raised her hand and looked at her fingertips as if to see a history of where they'd been. Her sense of touch connected her to the physical world, just like it did for everyone else. But for Lander, it was like having a laceration across a fingertip.

Lander had touched her with his gift and torn from her a new awareness of herself. While she avoided the term magic to describe his abilities, she had confidence in his capacity to unravel the mystery behind her fear of water and her reluctance around intimacy. She knew about the heat of a hand raised in anger. But the opposite, a caring touch, was unavailable to her until she learned to relax around men. It was possible he could help with that.

She ran two fingers along the underside of her collarbone. The skin was dry and smooth, and her fingertip glanced against its warmth. Brushing the silk shirt aside, she traced a line down between her breasts. Residual moisture from her shower added weight to her finger. The proximity to her breast triggered an increased sensitivity; the skin, steeped with a slight electric charge, awakened pleasure. Her nipple puckered against the lace of her bra. Touch was a powerful sense, and how horrible that for Lander it brought such pain. A chill replaced the flush of warmth.

Her next thought surprised her. Will Lander ever be able to touch me? Cassandra tasted sadness and wondered if she'd known pleasure in any lifetime.

As Cassandra emerged from the elevator, Ray looked up from his post at the security desk. "Ms. Sandra. Your friend's tip allowed us to catch the guys that were breaking into the garage."

Cassandra nodded and gave him a close-lipped half smile, but continued walking. She didn't recognize why this good news manifested as a sense of dread. "Have a nice evening, Ray."

She reached the corner just minutes after five and was disappointed that Lander wasn't waiting. She scanned the adjoining walkways, knowing how slowly he walked; he would have been visible approaching from any direction. By a quarter after the hour, concern enveloped her. She paced up and down the lane, only casually observing a dark stain in the cracked concrete.

After waiting for half an hour, she spotted a shiny object poking out of a crack between the concrete and asphalt. She bent and lifted a set of keys from the crevice. The Wrimo Hospital tag caught her eye for only a moment before she noticed the flakes of blood in her palm, causing her to jerk and drop the keys with a clatter.

Cassandra wiped the traces of blood from her hand, then, after rummaging in her purse, retrieved the keys and placed them into a stray envelope. With one last look at the alley, she walked back to her apartment. Something had happened, and her concern was visible in her frown. From the entry she saw Ray, and a theory darkened her mood further.

"Hello again, Ms. Sandra."

"Who did you tell?"

"Tell what?"

Cassandra's voice was rising. "Who did you tell about my friend helping you catch the thieves?"

"Nobody who would know that guy."

"You're a fucking idiot. Word travels fast. You have no idea what you've done! Now all I have is a blood stain and a friend who is either dead or injured."

"Where was the blood stain?"

"In the alley at the end of the block."

Ray looked down. "Shit, I'm sorry. A homeless guy got beat up at the corner a few hours ago."

"And basic human compassion didn't make you wonder if it was someone you knew?" Cassandra glanced around as if to find another person who could help her. "What hospital would they take him to?"

"They all take turns. It could be any of them."

"We're not done here. And you'd better hope he hasn't been seriously harmed."

Cassandra's tone with Ray masked her own disquiet. Dangerous forces now threatened her nascent relationship with Lander. She had run from fear before.

Chapter 25
Tuesday,
November 3, 2009 (5:30 p.m.)

D r. Aradice looked at the clock; his shift was over. He was tiring of the tedious hospital duties. The position afforded him access to the system and engendered a lot of good-will, but it was time to give it up. His upcoming book tour would provide a graceful exit and enough money to compensate.

He grabbed his bag from the shared office and started toward the parking lot, where Monica would be waiting.

At the end of the hallway, the nurse that he had yelled at was changing the dressing on a patient's arm. She looked up, then away too quickly.

He knew she used to work at Wrimo. *Could she have known Lander as an outpatient before the accident?* Despite his conspiracy-theory mind, he didn't believe she would have any way of knowing what happened after. But the fact that she'd been on shift when Lander evaded capture unsettled him. He would need to watch her.

Monica wasn't there when he arrived at the parking lot entrance. That did not improve his mood.

With time to make a call, he dialed his cell phone. A man started to answer, but Dr. Aradice cut him off.

"Where are you? Lander was just here at the hospital."

"I'm at home. You told me you had the hospitals covered."

"If only I weren't surrounded by idiots. He was admitted as being unhoused. Get down here and start walking the streets. Check shelters, anywhere they give handouts."

Dr. Aradice flipped the phone closed without waiting for a reply.

A car slowed at the curb, and Dr. Aradice climbed in.

"You're late."

Monica didn't respond, choosing instead to act distracted as she maneuvered the car out of the parking lot.

As she signaled to turn right, he said, "No. Not back to Wrimo. Turn left. We're going to drive for a bit."

After he'd directed her right and left a few times, Monica began crisscrossing a six-block area bordered by the Orpheum Theatre, the baseball stadium, and the arts district. As they idled at the light outside the Coffee Train, Monica asked, "Where are we going?"

"Nowhere. This is useless. Find a parking spot."

Monica turned onto a side street and pulled up in front of a parking meter. As she reached for her purse, Dr. Aradice put his hand on her arm. "You don't need money for the meter. We're just going to talk."

Dr. Aradice surveyed the sidewalk and roadway. They were alone. "Lander was just at the hospital. He walked out about thirty minutes ago. He was admitted as a John Doe, apparently homeless."

Monica looked frightened and chewed on her lower lip.

Speaking in a softer voice, he took a chance and reached up to touch her shoulder, directing her gaze into his eyes. "Everything is going to be fine. He's been on the street for over a week

160

and hasn't tried to contact us or his mother. Lander is broken and no threat to us, but we need to help him."

The last words about helping—a lie—hung in the air as a police siren wailed past on the street behind them.

"We need to bring him back to Wrimo for treatment. And we need to do it quietly. Will you help me?"

"Yes, of course."

At that, the doctor rested his hand on her forearm for a long moment before pulling away and smiling at her.

Chapter 26
Tuesday,
November 3, 2009 (7:30 p.m.)

Lander's walk home from the hospital was uneventful but slow and painful. He slept off the meds and woke just after seven thirty. Since the pain was the same whether he was lying down, sitting, or standing, his priority shifted to occupying his mind. In his current condition, he couldn't fathom crawling through the wall from his cubbyhole, so he walked to the front of the building and buzzed the super.

"Shit, Lander, you're not supposed to use this door." He swallowed hard when Lander stepped into the light of the vestibule. "What happened?" Lander knew his eyes were swollen, and that purplish-red skin covered a third of his face, particularly angry around his eyes and nose. The stitches above his lip completed the look.

"Don't lecture me. I've had a shitty day. I just want to distract myself and do your bookkeeping."

"Forget it. Do you need to go to a hospital?"

"Been there, done that. I'm all cleared and just need a few lifetimes, given how much it hurts right now."

A few minutes later, as he settled into the coding and organizing of the building's receipts, he wondered if he should have tried to find Cassandra. He looked across the desk at the phone, frustrated with the situation. He had her address, but not her phone number or any certainty of her last name. If he called the lobby desk, he'd get Ray. Would he help him? He had little doubt that Ray had told someone he was the snitch. If Ray knew he'd been beaten up, he'd either feel guilty and help or push Lander away. Lander had to try.

He picked up the phone and dialed 411. The operator gave him the number to Cassandra's building and offered to complete the call.

Ray answered in an overly friendly voice, reciting a script provided by the management company. Lander suspected that "Yo, what's happenin'?" would have been his personal choice.

"Are you able to connect me to one of your residents?"

"No, I'm sorry, this is not a switchboard. If you have the full name, directory assistance..."

"Ray, do you know who this is?"

With a call display showing only the name of an unknown building, it didn't surprise him that Ray had no idea.

"You blew it, Ray. I trusted you and tried to help. You pissed all over me."

"Who is this?"

"Come on, Ray. I'm that helpless hobo who's only good at noticing things. The police patted you on the back. The owner of the building might promote you. All this praise, while I was left for dead, bleeding in an alley."

After a long pause, Ray squeaked out a response. "You're Sandra's friend. The car theft thing. Look, man, I'm sorry. I was in a bar with two guys I play pool with. I told them about it. It was like a storybook from school, you know? Don't judge people by their appearances and all that."

"You're such a fool. They were playing you from the start. Why do they think they picked your building? What else did you tell them?" Lander paused, giving him time to digest how much they had used him.

"I need to get a message to Cassandra. They took all my stuff, and I don't have her phone number." Lander smiled to himself; it was only a lie by association. Lander could hear Ray typing before he recited the number.

"It's her cell. She doesn't have a landline. This is better anyway because she's not home. She found out someone had been beaten up. She guessed it was you and yelled at me—you two are a lot brighter at putting things together than I am. I'm really sorry about what happened. Do you want me to tell the cops about the two guys?"

"No, not yet. You'll just end up like me. Keep your mouth shut."

Lander hung up and hesitated before calling Cassandra. His life was such a mess. The thugs likely thought he was dead. Was he less of a target now than before? Was he putting Cassandra at risk by reaching out to her? He dropped his head to the desk and rocked back and forth until his nose brushed the surface, causing him to gasp in pain.

Cassandra sat on a Starbucks patio, wanting to be on her own. The inside tables were about half full and the air conditioning was uncomfortable. The late-afternoon November sun, low on the horizon, cast long shadows across the asphalt corridors between the office towers. It was still warmer than inside, and the settling darkness was comforting. But this still wasn't her town, and she felt isolated without a network of friends to enlist in her the search. Cassandra pulled her shawl around her shoulders and sipped on the steaming coffee.

She looked up and down the sidewalks. The streets were

quiet. A few people stepped through the pools of light that fell from streetlamps and seeped from store windows. She watched, half hoping, half expecting to see Lander shuffling toward her with his strange breathless gait. The first two hospitals she'd visited had no record of a Lander Gate being admitted. Both had at least one male homeless person, but wouldn't give her more details. She had one more stop. Mercy Hospital was in the other direction.

Warmed and reenergized by the coffee, Cassandra walked the three blocks to her next stop. Mercy was an older hospital. Cassandra couldn't pinpoint its exact affiliation, but the Christian icons above the entry door set the mood that suffering wasn't necessarily wrong.

A wide driveway and an arriving ambulance pulled her around the corner toward the emergency entrance. There were about a dozen people sitting in the waiting room in small groups. Further inside, beyond the glass electronic doors, Cassandra observed the medical staff, purposeful in their movements but not rushing. She imagined the pace might change at a moment's notice—something like her life.

A laminated sign with an arrow directed her to General Inquiries. She approached a thick-set man working at a computer behind a glass partition. Beside him, a man in overalls stood on a ladder, fussing with a surveillance camera. Beyond the windows, Cassandra could see curtained partitions, and her heart quickened when a grizzled man stepped into view. He was the same height and stature as Lander, and dressed similarly, but a different person. Maybe behind curtain number two, she thought, wincing at the game show analogy that seemed to trivialize her search.

Cassandra redirected her attention to the inquiries desk and stood at the window, waiting patiently for the man to look up. His head bobbed slightly as he typed. It took a minute before she noticed the thin white wires of his ear buds. Shifting on her feet, she wondered if she should knock on the glass. A nurse with a pink uniform and an aluminum clipboard entered from the opposite side and smiled at her. She looked at the man, then walked over to swat him on the shoulder. His head jerked up, an earbud falling onto his keyboard. When he saw Cassandra, he slid the window open.

"I'm sorry. You can't know how exciting these medical reports are."

"Better when scored to a great soundtrack," Cassandra guessed. "Why not imagine you're in an episode of ER?"

The nurse laughed at this and the man blushed, pulling the second earbud from his ear.

"How can I help you?"

"A friend of mine, a homeless person, was beaten up in an alley. I'm trying to find him. His name is Lander Gate."

Cassandra watched as the two looked at each other and then back at her. A change had occurred, and they evaluated her. Just a minute earlier, she'd been a plain woman standing innocently in a hospital foyer. Now, they were cautious.

He broke the stare-off. "I'm sorry, ma'am. We can't release information on our patients without proof of a family relationship."

The nurse bit into her lower lip.

A doctor came up from behind and startled the nurse. He thrust some file folders into her hands. "You two still here?" His voice was cast low and unfriendly. "Have you lost any more of my patients?"

Cassandra's presence diverted his attention, and she sensed he was evaluating her. His eyes scanned her head, lingering on her thick hair. He dismissed her face but paused at the open buttons of her silk shirt. She'd removed the shawl when she entered the warmth of the waiting room. The tight material swelled and gaped. Men were so predictable.

The doctor had a Richard Gere physical appeal, but she put little weight in looks. The changed mood of the two hospital staff indicated he wasn't popular. She imagined this man played off his position and good looks. If the rank-and-file hospital staff didn't like him, she would side with them.

He turned away to pick up a whiteboard marker and updated a wall chart. Apparently, she'd failed his desirability test and their interaction was over. Cassandra wanted to scream at him. She was so tired of his type.

Gritting her teeth and swallowing hard, she stepped closer to face the desk clerk. She needed to get back on track and find Lander. She was about to speak when a look in the man's eyes warned her to stop. The nurse also stared wide-eyed at her and gently shook her head.

Cassandra had to say something. At any moment, the doctor would question the sudden end to their conversation. Her mind raced to guess why his presence prevented them from talking about Lander.

"Thank you for your help," she whispered. "I'll see that those forms are completed and returned in the morning." The man at the computer, now playing along with her deception, reached into a drawer and handed her a blank hospital form. Cassandra folded it against the counter and slipped it into her pocket. The doctor put the cap back on the marker and was reading the suspended board.

Cassandra lifted the shoulder strap of her purse and turned to leave. She'd taken two steps when the clerk called out to her.

"I'm sorry, ma'am. You'll need this as well." She turned and walked back toward the clerk's outstretched hand, while the doctor departed.

The nurse stepped forward, speaking in a hushed voice.

"Your friend was here. I treated him." She stopped for a moment to make sure that no one was listening. "His injuries weren't life-threatening. His name came up with an alert linking him to Dr. Aradice, that creature that just slid through here. I helped your friend leave."

"How long ago?" Cassandra asked.

"He was brought in early in the afternoon. He slept for about two hours. Say another hour while I cleaned him and bandaged him... It would have been about five fifteen."

Cassandra checked her phone; it was almost eight. At the same instant, the phone chirped, and the display lit up. Cassandra didn't recognize the number or the name. She hesitated before pushing the answer button.

"Hello?"

They could all hear the strained, nasal male voice. "Cassandra? It's Lander."

"Are you okay?"

"I'm going to be fine." Lander's voice was hoarse and fuzzy over the small mobile phone speaker, but she sensed a strength in his words. "Go home. I'll meet you in the morning, seven thirty at the Coffee Train. Our usual table."

Cassandra smiled at this reference and blushed when she saw her two accomplices following the conversation.

"Where are you?" he continued.

"I'm at the hospital. There are two very helpful employees in front of me."

"No kidding. Please thank them."

Cassandra held the handset away from her ear. "They can hear you. It's all good here."

Chapter 27
Tuesday,
November 3, 2009 (8:07 p.m.)

L ander felt better having spoken to Cassandra. Now she could relax and end her search. He soon finished the backlog of bookkeeping receipts. His ability to use the technology had advanced rapidly. If only his understanding of the world kept pace.

Whatever filter concealed his past also masked his ability to go beyond critical thinking and establish opinions on social or political issues. He didn't know if he voted Republican or Democrat, or if he'd ever voted. He couldn't remember ever seeing a movie but could recall the plot lines of many popular— albeit older—films. To him, titles like *Harry Potter* and *Twilight* were nothing more than colorful posters in a bookshop. A search for Lander Gate on Facebook had not revealed a listing. From what he could see of people's pages, he wondered how the network had become so popular.

His opinions were shallow, as if he'd only formed them in the time since he woke up. He catalogued world affairs as he learned them, and was troubling that he didn't have an emotional reaction beyond basic empathy. If people died, he experienced a clinical level of sorrow. If there was a natural disaster, he was in awe of nature's strength. When it came to wars or challenges between countries, ideologies, or religions, he could weigh the different arguments but, like a child, was unable to take a stance.

Before he shut off the system, he contemplated the little blue "e" symbol on the screen.

His unfamiliarity with computers and the web led him to wonder how long he'd been sequestered at Wrimo. He knew about the "World Wide Web" but didn't understand the science that powered it. This mattered to him. There was something about his ability to connect with past lives that mimicked a web connecting people and ideas.

Lander used the mouse to circle the web browser icon. With a double click, the welcome page opened, and into the "search" bar, he typed *Wrimo Hospital*.

The home page had little information. The facility lauded itself for its excellence and included two pictures of the building's exterior. Under the *About Us* tab, an interior photo of a modern-looking lounge was accompanied by three images of smiling, happy people. Lander scrolled through the different tabs, hoping to find his pie-shaped white room. The room pictured in the *Accommodations* section looked like a student dorm with bright primary-colored furniture, a simple desk with a swivel chair, and a single bed set along one wall. It didn't resemble the room in his vision.

The *Leadership* tab brought up a list of names in alphabetic order, with Dr. Aradice at the top. The hyperlinked name invited Lander to go deeper. With a push, the screen filled with text, and a four-by-five picture in the left corner triggered apprehension in his chest. It was an older shot, about ten years younger than the man Lander had seen that afternoon. Back then, his thick hair had been cut short in an effort at academic pretense. His piercing green eyes looked into the camera. A starched white jacket pressed against a shallow single Windsor knot, a purple tie poking through like a flower bud.

The biography told Lander very little The man was Ivy League educated, a senior researcher, author, and practicing psychologist with a neuroscience and cognitive science specialty. He was based at Wrimo but consulted at two other hospitals. There were links to three articles in medical journals and a published textbook. His area of expertise was the unconscious and the treatment of delusions.

Lander concurred with Cassandra's earlier comment that the website did little to inform about the true nature of the facility. He unconsciously rested his hand on the outside of his pocket to confirm that the keys were lost, and that his attack in the alley had thwarted his plan to gain access to Wrimo. Then he remembered the paper bag the nurse had given him. Was it possible that the keys were in there?

With a click, he shut off the computer. His ribs ached from sitting up, and he wanted to sleep. From his hip pocket, he extracted two of the pills the nurse had given him and swallowed them with a sip of water from the utility sink. Then he returned to his tiny room, where the paper bag sat waiting.

He shook the bag, but there was no sound of keys rattling. He poured the contents onto the bed and fingered through them: the crystal, a few dollar bills and coins, a book of matches —though he didn't smoke—and still no playing cards. He was about to scoop everything back into the bag when a slip of newsprint caught his eye. It was about three inches square, crisp and neatly folded; it couldn't have been in his pocket.

He assumed it wasn't related to him until he flipped it open. It was an obituary, dated November 2008, for a young man named Lander Gate. *Apparently, I've been dead for a year.*

Cassandra stood next to her window, looking out at the lights of the city. In the park below, the wall she'd climbed was only dimly lit. She could just make out the shadows where the thick bolts rose out of the concrete. The halogen bulbs on one side were dark. She recalled seeing broken glass. *Someday a piece of artwork will be poised on that giant pedestal.* She wondered about the theme and how the controversy had arisen. Someone must have been a passionate advocate. Where were they now?

Cassandra absently stirred the soup she had reheated: the lunch special from the Coffee Train. *Was that three or four days ago?* She questioned if it was still safe to eat, but it was all she had. She tried to distract herself by reading the journal articles she had printed that afternoon. Being productive at her work wasn't typically a problem. Lander had changed that.

A few hours later, just like Lander, Cassandra looked up the Wrimo website. The profile on Dr. Aradice underwhelmed her as well. She looked at his green eyes and remembered how they had methodically scanned her. She remembered him looking at her body, lingering on her figure, likely weighing the options of her perfect skin and how she would feel beneath him. She clenched her teeth. And then he'd turned his face away from the inconvenience of her less than desirable facial features. A few minutes of pleasure had merit, but she guessed he wouldn't value a trophy that couldn't be displayed.

Cassandra shivered with revulsion at the thought of him touching her. She closed the web page and navigated to her own institute's icon.

She logged in and completed an online form: an official request to include the Wrimo Hospital in her research. These requests were commonplace and seldom scrutinized closely. Her employer would generate a letter of introduction to establish Cassandra's credentials and request the institute's support in her study. This could mean something as noncommittal as a coffee with a low-ranking clerk or, only slightly more valuable, an interview with the executive director. On other occasions, institutions granted access to their in house libraries and extensive patient histories. The confidentiality of the subjects is required. Access to Wrimo's patient files, even with the names encrypted, was what Cassandra hoped for.

The probability of gaining access was good. Neither Cassandra nor her institute had a reputation as a whistle-blower. In the competitive arena of government research grants, there were few secrets about who was working on what. Cassandra's work on the post-treatment of mental disorders wasn't likely to raise any concerns.

With the form sent, Cassandra shut off the computer and sat at the granite-topped island that separated her kitchen from a sitting area. Muffled music filtered through the wall from her neighbor. Usually, it was the TV, especially the commercial breaks, whose higher-pitched tones seeped through the cinderblock and concrete walls. She glanced across her small living room: when had she last turned on her TV? A thick layer of dust covered the flat screen. She wondered where the remote control was.

She dug in her purse and withdrew the key ring she had recovered from the alleyway. Additional flakes of blood chipped off in her hands as she flipped through the keys. She rinsed the entire set in warm water and dried them with a paper towel.

There were six keys. Three were industrial weight. A closer examination revealed the embossed words *do not copy*. Two smaller keys bore a furniture manufacturer's label—desk keys. The final silver key reminded her of a filing cabinet key, to the type of lock that popped out when you opened it.

Stamped onto a small copper disk were the Wrimo logo, the number 8, and on the reverse a faintly scratched word.

Cassandra looked closer; the word started with the letter *s*. Instead of reaching for her glasses, she pulled out a magnifying glass from a drawer beneath her bookshelves.

The word was *somnus*. Cassandra's ability to understand medical terms included a working knowledge of Latin. *Somnus* meant sleep.

The last item on the ring was a plastic tab similar to those issued by grocery store reward programs. Whatever logo had been printed on it was worn off; all that remained was the shiny white plastic. Cassandra sat back in the chair and turned the keys over repetitively as she would mala or rosary beads. As she repeated the word *somnus*, the two syllables rose and fell like a mantra. But what did it mean? Was it a koan—a Zen phrase meant to illuminate, but with no literal answer?

The face of Dr. Aradice reappeared in her mind's eye. His bio said that he specialized in patients recovering from a coma. A type of sleep. She wondered if it linked the keys to him.

Cassandra went to the window and looked again toward the benches and the plinth. A movement in the shadow caught her eye. She swapped the magnifying glass for a small pair of binoculars and focused the eyepiece. The glare from her kitchen light made it difficult to focus, so she turned it off, moved in the darkness back to the window, and rested the rubber tips of the lenses against the cool glass.

Two men walked out to the end of the rampart. One held a flashlight and peered into the hole where Cassandra had found the bag. She smiled, knowing all they would find was an empty niche and perhaps an annoyed rat or two. She could see them scanning the area at the surface, wondering if they had looked in the wrong place, hoping to discover another loose cover.

Even without sound or subtitles, she read the lips of the taller man well enough to decipher a curse. They took one more frantic look around, and their argument escalated. The smaller man held out his arms, palms upward, as if asking for understanding. The taller man whipped the back of his hand against the other man's face, sending him cowering.

The smaller man mouthed, "Wait!" He gestured off to his left, down the block from Cassandra's building. He shook his right hand and made an expressive gesture with his open palm.

Cassandra understood. His shaking wrist mimicked the jingling of key ring. He was pointing to the alley where Lander had been attacked. That's where they were headed next. If only she could set up a rendezvous with the police. But how to do it without implicating herself?

Ray.

She grabbed her purse and pulled a raglan sweater over her head, taking one last look out the window. The men were now halfway across the park. She bolted out the door and down the hall to the elevator, lamenting while she waited that her building lacked accessible stairs.

In the lobby, she cursed. Ray wasn't at his post.

Christ. Maybe it was better this way. *The less he knows...* She slipped behind the security desk and looked around. The electronics, video monitor, and control panels for the building were behind a roll-top enclosure. She reached for it, expecting it to be locked, but it slid upward. Luckily, Ray was still cutting corners. The monitor screen was divided into four sections. Each rotated through different views of the building. The right section included exterior views, where the two men she'd been watching stepped up on the curb after having crossed the road, almost out of the range of the camera. On the bottom left, the image showed the parking garage where Ray was walking toward the elevator bay. He was coming back to his desk.

Cassandra fumbled to pick up the desk-mounted phone and dialed.

"911. What is the nature of your emergency?"

"Police."

"Go ahead."

"This is building security for the Karsh Apartments. The two suspects in the beating this afternoon are back in the same alleyway, just south of our main entrance. They're looking for something."

"What makes you think this is a criminal act?"

Cassandra hesitated, unsure how to answer the question. One screen mimicked her indecision, rippling and going fuzzy before snapping back to clarity. "These are definitely the two that beat up the indigent man. We caught them on our video camera. Your officers were supposed to come and view the tape."

"Please stay on the line."

Cassandra scanned the control panel. The top-right camera covered the entrance to the elevator and a corridor leading to the fire escape. Ray had just walked back into view after checking the basement door. She had maybe two minutes. In her head, Lander's voice repeated a warning: *You don't want to be associated with me.*

She wanted to erase the images of her crossing the lobby to the desk to prevent Ray from knowing she'd made the 911 call. She randomly punched the *No. 2* preset. The screen filled with the lobby cameras. A rewind symbol appeared above a row of push buttons. As she pushed it, the image fluttered and back-tracked. After only a few seconds, she saw herself flit from the elevator, moving off camera, then reappear as she approached the desk.

At the bottom of the screen, a message asked if the recording should resume. She pushed the button and a second warning message appeared: *Erase previously stored data?* Cassandra punched *yes* and let the camera play for about ten seconds—enough time to erase the previous capture. She punched the square stop button, and the image flickered for a moment. A new message appeared: *Recording will resume in 10, 9, 8...* Cassandra slammed the roll-top cover down and grabbed her bag.

As the front door closed behind her, she heard the bell of the elevator. She looked up to see the darkened sphere of a camera mounted above the entrance to the parking garage. But from what she had seen on Ray's monitor, she figured that if she stayed close to the building, the camera wouldn't capture her.

Up at the corner, a police cruiser flashed its lights and came to an abrupt halt at the alleyway. One uniformed officer was out of the vehicle even before it had stopped, and the other followed out the driver's side. They moved quickly but cautiously into the laneway, calling out a command to someone out of sight. "Stand up straight. No sudden moves. Step forward into the light."

Cassandra slowed down, staying close to the edge of her building. She felt a wave of anxiety wash over her as she tried to blend in and avoid attention. *Single white females don't hover in dark alleys in this neighborhood.* A minivan taxi pulled up alongside her and three men climbed out.

As they stood by the open window, pooling their cash to settle with the driver, Cassandra darted across the sidewalk and slipped into the cab. The driver eyed her curiously but said nothing until the men moved away.

He settled back into the driver's seat and turned to her. "Where to, miss?"

"Circle the block and park on the other side of the street. Keep the meter running." The driver craned his neck to see what the activity was as he steered around the police car and passed the alleyway. It was too dark to see anything more than stray sabers of flashlights crisscrossing the walls.

The taxi circled the block and pulled up across the street. The police officer led two men in handcuffs toward one of the police cruisers. Cassandra shifted in the seat and, out of the corner of her eye, noticed the taxi driver was watching her instead of the unfolding drama . It made her uneasy. "We can go now. One more time around the block and drop me at the lobby of the Karsh Apartments."

As they pulled away from the curb, Cassandra looked back to see Ray standing out in front of the lobby. After circling the block again, the cab stopped; she paid the driver and stepped into the light at the entryway to her building. Ray caught sight of her.

"Hello, Miss Sandra. No shortage of excitement in this block the last few days."

"What's happening?"

"I don't know. They were already there when I came upstairs from doing my rounds. They arrested two men." Nick stepped forward and held the door for Cassandra. As they crossed the lobby, they were both surprised to hear a voice behind them.

A police officer had caught the door before it closed and walked up beside them. "I need to speak to the security detail that reported the suspicious men."

"That would be me?"

At the entrance to the elevator, Cassandra called out. "Good night, Ray. Night, Officer."

As the doors closed, the police officer repeated his question with a different emphasis. "No, I need to speak to the woman who made the 911 call."

Chapter 28
Wednesday,
November 4, 2009 (7:20 a.m.)

E ven though they had plans to meet at the Coffee Train, Cassandra was waiting in the lane outside Lander's apartment. She stood a few feet away as he straightened up from locking the metal door to his bunker.

He jerked painfully. "Where the hell did you come from?"

"A change of plans."

"But how did...?"

"Your call. Instead of a person's name, the display on my phone identified this building." She scanned from pavement to roof, her head tilting up. "I remember touring it before I chose the Karsh. It's old, and I'm suspicious of ancient plumbing. Maybe it's that fear of water again. Your super sent me back here. He's out front sweeping."

"That's supposed to be my job. I'm hungry. Are we going for breakfast?"

"Yes, sir! Follow me."

Cassandra was all business for the next four hours. First, they drove a short distance out of downtown to a busy bakery and café. Lander ate an enormous meal, and they spoke little of what had happened over the previous few days.

When Lander hesitated in front of a Target store, Cassandra elbowed him to keep moving. "What's wrong? Are you a Walmart shopper instead?"

"I don't know if I've ever been in either."

The bright lights and the cavernous roof made him nervous. Cassandra pulled him along from department to department. They purchased basics, including snacks, bottled water, T-shirts, and two complete outfits: one comfortable and casual, the other more businesslike—at least for Scottsdale-Phoenix—and comprising a pair of pleated pants, a tailored golf shirt, and a sweater.

Lander knew people were looking at him, but he eventually relaxed. For someone with an articulate memory and an eye for patterns, the store put him into visual overload. At one point, Cassandra had selected a shirt and Lander noted that the price was wrong; it had been discounted on a different rack. She argued with him, then agreed to check his theory. They walked back a few rows, which vindicated Lander. She nodded. "You only had a moment to see this rack when we walked by. Impressive."

After leaving Target, they drove a short distance up the interstate to a clean, independent courtyard-style motel.

Lander became curious. If Cassandra just wanted him to change his clothes, there were other options. She hadn't let him use the fitting rooms at the store; he guessed that his state of personal hygiene negated any benefit of putting on clean clothes.

After shutting off the engine, she turned to Lander. "Don't overthink this. You need a private place to get cleaned up. I don't want anyone to see you at my apartment. It might further implicate you in the police activity."

Or you're just being smart and not bringing a stranger into your home, he thought.

"Wait here while I get you a room."

Cassandra let out a nervous laugh when she returned to the car. "This is so cliché. The desk clerk is checking us out. Look!"

Lander turned as someone pulled aside the curtain in the small office. Despite the reflection on the glass, he could see two eyes focused in their direction. "It's as much about security as caring about your personal story."

"Or, more likely, he wants to see who I'm hiding. I considered registering as Mr. and Mrs. Jones. I should have asked if they rented rooms by the hour. But I didn't pay with cash. That threw him a little. I'm guessing most of their guests try to cover their tracks. I might make you a tax write-off yet."

They both laughed, and Cassandra moved the car around to the side of the building closer to the assigned room. Lander retrieved his shopping bag from the back seat and was about to say goodbye when Cassandra also got out of the car.

"I wasn't going to come in with you. But, it makes little sense to drive back to my apartment when we have more to do." Her face transitioned to a stern look, and Lander thought he was about to be scolded. "Can I trust there will be no weirdness?"

Unsure what to say, Lander lifted his arms to shoulder height with palms forward, implying he surrendered.

As the guest room door closed behind them, Cassandra pointed toward the bathroom. "Take your time." She held up a smaller Target bag he hadn't noticed and passed it to him. It contained a small pair of scissors, shaving cream, a pack of disposable razors, deodorant, and some skin lotion.

A flash of another random memory had him speaking before he even knew the details of the comparison. "I'm channeling Kim Novak in *Vertigo*," Lander said. "Maybe we were married in a previous life. Do you have hair dye somewhere?"

"That's our next stop—at least a haircut. Now get to it."

Cassandra moved over to a tiny built-in desk and set up her computer. "I have work to do."

Lander took his time. After trimming his facial hair with the scissors, he used multiple razors to hack through his scraggly beard, contorting his face to avoid the sutures.. He relaxed in a long, hot shower, twisting sideways to reduce the impact on his bruised ribs. He emptied the little bottle of body wash to scrub away as much of the grime as he could.

The fogged mirror cleared as he dressed in the new clothes. He tugged on the fabric, unsure of their starched roughness against his skin. His face, now visible over the sink, stopped him. He had no mirror in his coal chute and wondered when he'd last considered his reflection. He recalled glimpses in store windows, but those were ghostlike and multifaceted, picking up everything and everyone around him. It suited him to be seen that way—it was a confirmation of how his mind worked.

He looked again at his clean-shaven face, expecting recognition or a flash of his past. He couldn't always have been a scraggly, long-haired bum. But he saw nothing. Just his swollen black eyes and misshapen nose staring back at him. Using a facecloth, Lander wiped down the sink and counter, sending tufts of hair into the plastic garbage can. The big clumps collected easily. He didn't want the housekeeper to clean up the mess. Unfortunately, the cloth shifted more stubble than it picked up.

But as he stared at the dusting of hair fragments on the tiled white floor, a memory coalesced in his consciousness. Unlike his usual visions, this one had distinctive sounds—the chafing of steel shears and the crispness of hair being sliced. He sat in another white room, getting his hair cut. He lifted his arms, which, this time, were not restrained. A woman scolded him to sit still. He tried to rise, and a clump of hair slid across his forehead; he blinked as it caught in his eyelash and tickled. In his vision, he wiped away the strands, his arm colliding with the scissors. The point pierced his skin and he let out a small gasp of pain. The blood dripped onto the floor in vivid circles.

Lander's head snapped up, and only the motel bathroom surrounded him. The disorientation subsided as he blinked and wiped away the phantom hair in his eyes. He looked down. A tiny incision across the top of his arm oozed blood. But there were no scissors within reach, and the razors lay discarded in the wastebasket at his feet. He scraped at the remnant of the memory, but, like a dream after waking, the wisps of thought failed to coalesce.

He leaned forward, pressing his palms into the edge of the laminate countertop. As his breath slowed, he tried again to evaluate what had happened. This memory, he was sure, wasn't that old, and his mood had been playful. He had trusted whoever was cutting his hair.

The blood darkened the tissue he pressed against the cut, and Lander waited for it to scab. Jane had succumbed in this life to his touch. And now his own memory, emerging from the shadow of his amnesia, had torn the skin on his arm. Just how real could these experiences be?

The coolness of the tiles seeped into his feet. What was real for him? The detritus of his unhoused persona had been swept into the wastebasket. Now he stood there as if he was about to go play golf. Neither seemed right. Lander would be an outcast no matter where he was.

Unable to hide any longer in the bathroom, he inhaled and steeled himself for the reveal. The handle clicked as he opened the door. On the far side of the room, Cassandra's computer screen had gone into standby mode, and she was curled in a fetal position on the bed. She lay on top of the sheets but had slipped under the bedspread. Her head was crushed into the pillow and strands of hair that had escaped her elastic fell across her face.

He sat on the edge of the bed, careful not to disturb her, allowing the images of her past lives to drain into him. To accomplish this, Lander had to push past the puddles of abstraction that quivered in Cassandra's thoughts, waiting to coalesce into REM-sleep dreams. In most people, past-life memories are submerged and repressed. From time to time, though, these experiences arose as terrifying nightmares.

Lander flipped through Cassandra's history, looking for one that fulfilled his needs. A common theme in her past lives was a need for acceptance. He dwelled on this for a moment and decided this was true for everyone. Whatever he tapped into— soul, chi, karma—it screamed to him that everyone was connected. People grasp at individuality while being buffeted by the choices they make. They tumble in circles through repeated lifetimes and from time to time they may detect a sense of direction—as if pushing off from the side of a river. But, only briefly independent before the current asserts itself and pulls.

Cassandra stirred and stretched her legs, the cadence of her breathing interrupted. Lander lay down on the bedspread beside her. The pain in his ribs subsided, and the change in position allowed him to track the air moving through the back of his throat. He counted each exhale and started over again every time he reached ten. It wasn't about reaching a high number but about being attentive to the breath. He shared the air with the warm body beside him, trying to match Cassandra's pace, but her respirations were lighter. Despite this, Lander was awash in calm and safety. Like Cassandra, he felt a welcome sense of inclusion.

A vacuum started up in the adjacent room, bumping against the baseboards. The interstate hummed outside the window. The plume of an air horn, stretched thin at seventy miles an hour, traced a truck racing north. Each driver navigated the same road, each with their own destination. Lander exhaled, knowing how temporary it all was.

Cassandra shifted and felt the sweat from her legs sticking to her jeans. She didn't want to look at the wrinkled state of her blouse. She became aware of the weight next to her. Lander lay on his back, his steady breath vibrating through the base of his throat. She saw the smoothness of his face and his damp, matted hair. She lifted the bedspread and rolled off into the chilly room.

Her nap had scrunched her blouse on one side, and it needed attention. She rummaged in the closet and retrieved an ironing board and iron. As she unbuttoned and removed the blouse, she checked that Lander was still asleep. She'd never been shy, but who was this strange man? Settling on the need for modesty, she padded to the sideboard and swapped her wrinkled shirt for one of the T-shirts she had bought Lander.

As the iron warmed, she panned the room with an inquiring mind, evaluating the surreal landscape around her. Lander shifted and sighed, twitched his leg, and settled. He had lain down beside her and she hadn't woken up. How was that possible? And they had shared the top of the bed, only eight or ten inches apart, without her suffocating. This dissolving of the physical barrier that had separated them opened her to appreciate the intimacy of the motel room and her nascent relationship with Lander.

She wasn't afraid of him. And though she didn't understand him, there had been trust from the beginning. The iron at least resolved the major wrinkles before Cassandra gave up. As she returned the iron to the metal stand, Lander stirred.

He cleared his throat and spoke in a gravelly baritone. "Well, I hope it was good for you. Pass me a cigarette."

"Very funny." She held up the blouse to exhibit the still wrinkled front panel. "I'm trying to make myself respectable. But then again, being holed up in a motel room with you excludes me from that list."

"Come here." Lander said softly. "Don't worry. I won't take advantage of you." He shook his head. "Hold that last thought. It's all relative when you consider the weirdness we have already shared." Lander shifted to sitting and patted his hand on the bed beside him.

Cassandra experienced a moment of shyness. There was something about the proximity of the bed that made her wish it was a sofa or a bench. But if she hesitated any longer, it might show a lack of trust and break the playful mood. She was also imbued with the excitement of the moment. It was all a little daring; the skin on her arms rippled into goose bumps, and a slight flush brushed her cheeks.

He continued encouraging her. "There's something I want to show you."

"You show me yours and I'll show you mine," she teased, her voice quivering.

"If only that were possible."

Cassandra detected a note of sadness and came over to sit. She expected something to happen spontaneously but, just like when he was asleep, she didn't detect his power. Lander had his eyes closed, moving his lips in some silent recitation.

"Please let me show you this," he whispered. "Be open to it as a gift. No judgment."

He reached over to intertwine their fingers. Immediately, her body temperature soared as the room fell away. Her breathing quickened. Warm, rough hands pulled her close. As she grew helpless, she abandoned the need to be in control. Her role of spectator dissolved as she became pliable to an embrace. It wasn't Lander that held her. But, whoever it was, they shared a deep trust. Was it possible to feel another person so completely? Aware of Lander as a spectral bystander, she dropped his hand for a moment and raised her arms to slip the T-shirt over her head. Nothing would impede her hunger to be touched.

She couldn't distinguish what was real. The motel bedroom shimmered. Lander sat regarding her in one reality, while in the other, a man pulled her on top of him, sinking into the mattress beneath her weight. She tried to focus, to rise above the pheromones that ignited in her body. As a spectator, it was cliché to witness such an intense union. But she wasn't just watching. Her shortness of breath and the tactile response of her skin devoured her. She arched her back and, with a deep exhale, abandoned any need to figure out where she was or who she was with.

When the orgasm hit, nothing else mattered but the transcendent arc.

Cassandra opened her eyes and found that Lander had moved across the room and now watched her from the swivel desk chair. She let out a deep sigh and licked the dryness from her lips. Her voice cracked. "Now who needs that cigarette?"

She knew the T-shirt lay puddled on the floor a few feet from the bed, and her bra had slipped, exposing a breast. Lander had respectfully turned away. Her jeans were undone and pulled open, and the lace edge of her panties was scrunched against her pubic hair. She ran her fingers across her face, aware of the moisture on her fingertips. The muskiness told her where her hand had been.

"I found that memory as you slept. You are capable of deep love and intense passion."

Cassandra sat up. "I'm going to take a shower. It seems we got our money's worth for the room."

Chapter 29
Wednesday,
November 4, 2009 (11:15 a.m.)

They pulled up to a strip mall that stretched an entire block. In the window of a real estate office, a woman was inserting four-by-six photos into a hanging frame. Next door, a faded and curled travel poster showed an ancient bridge in a rural Italian town; the travel agency had gone out of business and flyers were collecting below the mail slot behind the glass door.

Cassandra held the door to the next shop in the row, a hair salon. Ammonia vapors assaulted them as they entered and Lander tensed—the similarity of the smell to antiseptic triggered a flashback of being in a medical facility.

Five brightly lit workstations lined a mirrored wall, and only one chair was occupied. This woman was the source of the chemical in the air. Her hair was wound in bright pink curlers and she was midway through a perm.

Cassandra spoke with familiarity to the woman at the entry desk, and Lander wondered what sort of story she was weaving. He thought of *Vertigo* again, when the actor James Stewart sets the stage for the last piece of Kim Novak's transformation, though Rex Harrison in *My Fair Lady* would have been more on point.

With the arrangements settled, Cassandra walked over and whispered in Lander's ear. "Will you be able to control the images? She'll be holding scissors. I don't think you would survive another hospital visit."

"Suggest that she wear gloves. Pay her a little extra and tell her I won't be offended."

At the sinks, Lander stretched back as the stylist reclined his chair to lower his head into a smooth porcelain slot. He felt vulnerable with his carotid artery exposed, but as the warm water sluiced through his hair, Lander relaxed and enjoyed the comforting caress of the woman's hands even through the blue latex gloves. The hairdresser's fingers, slick with the viscous soap, pushed into his scalp and tugged at the strands of his hair.

He sensed other life presences as she dipped in and out, leaning into the task. He noticed her closeness when her chest hovered inches from his face. The water splashed and dripped down the white insides of her arms, invading the gloves. He kept her images shuffling so no single memory or emotion dominated. There was a pungency to her deodorant that mixed with the botanical scent of the shampoo and a hint of coffee on her breath. She was in her late twenties, a stocky girl with gelled black hair and a fleeting smile. Her teeth flashed when she laughed, but she didn't hold the expression. Lander guessed this was the face she would reveal if caught in an unguarded moment: pursed lips with a hint of sadness in the eyes.

Lander wanted to give her the gift of being away from the dreary salon, even for a few minutes. He could do that, but he feared losing control. What if a violent memory took over? There were risks, but he had to try.

He exhaled and let his power coalesce. When it took hold of her, the hairdresser transitioned from washing hair to

sitting on the back of a motorcycle. The pressure of her fingertips on his scalp slackened and her hands stopped. Her chin
tilted up as her eyes closed. Only Lander could see her,
framed in the rectangular rearview mirror, as an apparition
with tousled and wind-whipped hair. The girl's body rose and
fell, buoyant on the drifts of a long-forgotten country road.
Lander shared in the pleasure of what they saw. The enormity
of the sky had allowed her spirit to soar above the vast fields of
corn.

Maybe it was the gloves or Lander's rising exhaustion, but
the connection slipped. In that second, she jerked away,
blinking and confused.

Cassandra, perched nearby on one of the empty barber
chairs, sat up with a look of concern. Lander dissolved the
connection and brought the girl back into the tiny shop. She
shook her head and smiled.

"I'm sorry," she said. "I must have drifted off for a moment."

"Daydreams can be quite intoxicating. but next time you
should wear a helmet."

The girl went wide-eyed. "How did you know?"

"A lucky guess. The way you tilted your head back
suggested a motorcycle ride on a summer afternoon."

"Actually, it was a fall day in Iowa. Late in the season, the
corn drying on the stalk for a feed harvest." The girl stopped
speaking and cocked her head to one side. "Where did that
come from? I've never been to Iowa, or in a cornfield, for that
matter." With a shake of her head, she resumed the final rinse
on Lander's hair; all the while, her eyes belied an uncertainty
about what had just happened. Behind her, Cassandra smiled,
and he knew she was comparing the gifts they had both
received from Lander.

When the hairdresser asked Lander how he liked his hair
styled, the question stumped him.

"I don't have an opinion." Unlike most of her patrons, he meant it. He had no memory of how he liked to have it cut.

"It naturally wants to part to the left. Who are we to defy nature?"

A soft snort from Cassandra's direction caused her eyes to flick sideways. Lander suppressed a smile.

Later, the woman finished with a little gel, whipped off the sheet, and announced the transformation complete.

Lander stood beside the chair, trying to recognize the person in the mirror. The clothes, the haircut, the scraped face, and his situation all belonged to someone else. Only the faded bruises anchored him. He surveyed the rest of his body and wondered if he was sitting in an alternate reality, where someone with Lander's powers was holding onto his wrist, giving him a glimpse at a past life. Any moment the connection would break, and he would find himself strung out on a park bench.

They thanked and paid the woman, and Cassandra pulled out of the parking lot, heading toward the motel. "I have to get some work done. Let's grab a coffee and crash in our room."

Our room, he thought, liking how it sounded. He also recognized his discomfort in ordinary situations, simply hanging out and doing nothing. One could argue that, as a person in a homeless situation, he did nothing every day. But scratching out an existence kept him busy. To sit in a clean, air-conditioned motel room, fed and safe and not being poked or questioned in some social-work experiment, was an unimagined luxury. He needed to relax and not dwell so much on why Cassandra was inserting herself into his life.

In the room, Cassandra gestured for him to stand behind her at the small desk. "Before I work, we need to set you up with an email account and a presence on the Internet. It'll help you with your research. Finding people is becoming easier because everyone flocks to Facebook and Myspace." Cassandra typed a few keystrokes, pausing to scribble something on the small desk notepad with the motel's scratchy pencil. "Your fake name is Michael Emory." She paused and looked at him, her head cocked to one side in expectation.

"What? Should I know who that is?"

"I thought I was being clever, M. Emory. Memory! That's what we're trying to find out."

She handed him the paper. "Here's the site to log in. Your username is your email. Your password is 'pastlife,' one word, all lower-case letters. Most people use Hotmail for email, but I like the new Gmail."

Lander understood on a superficial level what all that meant. He folded up her note and as he placed it in his pocket, he remembered leaving a few stray dollars in the pants from the hospital. They were still on the floor in the bathroom.

He retrieved the cash and placed it on the vanity before he stuffed the clothes into the wastebasket and washed his hands.

The obituary from the newspaper rested on top of the bills. Lander didn't know why he hadn't shown the clipping to Cassandra. The cascade of questions it created overwhelmed him. Death, being the end, normally simplified things, but in this situation, his being alive made it complicated.

The flimsy newsprint bubbled under the moisture on his fingers, and in the bright light of the bathroom, he noticed for the first time that someone had underlined the name and address of the memorial gardens where a service had been held.

Cassandra looked alarmed when he showed it to her. After rereading it multiple times, she flipped it over as if expecting there to be more information. "Where did you get it?"

"It was in the bag of my personal items from the hospital. It must have been the nurse. She was very helpful and, in hind-sight, there was something familiar about her. It was more than my having seen her at the shelter. When I used my skill to encourage her to help me, it didn't seem like she needed it. She was already a step ahead of me."

Cassandra typed the address into her computer. "We have a mystery and a short drive ahead of us." She jotted some directions on the motel notepad. "But only after I get some work done."

As Cassandra worked, Lander sought to distract himself from the escalating complexity of his life. He clicked through the channels on the TV. As there was little of interest, he switched it off. He slept for a while and, when he woke, read the tourist information magazine on the coffee table. Some of the featured locations seemed familiar to him. His brain absorbed everything else. Like the memory game with his deck of cards, he flipped between sections, seeing how quickly he could memorize the facts.

When he tired of this activity, he got up and slipped on his shoes. "I'm going for a walk."

Cassandra looked concerned, but nodded in approval. "I need an hour before we can find lunch."

At the door, Lander tucked in his shirt. "I won't go far. I need some air and exercise. Being inside and being fed every four hours is still new to me."

Outside, Lander moved slowly along the raised walkway. It was another sunny day, and the painted aluminum railing warmed his hand. He thought of going back to the room for a bottle of water but decided against it. A day before, he would have looked for a spigot on the side of a building. A housekeeper in a gray striped uniform passed him at the top of the stairs. She nodded a greeting, and he heard her cart rolling on to the next room for service. The motel parking lot surrounded the building and Lander lamented the bleak landscape. At least in his neighborhood, he had the park. Just beyond the hotel's entrance, cars idled at a light while others accelerated up the ramp to the interstate. Phoenix wasn't a walking city. It was a classic example of suburban sprawl. A person required a car for even the simplest of errands.

Why bother with sidewalks and crossing signals? Who would ever walk here? As if to defy his theory, Lander began a slow progression around the entire intersection. With each signal, he crossed multiple lanes of traffic, cautious of the drivers that wouldn't be expecting a pedestrian. Twice he had to sprint to clear the roadway before the lights changed.

In the shadow of the overpass, Lander stopped to catch his breath. Near the next corner, a small stack of cardboard squares littered the crushed gravel edge. He moved forward, picked one up, and flipped it over. In thick black lettering it read, *VET. Please help.*

The second one was printed on both sides. On the first side, it read, *Please Help, Cold and Hungry.* Lander flipped it over: *Please Help, Hot and Hungry.*

At the crunch of gravel, Lander looked up to see a man in a baseball cap approaching him. The shadows of the overpass and the brim of the hat revealed nothing but dark skin.

"Don't be touching those. They are my tools, and this is my office."

Lander handed him the signs. Up close, he recognized the man. He had been with the group in the alley behind the Coffee Train and had also sat near Lander once at breakfast. By the standards of the street, Lander guessed he was a moderate.

Lander had studied the social strata of the unhoused. They were more defined than many believed. The drunks didn't trust the mentally ill; the users tried to recruit the drunks so they could then steal their drugs. The pimps and pushers looked out for themselves. In another tier were the thieves and ex-cons, who came and went. They returned only if they weren't rehabilitated, and that didn't happen often.

This man was only an occasional drunk and periodic drug user. In any other lifetime or situation, his quick tongue and comedic timing would have landed him a job in sales.

The light changed to red and cars slowed. The man glanced between Lander and the roadway as if assessing where the most profit might come from.

"I tried cleaning windows once. Not enough fresh water. It made a big mess." He held up the *vet* sign. "When I see American flags or yellow ribbons, I always use this one." He pointed to another sign on the ground. "That one is good for families with young children." Lander bent over and picked it up. *My mother would still love me.*

"Now you know some secrets to success in this line of work. I've thought about setting up a school." He lifted his hands and spread his palms apart, creating a visual of an imagined sign. "Dave's College: Home of the Short Sale." He dropped his hands. "I know a short sale is something to do with houses, but it really describes what I do here."

Lander smiled. "I like the logic."

"Now how about a little *too-ition?*"

Besides the cash he had retrieved from his old clothes, Cassandra had given Lander some money after breakfast. He had felt weird accepting it. Rummaging in his pocket, he handed Dave a five-dollar bill.

"You must let me know where to register."

Dave laughed and was about to say something when he jutted his chin and focused on Lander's face. "I recognize you from somewhere."

"It's possible. We've had a few meals together."

Dave scrunched up his face and, like a bobblehead doll, flipped his head back and forth. "Yeah, you're the wheezy guy."

He abruptly stepped backward. "Shit, you're the rat that pegged the dunk tank boys. Some say you're dead. By the looks of your face, probably close to the truth."

Lander nodded. "Those three were into some nasty shit, more organized than you might imagine. Stealing and distributing prescription drugs was just part of it. They weren't doing any of us any favors."

Dave hesitated for a moment, considering what Lander had just said. "It's all cool. I had no dealings with them. Did you trade the info for this new look?"

"No. This is some other craziness. It's only a matter of time before the novelty wears off for my new patron." Lander didn't believe Cassandra to be that shallow, but he wanted to get back to the motel room. "I gotta go. I'll see you around." A few minutes later, he spied Cassandra leaning on the railing outside their room.

"Pleasant walk?"

"Not really. Just a lot of concrete and car fumes."

"Let's go," she said, when he reached the top of the stairs. Lander made a step toward the motel room door to get his things. She sensed his confusion. "You're coming back here later to sleep in a proper bed." She placed the key in his palm and led the way back down the stairs. "We've got a mystery to solve, but first we need something to eat."

They pulled out and drove beneath the overpass. Up ahead, the light turned yellow and Lander saw a figure moving among the cars. Dave approached Cassandra's window, pausing to peer through the reflection.

"Hey, dude, you inspired me." He shuffled through the corrugated cards, and with a smile, lifted a sign that read, *Patron Needed.*

Chapter 30
Wednesday,
November 4, 2009 (1:45 p.m.)

The empty parking lot at the memorial gardens was a welcome sight. A floral wreath on an easel announced a service that afternoon at three o'clock. Another soul had entered the cycle of death and rebirth, and Lander wondered if they had died horribly. It was hard for him not to think in this manner after all he had seen.

The double-height wooden door swung out on silent hinges as Lander held it for Cassandra. The lobby was cool and dark, not unexpected for a place of mourning, and they stopped to let their eyes adjust. A series of second-story rectangular windows spread shafts of light across the terrazzo floor. Quiet music filtered from a room to their right, where red carpeting and pews suggested a church but without the religious symbolism. Paraffin and citrus infused the air, deepening the sacred spirit. Two candelabras set with new pillar candles flanked the chapel doorway but had not been lit. It felt very much like a theater before showtime.

Lander turned to Cassandra and winked. "I wonder if they would rent this space for my performances. It's perfect."

Cassandra grimaced. "Do you think they have a directory,

like at an apartment building?" she whispered in a businesslike tone.

Before he could answer, a soft footfall drew their attention to a man in a dark two-piece suit who approached them.

"Good afternoon. May I be of assistance?"

Cassandra stepped forward. "We are looking to pay our respects to one of your..." With this, she faltered. "I'm unsure what to call them. Residents?"

"We call them our eternal guests. Please follow me."

The man led them through a door on the far side of the vestibule and stopped in front of a computer terminal. With a tap of the space bar, the screen came to life. "The name?"

"Last name Gate, first name Lander," Cassandra said.

"A second visitor today." The man spoke matter-of-factly as he typed the name.

Lander and Cassandra shared a glance. "Is the person still here?"

"No, it was earlier, when we first opened. I didn't speak with her because she knew where to go." As if dismissing the need for the computer, the man turned and pointed. "You will find your friend in the succulent garden columbarium." He handed Cassandra a map and pointed. "On the end of this wall near the Saguaro."

They thanked him and moved away. Once they were out of hearing range, Lander leaned toward Cassandra. "How did he know she was here to visit me if he didn't speak with her?"

Cassandra pointed to a camera mounted high on the wall. "A good security system?"

"Something isn't right." To emphasize his point, Lander swept his arms in an all-encompassing gesture. They were surrounded by a checkerboard of niches, each sealed with a carved stone or steel plaque and bearing a brass ring for holding flowers. "Thousands are entombed here, yet he knows my name and location."

"Most likely he watched where she went. I wouldn't imagine there's much else to do."

"I'd like to know who was here earlier."

Cassandra nodded as they reached the archway into the next garden.

Their destination was aptly named. The courtyard surrounded an assembly of succulents: prickly pear, organ pipe, and compass cacti all arranged in a central plot. The layout was dominated by a fourteen-foot-high saguaro cactus with two statuesque arms reaching skyward, the distinctive state flower of Arizona. They found Lander's plaque, the only one on the wall with a nosegay of fresh flowers. A simple etched metal plate identified Lander's dates of birth, December 9, 1973, and death, November 12, 2008, and included a quote.

There is a crack in everything God has made – Ralph Waldo Emerson

"That's another confirmation that I've been dead for almost a year."

"Look, there's something behind the flowers." Cassandra delicately reached between the stalks and withdrew a small envelope addressed to Lander.

Lander took the card and turned it over in his hand. "Is there a tradition of writing notes to dead people?"

"I'm sure in some cultures, but not so much here."

The back flap had been tucked inside, not sealed, and Lander extracted the contents. He held up a laminated card with a yellow sticky note that read, *You need to remember.* Lander peeled away the note to reveal a driver's license—his driver's license—complete with an awkward photo of a much younger but very recognizable Lander Gate.

"Why would someone leave this on your memorial?"

"They didn't just leave it. They left it specifically for me. Breadcrumbs. This scavenger hunt began with the newspaper clipping of the obit. If the nurse is behind all this, why didn't she just tell me?"

Cassandra ran her finger along the bottom of the ID card. "Look at the edge. It's been cut." Her thumb pressed against a splinter of plastic.

Lander recounted to Cassandra his discovery of a fragment of his file. "I wonder if this was in the folder when it got stuck in the shredder."

"It has a Phoenix address on it. Based on your age in the photo, it's probably your family home."

Lander let the street name and address roll around in his thoughts, but there was no tendril to latch onto. It was another piece of the strange puzzle of his life that he was trying to assemble without seeing the picture on the box. If the border pieces were important, then the top left corner piece would depict this moment: him standing in front of his own tomb.

Now, a mysterious ally was handing him pieces to the puzzle. He stole a glance at Cassandra, who was now looking out at the courtyard. He felt a tug of gratitude that she was helping him. *If what I have is a superpower, then at least I have a sidekick too.*

Chapter 31
Wednesday,
November 4, 2009 (6:00 p.m.)

C assandra was quiet during dinner. Lander wondered if it was the growing complexity of his situation, or perhaps his sexual exhibition earlier had overstepped a boundary. He had tried to talk to her about it, but she had blushed and shut the conversation down.

She chose a small restaurant with narrow aisles between the bistro-style tables. The menu leaned toward Italian with a salute to local flavors. Lander assumed one reason for her silence was the proximity of the other guests—it would have been difficult to talk about his talent or their circumstances without being overheard. Lander caught himself, not caring if his secret got out.

Their banter provided little new information about Cassandra. He learned of inconsequential things such as her favorite foods, books, and movies, but stumbled when she turned the questions back on him.

"I can't remember ever reading a book, but I know many of the storylines—for older books at least. The same applies to movies. Can't say I've ever been to a theater, but I know I've seen movies."

Cassandra perked up. She plucked a credit card from her purse and waved it at the server.

"We're out of here. I know what we'll do next."

Just before they rose to leave, Lander placed his hand on her forearm. He looked her straight in the eye and put everything he could into a sincere, "Thank you."

Her warm and genuine smile made Lander blush. His second thought was to pat himself on the back for controlling his skill. He'd come a long way in a few days. As if reading his thoughts, she dropped her gaze to his hand.

A large chain bookstore was their next stop. Lander hesitated at the front door. He'd tried to cool off in their air conditioning a few days earlier and they had asked him to leave. It was ridiculous to think they would recognize him now, but the memory was still vivid. When you only had a few days of memories, everything was top of mind.

Cassandra took his elbow and pulled him toward the door, but stopped short, letting her hand fall as if it had gone numb.

"Sorry. It's my nature to touch the people..." She hesitated. "The people I care about. That's the second time we've touched. Why didn't the drowning overtake me?"

"I'm getting better at controlling it. The best way to describe it is to visualize shuffling playing cards, where each card is a memory. A dealer can fan and snap through the deck. As long as I keep the visions moving in my mind, I can do the same, and the influence diminishes or vanishes."

Lander let out an involuntary wheeze when he inhaled to continue. "But it takes an effort. It's like being sucker punched. Thankfully, my recovery time is improving."

He shrugged and held the door for Cassandra. She deserved a better explanation, but he was distracted by the intimacy of her words. *People I care about.*

As he followed her around the bookshelves, she pointed to titles she had read. Lander took it all in, his powerful memory trying to keep up with the flood of data. She picked a few books and led him to the back of the store, where large black leather chairs encouraged them to linger.

"How about a paranormal thriller? As far as you're concerned, it could be filed under nonfiction." She smiled weakly and Lander nodded, willing to play along. She held up a paperback. "This is about a man who trades his eyesight for the ability to see what others cannot: ghosts and other creatures. That sounds like you have something in common." Cassandra passed Lander the book, and he studied the cover, admiring the dark mood it created.

"Memoir would also be good for you. It's about a person's memories. These people have captured aspects of their lives." She held up a book. "This woman was raised poor. Her parents were brilliant and had resources, but they made a choice to live outside the system."

He flipped over the book and read the back cover. "She grew up here in Phoenix."

They passed other titles back and forth before Lander dropped his head, suddenly very weary.

"Cassandra, I'm exhausted. It takes a lot of mental power to keep from influencing you, and the saturation of information in this store is overwhelming me." He fanned the books out on his lap. "You pick—assuming you will buy it, since I don't have any money."

"My mother always warned me against deadbeats who can't pay, and you really are the—" She stopped, realizing that she was about to make a joke about him being destitute. "Lander, I'm sorry. That was insensitive of me."

As they walked toward the cashier, Lander considered

what had just happened. She'd bathed him, clothed him, fed him, and was now pretending he belonged in her social strata. While he acknowledged that being around a dirty, smelly, and slightly older man might be unpleasant, would it be impossible to meet him at his level?

On the drive back to the motel, Lander played with the satellite radio controls. "This is staggering. So much happened during the years I was at Wrimo. I've seen nothing like this before."

Cassandra considered this. "How long were you in there?"

"Based on the little I could tell from the file folder, I became an out-patient about ten years ago, though I've been isolated or institutionalized for the last five years, both at home and at Wrimo. And don't forget, I've been dead for a year as well."

Cassandra didn't respond to the joke. "That explains a lot. Technology has changed. Do you remember if you ever owned an MP3 player?"

"An MP what?"

"Never mind." Cassandra reached over and turned down the volume. "I want to talk to you about something. I received confirmation today that Wrimo will take part in my research. I didn't plan on using them, but it would be a great opportunity to get inside and see if we could learn more about your case."

Lander was shocked and spoke without thinking. "You did that without asking me?"

Cassandra nearly swerved off the road. "Are you kidding me? After how much we've shared these last two days? Did I have to come out and say I would help you?"

Lander looked away, needing air. He rolled down the window. "I didn't ask for your help." He wasn't sure if she heard him. The cool currents wrapped around him and his brain amplified the sound until it was like static on a radio. It protected him from having to think. *Is this how most people's brains are when they're tired and out of focus?* The constant bombardment of thoughts was exhausting.

His situation had changed. In the days since he'd found himself on the street, he'd done nothing to learn about his background. Ignorance was easy, and there was no burden of taking responsibility. That changed when Cassandra inserted herself into the quest for answers. He was afraid of what he might find. His gut told him there were more sinister elements at work than just a circus-freak homeless man.

The car pulled into the motel parking lot and Cassandra stopped abruptly in front of their room. She undid her seat belt and turned toward him.

"You can't hide from this. The street will kill you. That beating the other day is one more thing that is wearing you down." She stopped to catch her breath. "You have this incredible skill. It's magical. Who can explain it? I sometimes wonder if I'm dreaming—it would be just like me to conjure up a man who is weaker and more desperately isolated than I am. We have to find out more."

She slouched back in her seat as Lander opened the door. He was still processing what she had said. "Okay, one step at a time. Do we have a plan for tomorrow?"

"A partial one at least. I'd like to see that scrap of a medical folder you found. And then let's see where the address on the driver's license takes us."

———

Cassandra had been tempted to go with Lander to the room. They had both cooled down after their argument. It would have been easy. *It's our room!* There was no reason not to join him. He'd seen her practically naked and in the throes of a fabulous climax. There wasn't much left to hide. It was an interesting dynamic for a first date.

Her analytical mind wanted to label and classify that earlier, heightened experience. Was it sex or masturbation? And Lander's participation was difficult to define. He hadn't touched her sexually, but he'd certainly overstepped in the role of a voyeur. Either way, it had been lovely. She felt a tremor of anticipation; if given the opportunity, she wanted to explore further.

But, modesty aside, there was another reason she didn't go with him. She was more aware of the cognitive work he had to do to keep her from painful memories. She hated hurting him and wanted to be near him, but this tired him.

She sighed deeply. "I love impossible relationships."

Lander's situation reminded her of a passage in Dr. Lampkin's thesis. Our definition of "normal" is too constricting. The mores of our culture set a code, and those who are labeled as "normal" are just better at fitting in. Their choices allow them to blend in. Acceptable behavior is not an indicator of a person's mental stability. Biologically and genetically, there could be multiple wiring problems that are masked. She was intent on helping Lander find peace.

Cassandra marveled at how his skill enabled him to discern what people were capable of because of their previous lives—especially given his inability to look into his own past.

He had told her that afternoon, "I believe it takes many lifetimes for a person to change. I see firsthand, like a textbook case study, the slow progress as a soul recycles. In the meantime, all around us, normal people hide their fantasies and desires for excess. They put on a good show until something cracks and the truth seeps out. All you have to do is turn on the news to learn about somebody who has given in to an impulse."

Cassandra knew all about acting properly—but what if

someone were to observe her in an unguarded moment? She smiled, imagining an audience to her naked strutting in her apartment, awkward solo dancing, or her periodic sinister thoughts. What if her internal switch failed and she couldn't suppress an outburst? Lately, this had seemed likely.

Chapter 32
Thursday,
November 5, 2009 (7:30 a.m.)

C assandra picked up Lander from the motel at seven thirty, and they drove into the wealthy community of Paradise Valley, between Phoenix and Scottsdale, for breakfast at a luxury resort. She craved a particular style of Swiss muesli that nobody else offered.

As they ate, Cassandra settled into a rhythm that Lander recognized as her researcher mode. Between spoonfuls of her cereal and bites of his breakfast burrito, an interrogation began.

"I need to put all this together." She rummaged in her satchel purse and pulled out a small Moleskine notebook and an expensive-looking white pen. She pushed her half-finished bowl aside to make room. The spine of the notebook cracked as she flattened it against the table. "I'm always overwhelmed by what I don't know when I am first assigned a research project. In your situation, we know quite a lot. And I'm betting you haven't even told me everything."

Lander wondered if this was his cue to speak. He nervously folded his cloth napkin, first as a square, then as a triangle. When he dared to look up, Cassandra regarded him with wide, empathetic eyes. She understood these conversations made him

213

uncomfortable. For his part, he would not walk out on her this time.

Cassandra drew a circle in the left margin, then let the pen continue to trace the perimeter, the line getting thicker and less circular with each pass. "We need to identify goals." She lifted her pen from the loop and populated a series of bullet points. Lander leaned across the table to follow along as her scribbles filled the page.

"Here's my list: origin of your disorder, Wrimo's role, Dr. Aradice, life before ten days ago, home address, special skill, health." After the last item, she drew a dotted line back to the bullet point above, then wrote "side effects" inside the line. "Your shortness of breath—does it get worse the longer you're accessing someone's memories? Or the closer you are?" She looked up, her pen tapping the page.

"A combination, but physical contact takes the most out of me. It's like my lungs get smaller and smaller. I can only take tiny breaths, and they're not satisfying. On the days where I've done several readings, it takes longer for me to recover. I have a theory that each time I do it, a little piece of me dies—or less of me lives."

Cassandra bobbed her head from side to side as if deciding to record these details. Apparently not, because she dropped the pen and assigned an action to each finger. She held up her right thumb. "Wrimo." The index finger. "The address on your driver's license." And, carrying on across the hand, "The library for any local records on you or your family, Dr. Aradice, and the research project he is working on." She ran out of fingers on the right hand. "Item number six. Experiment with your abilities."

Lander looked up. "Test my skills? I would have thought you'd seen enough yesterday." It seemed like a suitable moment to pursue this topic. "Are you upset with me?"

Cassandra went wide-eyed. "Absolutely not! It just makes me sad to see how little I have grown emotionally in this life."

"I didn't intend to show you what you didn't have. I wanted you to see what's possible. You've been there."

Cassandra closed the notebook, pulled her bowl back to the center of the placemat, and folded her napkin before placing it on the table.

"Before our meeting, religion was only a philosophical inquiry for me. A mash-up of concepts that influenced me but didn't require a commitment to a particular path or ideology. I didn't believe in heaven or hell. Now you've provided compelling evidence to support the rebirth argument. Buddhists propose that everyone has godlike qualities. I like this assumption. I also believe we start with a *tabula rasa* and then, for the rest of our life, we're buffeted about by our choices. Occasionally there's bad luck. Shit happens, especially when you wander into a confluence of someone else's negative streams." She used her hands to suggest two objects almost colliding but slowing and then missing as they pass. "The purpose of life is to navigate through it and, metaphorically, to be in a better place at the end than when you started."

She sipped her coffee. "You rocked my world, but this isn't my first rodeo, dealing with unusual people or being challenged intellectually. Though, I admit, this time it's a lot more personal." Cassandra shook her head, as if to convince herself.

"If it's any consolation, I feel the same about you. In the last few days, you've forced me to study this power and to understand what I'm capable of. Last night, when you spoke of looking backward into my life, I got scared. I think I may have been through this before and I wasn't able to handle it—which has brought me to where I am today."

"One step at a time," she said in a reassuring tone. "Wrimo confirmed out appointment for tomorrow morning. That leaves today to do some digging. Let's get a few things done this morning and see what happens."

They drove back downtown and Cassandra pulled up in the alleyway behind Lander's building.

In just twenty-four hours, Lander had changed. The alley seemed less familiar. As he unlocked the hatch, he moved carefully: he didn't want to get his new clothes dirty, and his ribs still ached. The moist smell of sweat and mildew that rose from the oily blankets on his bed assaulted his senses. He tiptoed around the room, fishing out the file folder from its hiding place. He had also stashed about twenty dollars, which he pocketed.

As he was about to leave, a white object near the interior hatch caught his eye. A note from the super: *Checking that you are okay. I was worried about your injuries.* Lander stuffed the note in his pocket.

Before climbing back up onto the street, Lander wondered if this might be a farewell to his hovel. He didn't expect Cassandra to support him forever. But would it be enough to build a life? It encouraged him to have learned that his skill became more manageable with training. Could he parlay it into a business? *Lander Gate, PI—Solving Crimes in Any Lifetime.*

If he dug even deeper into a person's memories, could he find content related to their current life? That would make him a mind reader. This, however, seemed impossible, even relative to the absurdity of his bizarre situation.

Lander locked the hatch and climbed back into Cassandra's car. He read off the address as Cassandra punched it into a device on the dashboard. A second later, a feminine metallic voice offered them directions. Halfway down the block, it wailed, "You are now off course. Finding new route."

He laughed. "If only it were that easy."

Chapter 33
Thursday,
November 5, 2009 (10:15 a.m.)

They entered a neighborhood that resembled one of the many subdivisions that had blossomed around Phoenix in the late eighties, a city whose population grew as thousands of acres of bulldozed desert became pink and beige stucco-clad single-family dwellings. The growing population's thirst for water and the displaced indigenous wildlife marked only the beginning of the ecological changes. A million lawn sprinklers, patio misters, and sweaty citizens raised the humidity level. The microclimate grew hotter as the skin of concrete and asphalt that stretched over the ever-expanding urban sprawl retained heat deep into the night.

The address on the driver's license led Cassandra and Lander to a small ranch-style house that, at one time, had been covered by textured white stucco, but was now faded and gray. A xeriscape garden, where pockets of scrub grasses and resilient weeds pushed up through the thin layer of gravel, separated the house from the road. An air-conditioning unit straddled the brick-colored tile roof, and just below, dusty weather screens covered the windows. A carport on the side of the house was empty of vehicles but uncluttered. Two tires

stacked in the back corner propped up the frame of a disman-
tled motorcycle. The concrete pad was stained black with oil.

Cassandra was the first to speak. "Any memories?"

"Nothing yet. Pull up a little closer." Lander didn't know
why he was being cautious—a hunch, perhaps, based on the
computer alert at the hospital. Would someone expect him to
come back to the old neighborhood?

Cassandra drove past the house and parked at the end of
the block. They climbed out of the car and, without speaking,
walked back toward the address.

Two houses to the west of their destination, a woman in her
seventies was having difficulty pushing a blue two-wheel recycling bin through loose gravel toward the curb.

Lander glanced nervously up and down the street and
focused for a moment on their parked car as if willing it to come
and pick him up. When he slowed his pace, Cassandra raised
her hand as if about to poke him in the side, but she let her
hand drop.

"Come on. There may not be another chance. Let's see
what she knows," Cassandra said.

"Good morning," Lander said to the woman in greeting,
holding up his hands in a gesture offering aid. She stepped
back, and Lander completed the bin's journey to the sidewalk.
"May we ask you a question?"

With mild suspicion, she nodded for Lander to continue.

"How long have you lived here?"

She crossed her bony arms over her chest. "Since 1985.
What are you selling?"

"Nothing," Lander replied, a little too abruptly. He softened his voice. "We're looking for an old neighbor." Lander
pointed at his old house. "Members of the Gate family."

The woman followed his gaze and lingered on the house
even after Lander looked back at her.

"What's your business with them?"

Lander sensed the woman's mistrust—not just of him but of everyone. It was a by-product of being an age group that was too often victimized. He realized how important she could be to him, to their investigation, and edged closer, hoping to find something useful in her past lives to build her trust.

Even the most basic information would be helpful. Did she know her neighbors? His family? Had they lived there long?

He needed to shuffle the imaginary cards faster, but nothing useful presented itself. Could a person cycle through so many lives with so little happening to them? It was taking too long. With the street busking, the foreplay of the pantomime gave him time to dig. He was losing her.

Lander wished he had coached Cassandra. As his sidekick, she was supposed to distract his subject and give him more time. She stood just out of the periphery of his vision. He didn't risk a glance for fear of losing the little ground he had gained. Mere seconds of silence between strangers felt awkward, and his standing there doing nothing didn't help. But he got a sense she wanted to trust people, which might be all he needed.

"I'm a relative, and I used to come and stay with them. I think I remember you." He scanned the fence and gate behind her where the recycling bin had come from. A faded white sign with black lettering warned, *Beware of Dog*. Someone had tried to add an *s*. "You had two dogs," he probed.

Her eyes widened, and she looked back at him. A smile creased her lips, and she began a gentle nod. "Yes, the boys used to come over and play with them. At least when they were younger. Before the trouble with the older boy—Lander, I think his name was. Though I don't remember there being three of you."

Cassandra had moved up beside him, and he saw her twitch at the mention of Lander's name. Her training as a researcher and interviewer couldn't suppress her excitement that the woman was opening up. But Lander wasn't ready for his big reveal. Would she recognize him? His hand dropped to his pant pocket and traced the rectangular edge of his driver's license: his only proof of who he was.

"That's about the time we stopped coming."

"You must be on the father's side. After he left with the younger boy, nobody ever came to visit."

"Yes, that's how we lost touch. Whatever became of Lander?"

"In and out of the hospital. Then he died."

Hearing those words still pummeled him with emotion. Her saying it so matter-of-factly made it real, more so than seeing the clipping or even standing in front of the memorial niche. But throughout the exchange he kept his face neutral. He didn't betray the effect her comment had on him.

Then a floodgate opened, and a wash of images assaulted him. It was as if he had wrapped his fingers around his own wrist, inflicting his own power on himself. Each memory assaulted him like a spark burning where it landed, riddling his entire being with pain. Any talent he had achieved with others, at controlling the flashes or adjusting their intensity, failed him in his moment of need.

Cassandra could see he had drifted away. The pause had become uncomfortable. She took a half step forward, which drew the woman's gaze away from Lander, and asked her a question. "Did they say what he died of?"

The question was too direct, or the woman had tired of standing. The result was the same; she lost interest in their conversation, turned, and shuffled away. "Thanks for the help with the bin."

Lander's mental fog cleared, and he realized a change in tactic was required if they were to learn anything. "I didn't die," he said, in a slightly higher-pitched tone, hoping to sound less menacing.

A second mention of death grounded the woman, and she stopped, the suspicion in her face shifting to fear. Lander reached into his pocket for the driver's license and offered it to her.

She raised the driver's license close to her face and stared at the picture. After a few seconds, she shifted her eyes to Lander, and then back to the card. She swallowed hard and took a step back as she recognized the similarity in the two faces.

"Please help me. I have limited memory of those years. I'm trying to sort out my past."

"They said you died. No memory? Maybe you did die, a little." Her words trailed off as she tried to reconcile what they had told her.

Lander looked at Cassandra and they both waited, hoping the woman would continue. Thankfully, she seemed to accept the basic facts about Lander's situation. It would have been natural for a person to want to extricate themselves from the conversation.

"You were never right in the head. Or too right! They said you were brilliant. All I ever saw was a nervous kid, terrified of people. I'd see you around the neighborhood, always alone, normally on a bicycle. You moved in when the houses were new—you were just a teenager. Your parents kept to themselves; your brother, a couple of years younger, seemed normal." The woman shifted her weight and adjusted the soiled apron tied at her waist. Her use of the world *normal* disturbed Lander, but he kept his face passive and open.

"Your father moved out, taking the other boy with him. Your mother tried to cope, but rumors on the street were that she couldn't afford the special care you needed. Then one day, an ambulance showed up. They took you away. Then the word was you died; most of the neighborhood said it was suicide. Your mother took it hard, and it surprised us she didn't move away. She seems to be okay now."

"Does she still live there?"

"Yes. She has a little red car. Doesn't look like she's home. She rents out a room, and her new tenant drives a motorcycle— looks like he's out as well."

It was now Lander who needed space. He was standing only a few yards from his family home and at any moment his mother, who thought he was dead, might pull up. He was not ready for that encounter.

"Thank you. You've been very helpful. If I could ask one more favor. It will be a shock to my mother, and I want to make this as easy as possible. Please don't tell anyone we've spoken."

They thanked her and walked toward the car. As they pulled away, the old lady leaned against the side of the house, watching them.

They had driven for about ten minutes, and Lander hadn't spoken or moved.

"Your out-of-body experience when we first started talking to her was bad timing. I thought we'd lost her."

When Lander didn't answer, Cassandra had to look to make sure he was present in the car. She reached over and turned off the car radio, not in the mood for Justin Bieber. She also hoped this might prompt Lander to share his thoughts.

Sensitive to Lander's stress, Cassandra recognized he needed a distraction. "Can you check my messages for me?" She passed him the small square device, and Lander fumbled with it while trying to follow her directions to use the keyboard, all the while squinting into the tiny backlit screen. Cassandra was growing concerned about her work deadlines, and Lander confirmed from the tone of the messages that she should be. Two messages focused on an overdue interview, and the last requested an explanation for her inclusion of the Wrimo Hospital in her study.

When they finished, Lander turned the small device over in his hand, examining it from all angles. "Why do they call this a BlackBerry?"

Chapter 34
Thursday,
November 5, 2009 (11:30 a.m.)

Cassandra dropped Lander off on the corner by the Coffee Train, and they agreed to meet in the lobby of her building at six o'clock. Lander guessed that with his new look he wouldn't be recognized and could drift safely for the afternoon. The word was out that he had given up the Dunk Tank Drunks. Regardless of how bad they were, he had broken the code of the street. As a result, he would be even more isolated and would have to watch his back. Some would believe that one beating wasn't enough.

In the café, Katherine was nowhere to be seen. Lander ordered lunch and moved to his usual table on the patio. Business was steady. He scanned the regulars, accessing his memory of cataloged information about their habits and lifestyles. This helped him relax; it was his version of normal.

A young girl about seven stared at him. He recognized her but couldn't remember when he had seen her. Lander admired how calm she was, even after sitting for a lengthy period. She seemed to be entertained by the people and activity, which he thought unusual for a child of that age. More than that, her facial features appeared to be taking part in an internal dialog. But with whom?

Her mother was turned away, her voice rising and falling as part of an animated cell phone conversation. From what Lander could hear, the topic was husband bashing, a common theme among the mothers in the café. Lander guessed she was talking to a sister. There were a lot of references to "Mom."

The girl slid down from her seat and approached Lander. "I like your haircut. You look friendlier now."

Lander didn't know how to respond and tried to hide his surprise. Apparently, she'd been watching him. He didn't want to encourage her but also didn't want to seem impolite. If this scene had played out even two days earlier, with Lander the street person, alarm bells would have gone off for anyone observing the interaction, and they would have locked him up as a pedophile. Now he looked harmless in his shiny fresh clothes. He mused it wasn't a very intelligent way to judge people.

One goal on Cassandra's list, Lander mused, was experimentation to learn new things about how his skill worked. This was his first chance to be close to a young child. He had learned a lot in a brief period about how to control the gift, but he needed to be careful. What if it was dangerous or magnified the emotions in a child?

She tilted her head and puffed out her cheeks, expecting a reply to her earlier comment. His silence had gone on too long.

"Thanks. I also feel better. A friend helped me."

"I have friends that help me. They tell me funny stories and help me when I'm scared. I met a new one this morning. She told me about you and said you'd might be here this afternoon."

Lander looked up to see if the mother had noticed her stray daughter. She was now leaning on her arm, still facing the other direction, listening and responding with periodic phrases. "Uh-huh, no. He didn't!"

The girl cleared her throat, aware that Lander's attention had shifted.

"What did she say?"

"She asked me to give you something."

"*Who* asked you?" said Lander, drawn back into the conversation.

"My new friend." The girl walked back to her table and rummaged in a canvas bag. She extracted a small nylon sachet. Her tiny fingers pulled apart the puckered enclosure and withdrew something delicate. She placed it on the table beside her then returned the pouch to the canvas bag. Her mother glanced over her shoulder to check on her and, seeing nothing of concern, resumed her call.

Picking up the item between her thumb and forefinger, she walked back to Lander. He held out his palm and she let the object drop.

"Smell it," she coached him.

He brought the object to his nose as he crushed the dried leaves and petals to release the aromatics. Lavender. He looked back at the little girl.

"Jane wanted to thank you for helping her," she said. "It's nice when friends help each other."

The comment stunned Lander. He wanted to blurt out, *How did you talk to Jane?* Was the girl aware of what he had done?

"Where did you get the lavender?"

"My mom. She puts it around the house, in her purses and shoes. Someone told her it keeps scorpions away."

"And where did you meet Jane?"

"The doctors call it my imaginary place."

"The doctors?"

"Yes. They're telling me not to go to there, and if I do, to ignore the people. But that's not nice. I'll just stop telling them about it. But I can talk to you about it, right?"

"Why am I different?"

"Because that's where we first met." She stopped speaking and looked at him. "You don't remember, do you?" She waited, but Lander looked at her with no change of expression. He was trying.

She sensed the lack of progress. "It was just over a week ago. I knew something was different about…"

"Natalie, don't bother that man. Come back here." The mother's call had ended.

"It's absolutely fine," Lander said, looking toward the mother. "We were talking about how important it is to have friends." He realized that channeling Mr. Rogers came across as creepy. But she didn't even acknowledge that he'd spoken.

The mother bustled about, picking up her packages. She extended a hand to Natalie, who reached up and placed her tiny palm in hers. As they walked away, the little girl looked back and chirped, "Next time, just make sure I see you here and not the other place. This is where you belong."

It was Lander's turn to be confused. The exchange with Natalie had been more like one of his past-life experiences than a real-time conversation. Was he hallucinating? The cups and plates still lay discarded where they had been sitting, and the dried lavender drifted from his palm to the floor, confirmations that Natalie had indeed been there.

It was only then he realized that the little girl had been a few feet from him, her hand only inches away, and he had sensed nothing. Was it because she was so young?

"Aren't you a sight?" Katherine approached with a tray to clear the table and interrupted his thoughts.

"I guess my disguise isn't as good as I thought."

"No, it's good. Out of context, I wouldn't have figured it out. Even as it is, I did a double take. Your posture hasn't changed, and this is your usual table. It's like someone hosed you down but hasn't given you the full Henry Higgins training."

Lander sat up, adjusting his position in the chair, aware of the accuracy of her comment and how much he slouched.

"Maybe it is a new start. Things are getting complicated..." He paused for a second to gather his thoughts. Earlier, he'd meant to ask Cassandra for assistance. "Can you help me? I found out this morning I have a brother. We were separated about twenty years ago. I need access to a computer to find more information on him."

"The library has public computers. They can help you, but you'll need a membership card. Let me get you mine. You can borrow it. It'll give you two hours online."

"Will they let me in?" Lander hoped she would offer the laptop he'd seen her using.

"Yes. I'm surprised you haven't been there already. They have a lot of services for the people experiencing difficulties. It's a place of refuge. One of my customers is a librarian. He often complains that people dismiss the library as losing relevance because of the growing popularity of electronic books and the web becoming the world's largest encyclopedia. But the library isn't about books. It's a gathering place, part of the community."

Katherine brought a flimsy plastic card to the table. "Take the northbound tram to Culver Street; the library is on your right. You can get that back to me in a couple of days." She reached into her pocket and withdrew some crumpled bills. "Bus fare?"

Lander shook his head. "I've got it covered. At least Cassandra has it covered."

He would have returned to the office in his building if it weren't for the super's strict rules. Even all cleaned up, his friend likely didn't want to explain who Lander was, his lodgings in the basement, or his access to the residents' accounts.

Lander had not yet used the light rail system and nervously approached the machine that dispensed the tickets. After the device sucked in his bills and a ticket popped out, he felt more official. A few minutes later, Lander boarded the modern streetcar, entering through the front door.

The handrails helped him make his way to the back of the tram where he spied some empty seats. In the rear section, six people had computers on their laps and were typing away, deep in concentration. There was a sense of unity among them, but nobody was talking to anyone else. His questioning gaze prompted an explanation from a middle-aged woman as Lander took an empty seat beside her on the sideways bench. "We're taking part in National Novel Writing Month. This is a write-in." She circled her finger in the air. "Everyone has pledged to complete a fifty thousand–word novel in one month: November. We pick unusual places to meet. Today we met to ride the train and write as a group."

"Fifty thousand words. That doesn't seem very long. How many words are usually in a novel?"

"Closer to one hundred thousand. Fifty is more than a novella, but it creates a first draft to build upon."

"What's your story about?"

"It's a diverging timeline, speculative fiction or urban fantasy, with romance thrown in." She stopped and looked at Lander, knowing her description meant nothing. "I'm sorry, that's geek speak. It's essentially a romance, but it takes place in a society where paranormal things can happen. It spotlights how the tiniest choices we make can act like a pinball bumper, sending us careening in different directions. For example, if a person stops to tie a shoe seconds before a hammer drops from a scaffold while another person uses a computer to get directions instead of asking a stranger, then those two people would never meet. That's where I am right now: tracing two people who are meant to be together while circumstances prevent them from connecting—though they come close many times."

"I think I understand. Your story follows the two people on their diverging yet nearly colliding paths. How do you know they are supposed to be together?"

The woman hesitated for a moment. "They were together in a previous life."

The phrase *previous life* caught Lander's attention, and he leaned in closer, intent on accessing the familiar swirl of images now emanating from the writer. She was composing the story from somewhere deep inside. He found some interconnected images from her past lives that related to a relationship denied in just that manner.

The imprints had a level of detail that surprised Lander. In her story, the two had repeatedly encountered each other, but the circumstances never brought them together. They'd hesitated a second, more than might seem reasonable when they brushed against each other on a crowded boardwalk, uncertain if they knew each other. There was another time when she had tended his wounds in the Second World War, but he had died before they connected. She was killed only days later when her medical unit was bombed.

Lander contemplated the portent of what he saw. Except for Katherine, whose past lives had stayed within her family, the connectivity of people through past lives had seemed random. But with this woman, he could see there were two intertwined beings who shared a proximity in at least three lives. How were the bonds created between these continuities that had them being reincarnated in similar situations? This contradicted the ideologies that embraced rebirth. Lander was ready to accept the concept that the karmic seeds that are formed from a person's actions can ripen and blossom in seemingly endless ways.

There was also the question that the two beings almost recognized each other. Their conscious minds would not have the ability to access these memories, yet even in different lives, a hint of recognition surfaced when the two met. This could only mean that there was something deep in everyone that was carried forward. Lander was reluctant to call it a soul but couldn't deny its existence, for how else would these imprints span multiple lifetimes?

The girl had resumed tapping on her computer, and the longer Lander sat, the faster her fingers operated on the keys. She was unknowingly accessing her past-life memories with greater clarity because of Lander's presence. Her conscious brain believed she had tapped into her muse. The look on her face suggested that this was a joyful frame of mind for a writer.

He considered pushing her a step closer. All it would take was his short-sleeved arm brushing against her as the tram sped up after the next stop. What if, at this moment, one of the other riders was her past-life shadow? Should Lander move up and down the car and find him? His intervention might finally bring them together.

Lander redirected his focus and found a memory in which they almost connected. Before he knew what he was doing, he said, "You'll find him among horses, but not as a rancher or a cowboy."

The girl leaned back, exhibiting a little fear and a lot of

awe. "I just decided that my character is an artist. He sculpts horses. How did you know?"

"Just a lucky guess. I'd better let you get back to writing."

A chair opened farther up the tram and Lander moved forward. But before he took the seat, the tram arrived at his stop.

Chapter 35
Thursday,
November 5, 2009 (2:45 p.m.)

T he Burton Barr Library on Central was an impressive edifice, a square block of iron and steel with curved ends. Lander would later tell Cassandra that it felt like walking into a giant four-story Bose speaker with its corrugated sides and stainless-steel trim. Lander had seen such speakers at the Coffee Train.

Inside, the scale of the building was disorienting. A narrow chute extended the entire height of the building. The floors hung as if suspended in an embrace between the main staircase and the elevator shaft.

A familiar voice drew away Lander's concentration. At the information desk, a woman whom Lander recognized as a friend of Jane's was asking a question. In response, the librarian pointed at a pull-up sign with an arrow. It featured a logo Lander recognized as an organization that offered counseling and training to the unhoused, among others. On this day, they were offering drop-in sessions. Lander imagined the reaction he would get if he asked for help with his supernatural power.

When she turned, he could see her swollen eyes and the sadness etched into her features. The death of Jane must have been weighing on her, Lander concluded. She looked directly at him, but her eyes moved past. The disguise was working.

As she moved away, Lander took her spot and was directed to the computer lab on the second floor. "If the workstations are full, use your library card to put your name in the queue at the kiosk at the top of the stairs. The line moves swiftly at this time of day."

Katherine's library card gave him two hours of access. And Lander's knowledge of computers increased as he used them. In the apartment office, he had hesitantly poked at the keyboard, not unlike how he did with Cassandra's cell phone. His mind understood the potential of the machines; he just needed time to learn.

He rested his finger on the *enter* button, about to begin a search. Perhaps because he was new to the technology, he didn't take for granted the power that lay before him. With a simple tap of a key—so different from his own touch—there would be consequences. Knowledge was its own form of magic.

Lander began by entering his family name. The computer wanted to add an *s* to the end. Gates was a popular last name. There was a massive amount of information available on the founder of Microsoft. When he refined the request to exclude the *s*, he then had to navigate around the more literal use of the term, such as companies that made or repaired gates. Even then, the number of people that came up made things difficult.

He didn't even know the first name of his father or his brother. Without basic family information, he had limited criteria for his search. What did his father do for work? Did his brother have any interests that might be in the public record— sports teams or academic pursuits? A few more answers from the neighbor would have helped.

He logged in to his email account with no expectation.

There was a machine generated welcome from Google and a message from Cassandra. *Hi... this is me. If you need me.*

Next up, he created a Facebook page under his alias and when it asked for this picture, he followed a screen link to the picture file on the computer he was using. A bewildering number of images accumulate on a public computer. He fumbled with the mouse and looked around self-consciously as an image of a large-chested woman peeling off her bathing suit filled the screen. Thankfully, the next picture was a landscape of the Grand Canyon. He chose a shadowy silhouette for his profile picture; a man in a baseball cap, the brim catching a starburst of light from the camera lens. He hoped it wasn't someone famous.

Facebook wanted to know his interests. This was a tough question. He didn't know if he had ever had any hobbies. He started with an easy one: *coffee shops*. Then, feeling emboldened, typed in *past-life regression.*

Apparently, it was a popular theme because multiple groups popped up. Lander didn't have enough time to dig into these, but he mentally bookmarked the page. After selecting one, it prompted him to become "friends" with the members.

Lander clicked through the profiles with growing curiosity about the frame Facebook placed around a person's life. It exaggerated the minutiae for those people who had an insatiable appetite to record every time they stopped for a coffee. In comparison, the moments that Lander accessed in a person's mind were significant. He wondered if his view might become cluttered with the trivial things people did every day.

Facebook also chronicled just one life, noting a date of birth and, eventually, a death. When Lander shuffled through a person's past lives, the placeholders that defined the start and end of each life dissolved, leaving him to interpret a vast timeline strung with experiences that straddled a multitude of lives.

It was like a video game with unlimited lives, except the replay was always a different storyline.

Lander revealed the stories that lay beneath a person's subconscious but could leak into the present. He wondered what caused some influences to manifest in a current life while others didn't.

For his next inquiry, Lander directed his focus to the high school near his house. He learned that many of the sites offering "reunions" required a credit card. A dead end. After that, he trolled through Facebook groups that were linked to the high school. He estimated the year his brother would have graduated and widened the search to include a range of ages. He found two people with the surname Gate who had attended during that period. One had a picture—he was African American—and the other had only a symbol for a photo but included an email address.

Lander sent a message to the second name, leaving an innocuous note that he had been a schoolmate and was updating the high school's alumni list.

When he was blocked by a password requirement for government listings, he redirected his search to the school newspaper. He found the web page, but the online issues were for the current year only. The local city newspaper wasn't helpful, either; it went back only five years. A pop back to the information desk confirmed that a more complete database of local and national papers was available on microfiche.

He also searched for his own name. Apparently, his death hadn't been newsworthy.

Lander, frustrated by the lack of leads, headed back downtown before meeting up with Cassandra. He declined to board a much busier tram than the one he had arrived on, unwilling to deal with the proximity of so many people. A proliferation of Phoenix Suns jerseys indicated a game that night.

By habit, he thought about the free dinners about to start. Typically, he'd be getting in line by this time. Wednesdays and Thursdays were the best days of the week. It was the most convenient evening for volunteers and the food was better. Tonight, he wouldn't have to worry. Cassandra was his meal ticket, though he bristled at thinking of her that way.

Lander arrived back at his building about four. He waited by the door for someone to leave and slipped in before the lock engaged. As he approached the office, he heard voices. One belonged to the super and the other to a tenant with a complaint or perhaps the super's boss.

Lander was about to turn around when the unfamiliar voice congratulated the super. "You have the most up-to-date and accurate record keeping in our entire system. I wanted to invite you to help train the other superintendents."

Lander stifled a laugh and wondered how the super was going to get out of this one. He paused in the hallway and listened.

"I'd love to help, really, I would," the super stuttered. "But I have to admit something. I'm terrible with computers. I asked a friend of mine to teach me. He set up the system and is still training me."

"Listen, Sam, I'd like to meet your friend," the original voice replied.

"It's not a good time. He got hurt a few days ago, beat up pretty bad in the alley. I don't know when—"

Lander saw this as his cue and, with a flourish, he swept into the room. "Hi. Oh, I'm sorry. I didn't know you had company."

There was a moment of awkward silence. The stranger expected an introduction. Sam couldn't see past the makeover and wasn't even sure who Lander was.

"I'm Lander, Sam's friend." He turned his back on the

visitor for a moment and winked at the super. "I'm sorry. I'd shake your hand, but an injury makes that difficult." With that comment, Lander placed his hands around his ribs. His injury was a convenient excuse to avoid contact. The flesh around his eyes, now only a lighter shade of blue-gray, completed the picture.

"Yes, I just heard. Did they catch who did it?"

"I don't know. It was a shock. In the middle of the day and only a block from here."

The man, who still had not introduced himself, shook his head in empathy and disbelief.

The super had regained his senses. "This is the friend who set up the bookkeeping system."

Lander spent the next half hour showing them his process for filing and his rather peculiar way of remembering the codes. As he spoke, he tested his earlier hypothesis that if he concentrated on something other than the people within his zone, it blocked his strange power. This was proving useful.

"Thanks for the note last night," Lander said to Sam after his guest had left. "As you can see, I've had a little help." Lander glossed over the details of his meeting Cassandra, mentioning only how she had befriended him and was helping him research his past.

"Do you think you'll be using the cellar again?"

"I don't know. If you don't mind, I'd like to hang on to it for a bit longer—who knows if the novelty might wear off and I end up back where I started."

The two chatted for a while longer, and Lander agreed to put together a training manual. The super said that he'd be paid, but he needed his social security number. Lander didn't know if he had one. He made a mental note to ask Cassandra to take him to the Social Security office. That could be complicated, especially if he was listed as deceased.

As he was about to leave, the super called after him. "Look, Lander, 305 is sitting empty and won't be reoccupied for three weeks. I haven't called to have it cleaned or the rental furniture picked up. I'll throw a set of sheets and a towel inside the door. Use it for a week—just keep it clean."

Lander thanked him and pocketed the ring with the two keys on it. He laughed to himself as he walked away. Things were looking up. In just forty-eight hours, he'd moved from the coal room to the third floor, and now he had a key to the front door. A shiver followed the voice in his head. *All the higher to come crashing back to the street.*

As Lander approached Cassandra's building, he looked around for anyone who might recognize him. It was a quiet time of day; most of his old associates would just be finishing dinner at one of charity kitchens. He rapped on the glass door to get Ray's attention.

The intercom clicked, and after a burst of static, Ray said, "If you're here to visit a resident, use the directory and have them let you in."

"I'm here to see you first. Open the door."

Ray walked around to the front of his desk and looked closer. The reflection from the glass made it difficult to see who was there. Lander pointed to his bruised eyes and the Band-aid across the bridge of his nose. It took a minute, but Ray figured it out and opened the door.

"I'm sorry, man—"

"Shut the fuck up, you weasel." Lander wanted to play the tough guy with Ray. "Look at what they did to me. This will be you next time if you ever cross me again."

"I'm sorry," he stammered. "They arrested the guys."

This was new information to Lander. "When?"

"Yesterday. I'm sure your girlfriend had something to do with it. A woman phoned from my desk to report that the two men were back in the alley. They confronted them, and found drugs, stolen property, and blood on their boots. They wanted to compare the blood with yours, but they couldn't find you. I kept my mouth shut on that one."

Lander wondered why Cassandra hadn't told him. "And it's best you just forget knowing me for a while."

The elevator chimed, and Cassandra walked into the lobby. "Good evening, boys."

She wore a high-collared black cable-knit sweater, tight gray jeans, and mid-calf suede boots with matching gloves. Lander murmured appreciatively, and then hoped Cassandra didn't hear him.

As they walked toward her car, Lander said, "That's a good look for you." He stopped and held out his arms, as if wanting her to return the compliment. "I'm sorry. I should have gone home and changed." He paused for effect. "Oh, that's right. I don't have a home or any other clothes."

Cassandra swatted him with the gloves. "We'll get you some more things tonight. After we've visited your mother!"

Lander nodded in agreement, though his gut sank. *It's too soon,* he wanted to say. *I'm not ready.*

Chapter 36
Thursday,
November 5, 2009 (6:05 p.m.)

T he drive back to Lander's childhood house through the heavy evening traffic was slow. They glided down the block and could see the tail end of a red car in the carport.

"She's home." Lander's voice cracked, betraying to Cassandra the anxiety that had welled up inside him. At the top of the driveway, a man in black leather bent over a motorcycle.

"Keep driving," Lander instructed. He couldn't shake a premonition that something wasn't right. "I think I should go on my own. So far, there's nothing to associate you with me. If things go weird when I meet my mother, it may be best you're not involved."

"If things go weird? I think we're past that."

"Weird may not be the right word. Dangerous." He let the word hang in the air between them. "It's more than just in my gut. This mess is bigger than just one missing patient. I can't shake the incident at the hospital. Why is Dr. Aradice setting up alerts for me?"

Cassandra circled the block and stopped five houses away. Lander opened the door to climb out.

"Wait for me on the next block. There's a two-story house, the only one on the block. It backs onto my old house. There's a shed that makes up part of the fence with a door into the neighbor's yard. My dad let them store their lawnmower there in exchange for not complaining about the shed being on the property line." Lander paused, as if hearing his own words for the first time. "And don't ask me how I know that."

Lander bit his lip and closed his eyes against a sudden onslaught of memories that came at him in strobe-like flashes. He could see role-playing games in the backyard, hide and seek, prisoner of war escapes, and a dark hiding place. He blinked to clear his head. Cassandra stared at him, her expression somewhere between confusion and compassion.

As Lander approached the house, the man with the motorcycle stood up, wiped his hands on a rag, and impassively watched him move up the walkway. Lander nodded just as he rounded the corner, out of sight onto the front stoop. He pressed the small white button and heard a muffled chime. Footsteps approached, and there was the scraping sound of a small chain being moved.

The door opened, and an older woman stood back from the door. She was tall, with sunken flesh around her cheeks and collarbone. Her skin was unadorned by makeup and dark after years in the sun. She'd pulled her rope of wiry gray hair into a ponytail and wore an unbuttoned knit cardigan over a man's denim shirt. The sweater hung low over her light tan cotton pants. "May I help you?"

Lander swallowed, and the words came slowly. "Mrs. Gate?"

"I haven't gone by that name in over twenty years. Who are you?" She leaned out and squinted. An accumulation of moth wings muted the weak bulb in the overhead light, making it difficult for her to see Lander's face.

From the side of the house, the man in black appeared. "Rosalie, is everything okay?"

"I think so, Charles. Thank you." She returned her gaze to Lander, as if seeking validation, and asked the same question again. "Is everything all right?"

She was stronger and more self-possessed than Lander had expected. He didn't know why he'd imagined someone frail. Perhaps it was from the neighbor's comments, and his own belief she was as much a victim in the whole situation as he was. He admired people who suffered but did not act like a victim.

"May I come in? I need to tell you a story, and I want to pick my words carefully."

She considered this for a moment. Lander realized it was a lot to ask, letting in a stranger at your door. She stepped back, swinging the door wider in invitation.

"Would you like tea? I just put the kettle on."

"No, thank you. I shouldn't stay long, but I hope to come back."

This interested her, and she moved, allowing him to enter. Lander stepped over the threshold but at once shifted away, desperate not to let his proximity influence her.

The entryway opened into a larger room. There was faint light from the doorway to the kitchen at the opposite end, and it cast shadows across an angular brown sofa and two chairs with wooden frames. A bookshelf on one side of the room held pictures and some ancient pottery pieces. His mother reached under the shade of a standing lamp and, with a click, a wan yellow light partially illuminated the room. But other than the predictable layout, nothing seemed familiar.

"Will you at least sit?"

He took the sofa, sitting upright on the edge like a child trying to impress an adult. She sat across from him, composed, her hands folded in her lap, silent and ready for an explanation. The lamp, now behind Lander, cast his face in shadow.

"Two weeks ago, I woke up in an alley downtown. I had no memory of anything before that moment. A Wrimo Hospital patient bracelet that had been cut off my wrist was caught up in my clothes."

Lander could see Rosalie silently repeating the word Wrimo. Her lips turned down as if tasting something sour.

"I was weak, exhausted, and unable to think. The bracelet was the only clue to what might have happened. I imagined I had wandered away from the facility. It took me a while, but I located Wrimo. It was after hours, so I waited until morning. I slept in the alley next to their dumpster. Among the debris, a strange serendipity: I found a partially shredded medical file. It made little sense, but I decided I was safer outside Wrimo than in." Lander paused.

"And what has this got to do with me—or a woman once named Rosalie Gate?"

Lander couldn't contain the emotion that was welling up inside him. He needed space or to leave. He rose and walked to the bookcase. Swallowing hard to steady his voice. "Do you have any children?"

"I had two boys. They would be grown up now."

"Would be?"

"One died as a young adult; the other left with his father over twenty years ago and I never saw him again."

Lander picked up a small silver frame with a picture of two boys. Lander looked into his own eyes from so long ago. He was holding the handlebars of a bicycle; his hair was plastered to the side of his head, and Lander had a sense memory of being out of breath. His brother leaned against the corner of the house, looking away. Lander tried to relax, to let the image connect with him. He remembered riding that bike, riding as fast as his legs could pedal. He laid the frame flat on the shelf and turned to her.

"If one of your boys came back, would you welcome him?"

"What do you mean?"

Lander stepped back into the wash of light and, for a second time that day, held up his driver's license as if it were an official badge.

"Rosalie." He paused. Even without his memories, the name felt awkward. "Mother. It's me, Lander."

She rose by pushing heavily on the armrests. Her eyes darted back and forth between his face and the small card. A look of frustration passed across her face. She fumbled in the pocket of her sweater before extracting a pair of black-rimmed eyeglasses. Lander stepped forward and met her halfway. She took the card and looked at it, pausing longer than needed to read the basic data listed.

Then she looked up and met his eyes. "But you were dead. We cremated you."

Lander shook his head. "That's not what happened."

Rosalie handed him the card back, walked over to the bookshelf, and picked up a different picture frame. It showed a much younger child holding a bright blue lunch box, the yellow shoulder straps of a backpack visible over his white-collared shirt. As before, she looked from the photo to Lander and then stared at the floor. Her head was a metronome of doubt.

"I'm sorry, I can't remember anything from my past or I'd tell you something that only I would know.'

Her eyes were glassy, and a tear dropped onto her cheek. She gazed at him. "It's not that I don't believe you. I shouldn't. It's preposterous. But what you're saying feels true." Rosalie's eyes grew wide, and a smile formed on her thin lips as she accepted what he'd revealed. She slowly reached for him and they embraced. Lander's emotions spilled over and he also cried. Her presence infused him with feelings of protection and comfort. Somewhere buried beneath the warmth that enveloped him, a small voice questioned why his ability hadn't manifested.

Out on the street, the screech of a car stopping pulled them apart and brought Lander to the window. A dark sedan idled at the curb. Charles, the biker roommate, stood waiting, and he pointed up to the house.

"Damn, he must have called them." Frantic to run, Lander came close to his mother. "There's something wrong about everything that's happened. These men have come to take me from you again. But we're not finished. I will find you."

He moved toward the kitchen, his head swinging as he considered his choices. Run out the side door through the carport, or out the back door led to a fenced yard with houses on all sides. Could he get to the shed? That was his original plan, but he wouldn't move quickly enough. And even then, the shed might be locked None of his options were good.

His eyes came to rest on the half-open pantry door at the edge of the kitchen, and a memory arose of a dark and secret place. "Is Dad's tunnel still there?"

"Yes, but it hasn't been used in years."

"Tell them I went out the side door, through the carport. It will be understandable that you're confused and not ready to believe me. But hear me on this—you can't trust Charles."

Lander moved through the kitchen to the pantry door. Pushing aside a bag of potatoes, he peeled up a floor mat and fumbled for the latch on a trap door. It creaked as he opened it, and dust lifted into the light. Propelled by a distant memory but unsure of what he knew, he lowered himself into the chute, pulling the door closed above him.

His father had built a tunnel from the house to his work shed. It served no purpose other than as an engineering experiment, and it had been a fun place to play. The darkness pressed against Lander as he felt his way forward. Behind him, the sound of boots on the kitchen floor and muffled voices pushed him onward. He gagged on the dirt and dust that threatened to suffocate him. When it was built, the passage had been lined with boards. But what followed had been twenty years of neglect. Many of the boards had collapsed, and small cave-ins made the going slow.

Lander let his instincts guide him. He'd completed this trip a hundred times, but in a much smaller and younger body. It was this sense that told him he was nearing the end. His finger stubbed against the step of a ladder, and he moved up, pushing on the trap door with a loud creak. The clatter of falling garden tools followed. He stopped and listened. All was quiet. He pushed the lid up again and savored the cool air that pulled him out of the tunnel. He cast a glance back at the house through the shed's grimy window.

In the illuminated kitchen stood Charles and his mother. She appeared angry, gesticulating with her arms. Another man came into view, but his face was in shadow. He gestured for calmness before stepping into the light. It was Dr. Aradice.

Chapter 37
Thursday,
November 5, 2009 (6:20 p.m.)

L ander almost lashed out at the garden tools around him. He knew he hated Dr. Aradice, but he didn't know why. Across the yard, through the frame of her kitchen window, Lander's mother and the doctor were in a standoff. Rosalie had her hands on her hips, glaring up at the taller man. Dr. Aradice stood straight, his head angled up in a haughty, dismissive gesture, as if waiting for her tantrum to end. Charles had left the room.

A creak from the side gate alerted Lander to someone approaching. Dropping to a crouch, he used his cuff to wipe back the grime on the window. The light from the carport silhouetted a form that had to be Charles. The figure stepped into the backyard and scanned the perimeter.

After Charles retraced his steps to the carport, Lander crept out of the shed into the neighbor's backyard. He followed the fence, stopping every few steps to listen for any sound that Charles had found him. When he emerged between the houses onto the sidewalk, Cassandra pulled forward. He climbed in.

"What happened?" she growled at him. "A little homeless

makeover?" Lander was only partially aware of the dirt and cobwebs that clung to his now bedraggled and torn clothing.

Lander wasn't in a joking mood. "Drive! Get us out of here, but don't draw attention." Lander hunched down in the small front seat. As Cassandra pulled up to the corner, the dark sedan passed them. Dr. Aradice, only glanced at Cassandra; her tinted windows hid both from view. A few blocks away, he straightened up.

"I knew something wasn't right. The guy with the motor-cycle was a plant. He must have called Dr. Aradice after guessing my identity. He came to the door and pretended to check on my mother. I had only just revealed who I was when the posse showed up—that white pickup truck and then, only seconds later, Dr. Aradice."

Cassandra's eyes grew wide at this revelation. "From over here, all I heard were the screeching tires."

"A lot of drama. They were careless when they tipped me off with their noisy arrival."

"Did your mother recognize you?"

"Yes, but not at first, which was helpful. It's a good thing she likes dark rooms and doesn't wear her glasses. I had time to set up the story of my return. And, thanks to you, she invited me in. That wouldn't have happened had I still been typecast as the bedraggled homeless person. I lost weight during my hospitalization," he explained. "Add to that the swelling and bruising. But when she put on her glasses as I stepped into the light, she realized it was me."

Lander reached for a bottle of water and took a drink.

"It's a good thing I didn't go in with you. Both of us wouldn't have got away. You were right, your situation might be dangerous."

Lander detected a quiver in her voice on the word *dangerous.*

They drove for a few blocks before Cassandra broke the silence. "You don't think they would hurt her, do you?" This last comment made Lander pause before taking another sip of water, his mind racing ahead to what he should do next.

Cassandra offered a comforting idea, answering her own question. "I doubt it. She's their best chance of finding you. I bet they'll try to make her feel safe. Encourage her to reconnect with you."

Lander didn't respond, choosing instead to stare out the window. When Cassandra sped up onto the highway, he roused and shifted in his seat. As he smoothed his shirt, dirt crumbled between his fingers and dusted his lap.

"Sorry about the clothes. They're filthy."

"Don't worry. Let's get you a few more things, and then we can figure out where you'll sleep tonight."

Lander told her about the super's offer, and Cassandra nodded in approval.

They picked up a new outfit, then made a quick stop for dinner and a small supply of groceries. He insisted on paying for the latter with the money he had retrieved from his apartment. They also dropped into a sporting goods store and bought a pair of pocket binoculars for surveillance of his mother's house. Cassandra teased Lander about becoming spies. He laughed it off, but tensed at the realization this wasn't a game.

Lander took the soiled clothes down to the laundry area. As he entered, he couldn't help but cast a glance toward his hiding spot in the utility closet. When his wash cycle had started, the urge to look became irresistible. With the door open, he could see the deck of cards. He hadn't remembered them being so dog-eared and stained. He left them where they were and closed the door.

As he waited, a man entered the laundry room and scooped

his belongings out of a dryer, nodding politely at Lander. This tiny sign of acceptance wasn't lost on him.

He let himself into the office and turned on the computer. A quick survey of his email showed no messages or new friends on Facebook. Happy for the distraction, he began typing up a training procedure to categorize and submit receipts from building operations.

Lander's untrained typing slowed him down, but he found the work easy, and time passed. With a break to move his clothes to the dryer, both jobs were soon complete. He printed the partial document, grabbed a sticky note, and scribbled a message to the super for his approval.

Apartment 305 was a one-bedroom unit that faced the laneway. Once Lander had the basic layout memorized, he shut off the lights, preferring to move about in darkness. Perhaps he shared a preference for dimly lit rooms with his mother.

The apartment windows framed the residential building across the lane. He wished he hadn't left the binoculars in the car. He liked to peer into people's current lives. It was so much easier than their submerged past lives. He wasn't motivated as a typical voyeur seeking flashes of nudity or carnal exchanges—though he wouldn't, he supposed, look away. Rather, it was the mundane and unguarded moments that attracted him and challenged his definition of what was normal.

A movie clip played in his mind. A beautiful blonde woman stared at him and spoke to an off-screen character. I'm not much on rear-window ethics. The imagined face morphed into Cassandra's, and he wondered what she was thinking about right now.

From across the lane, he could see the building's second, third, and fourth floors, as well as a clipped view of the fifth. He could see bursts of light and wide splashes of color from many televisions. In the apartment across from his, a man paced while talking on the phone.

A sliver of yellow light drew his eye to the right and up one floor. A door opened and closed, revealing a silhouette, before a wash of black neutralized any chance to see more of the room. Lander ducked back, at once suspicious that someone might be spying on him. The residence across the alley remained in darkness as he strained to detect changes in the veil of black. Lander imagined movement. Was he being watched?

He found this difficult to believe, and his conspiracy theory of just a moment before unraveled. His presence in 305 was too random for his enemies to have anticipated, let alone set up surveillance.

Lander stayed back from the window, well beyond the apron of light that reflected into his room. He continued to catalog the activities that played out in the opposite windows. The movie he'd remembered a moment earlier resumed its playback. We've become a race of Peeping Toms. What people ought to do is get outside their own house and look in for a change. It was an Alfred Hitchcock film from the 1950s, Rear Window. Lander didn't remember seeing it but he recalled the dialogue. That's a secret, private world you're looking into out there. People do a lot of things in private they couldn't possibly explain in public.

The morality of looking into anyone's life, past or present, was questionable. It was troubling how a viewer placed their own judgment on a scene as it unfolded. A misread cue might change the mood and meaning of an event. Filmmakers, for example, were skilled in directing the viewer to a predetermined mind set.

Lander looked again at the man on the cell phone. He now sat in profile at a table near the window, leaning back, his right ear pressed the phone. His left hand lay palm down on the table. If the soundtrack to this scene was sad music, the viewer would believe he'd received bad news. If a bass guitar played low, sinister notes, then the man would become cold, detached, his words caustic. Perhaps he was simply having a mundane conversation that went on too long. The man's face showed little of anything. This led Lander to question, and not for the first time, what beliefs he brought to a situation when he peered into past lives.

He had extracted a passionate interaction from Cassandra's past. As an outsider, he viewed two consenting adults in love. But what if one of them was faking it? He dismissed this notion, however, believing, at least for the moment, that Cassandra's experience had not been that of a bystander. If he had chosen a scene where she wasn't a joyful participant, she wouldn't have reacted the way she did.

Lander tired of the voyeur game, and his suspicion subsided. He concluded that his building was equally interesting to the residents on the other side. It was possible that someone watched them for the same reasons: to understand people, or to a cheap thrill, but not just to watch him. He remembered the amorous young couple in the laundry room and, for the sake of any curious neighbors, rather hoped that they kept their blinds open.

Chapter 38
Friday,
November 6, 2009 (8:45 a.m.)

The security desk was vacant when Lander arrived at Cassandra's building the following morning. He buzzed her, and she let him in. He paused in the tile entryway to her place, uncertain if he belonged beyond the threshold, until she encouraged him to come in. Her apartment was tiny, not much wider than her sofa, and dominated by her desk. Lander settled on a barstool in front of a kitchen island, and they chatted as she finished getting ready.

Lander admired her as she flitted around the room in her robe, catching a swipe of a leg when she bent forward. She seemed preoccupied and unaware of—or unconcerned with—with the effect she was having on him.

A simple plan had emerged. They would present themselves at Wrimo for their ten o'clock appointment, with Lander playing the role of her research assistant, and see what happened. Cassandra was loading her briefcase with a coil ring notebook and her computer, but she paused to look at Lander.

"Why are you looking at me like that?" he asked.

"I'm wondering if I should go alone. What if you're recognized?"

Lander considered this for a moment before reaching into his pant pocket to pull out a pair of eyeglasses.

"I found these on my travels. They're a weak prescription." He slipped them on, leaving them at the bottom of his nose. "Very professorial, don't you think? They'll know Lander as a man slouched in a wheelchair with bedraggled hair and a beard. I have enough memory to recall that, as a patient at Wrimo, I wasn't on display very much." As if to act out his new role, and remembering Katherine's comment about posture, Lander shifted to sit more upright in his chair. Next, he adjusted the glasses up to his eyes then placed a plain baseball cap on his head before turning to Cassandra and smiling.

Cassandra nodded in agreement as he acted out the transformation. "I'm not sure about the cap. It's the smile that completes the disguise. Out of context, all of it together, I think it will work. Except for Dr. Aradice. We'd better not bump into him. Our second challenge is to find the rest of your file, if there's anything left of it, without attracting attention. Our inquiry will need to appear random."

Their visit began with a low-ranking intern who explained the institute's rules and operating procedures for visitors. Unfortunately, they were not offered a tour but taken to a sterile room that housed floor-to-ceiling paper-bound case histories. Lander had been counting on a reconnaissance opportunity to restore lost memories.

The intern described their tagging protocol, similar to the Dewey decimal system, which cross-referenced the affliction or condition with the patient's name. He handed Cassandra a small notecard with a guest login code to access to the computer. Efficient but old-fashioned. Written records were disappearing at most facilities.

Both of them were aware of the camera perched in the top corner of the room, and Lander passed a note suggesting that their conversations might also be recorded. Cassandra wrote back that she didn't believe this but couldn't be sure. Cassandra explained to Lander that the system would log their computer queries, so she began with files that dealt with post-outpatient treatment, consistent with her research project.

They were dutifully playing their roles when two men entered, the younger with a stack of ten or twelve files. The older had the air of a bored trainer as he spoke to his associate. "We use this room for research and often provide access to outside consultants." With that, he nodded in greeting to Cassandra and Lander before pulling a key ring from his belt to open a locked cabinet at one end of the room. "They only have access to the files on the shelves. The longer-term files that still contain patient information are stored in these cabinets. We are slowly scanning and encrypting the names, then disposing of the paper copies. Soon, it will all be on the computer."

He turned to Cassandra and Lander. "Are you finding the information you need?"

"Reasonably. These case histories are dated," Cassandra replied.

"We are behind in our technology. And, sorry, this room isn't very inspiring."

Lander nodded, though he mused that it was better than the bare concrete and brick of his coal chute.

The two staff spent the next few minutes inserting the files into different drawers while cross-referencing them on a computer terminal. When they were done, the man pushed in the lock with a solid click. "We're finished with this for today." He paused at the exit. "Good luck with your research." He then lowered his voice to a conspiratorial whisper. "If you're wondering, I find it creepy to be watched. That camera doesn't work."

Cassandra and Lander looked at each other and smiled. As

soon as the door clicked behind the departing staff, Cassandra shuffled over to the computer he'd been using. "He didn't log out."

She began tapping away. "This is where we'll find what we need. Pass me my purse." Lander handed her the purse, and she rummaged for a moment before pulling out a tattered envelope. She tilted it upside down, and a set of keys clattered onto the table.

"You found the keys?"

"Yes. See if the smaller key fits the cabinet."

Cassandra typed as Lander tested the key. With a satisfying thump, the lock ejected.

"Your case file is #GL 271990b. Unlike these records," she said, pointing a finger at the shelves, "those will be filed alphabetically by the code."

Lander pulled off his fake glasses and dug through the drawer. He found the location, but looked up with a blank, questioning face and pointed to an empty hanging folder. He rummaged in Cassandra's briefcase and produced the remnants of his copy of the file. The format was the same as the others in the drawer. There was no doubt it should have been in the cabinet, not left shredded in a dumpster.

"Why would I still be in the active patient database if they destroyed the file?"

"Because nobody ever closed your case. Come look at this."

Lander slid around behind her.

The computer program divided the online file into three sections: treatment history, insurance or financial, and biographical data. It listed Dr. Aradice as the lead on the case. Cassandra scrolled through the computer records. They picked up where the paper file ended. As if to draw attention to the missing data, there was a placeholder where the scans should have been.

What they saw described a troubled history. Periodic hospital admissions, more than one assault, a suicide attempt in 2005, then another in 2008.

About a month after he became an inpatient at Wrimo, there was a notation in the file: *deceased.*

After that, the file was encrypted and a check box selected: *no external online access.*

"This raises serious questions about my mental competency. And my temper. Maybe we shouldn't be alone together."

"Don't overthink it." Cassandra then pointed to a date, her manicured nail making an indent in the flexible material of the LED screen. "Any thoughts on a password?"

Lander remembered the writing on the back of the key fob. Just as he flipped over the key ring, Cassandra said, "Never mind." She tapped at the keyboard. A confident beep confirmed success. "It makes sense. Dr. Aradice was listed on the prescription pad. These must have been his keys. His password is *Somnus.*"

The screen jumped to a new menu, where a message popped up: *Welcome, Dr. Aradice.* Cassandra pointed. On the right-hand side of the monitor, they could see that the system remembered the last ten files that had been accessed. Lander's name was the third down.

They opened the file, and the log entries continued. What excited the two of them was their access to a section of personal notes. Besides the routine entries, Dr. Aradice had logged observations and speculation. As a trained scientist, Aradice couldn't shake the habit of recording everything, regardless of how incriminating it might be.

The first entry of interest was a rant about the stupidity of his staff and a freak accident. They had given the patient a high dose of an experimental schizophrenia drug. It was under development and not approved for use on humans. Dr. Aradice had been on his way to the animal lab when he stopped to see Lander in his weekly session. The patient's agitation had reached a point where the doctor felt it necessary to have the staff administer an antidepressant. In the log entry, he described how he had told the nurse it was *on his desk*. The staff member misunderstood—it was the requisition that was on his desk, not the drug itself. Unfortunately, there *were* two vials on his desk, of an experimental drug destined for animal testing. Lander was injected with the experimental serum and released. Later that day, he collapsed in his home. Paramedics reported no vital signs and wanted to declare him dead at the scene.

At the hospital, they restarted the heart but could not find any brain activity. They turned life support off, and Lander was declared deceased.

"He must have manipulated the hospital records and smuggled you back here."

"My mother buried a John Doe."

From this point forward, Lander was never readmitted, but was assigned a case number, and only Dr. Aradice had access to the medical file.

For the next twelve months, the file had regular entries. Lander's condition ran the gamut, from unresponsive to awake, with varying levels of consciousness.

When awake, Lander was not coherent. He presented with aphasia. Both his language and emotional responses presented as if they were a secret code that no one couldn't decipher. Dr. Aradice believed Lander understood what was being said and was cognitively sound, but that he was incapable of expressing himself.

A separate thread of notes referenced two staff members who had contact with Lander and reported unexplained anxiety. Dr. Aradice wrote about these incidents, but with offered no conclusions. At one point, he theorized an airborne hallucinogen. There was a tiny branch of medical research on pheromones and the idea that their effects could be manipulated. He logged further tests and interviews with subjects exposed to Lander. Often during this period, the subject was kept sedated.

Cassandra continued to scroll before stopping on a brief entry from a month earlier: *Test Failed. Patient again comatose.*

Cassandra turned to Lander. "He doesn't say what the test involved. That's suspicious."

There was a gap in the chronology, then an entry dated the beginning of the previous week, which included a strange notation, unusual because it wasn't clear how it related to Lander: *Staff explain four patients were released AMA without insurance. Should have only been three.*

Cassandra sat back and pointed at the note. "This is exactly what I'm researching: facilities that kick people out when their insurance expires but pretend that the patients left on their own, 'AMA'—against medical advice. And what does it say about this place that they kick out an extra person by mistake when they're cleaning house?"

She ran her finger along the screen and tapped the down arrow on the keyboard. Lines of text scrolled up and off the screen. "The log entries don't stop. They've increased over the last ten days. Now there are multiple notes per day."

The notes were vague, commenting only on the subject's level of consciousness. A common entry read: *normal—sleep, wake, night, day cycle, unremarkable.* This changed with a log dated four days prior: *repeated agitation, increased brain activity.*

They looked at each other, both realizing that the doctor

still had a patient. Cassandra leaned back in her chair and crossed her arms. "Who was it that just four days ago had been in a state of extreme agitation?"

"Who is he studying, and why are they in my file?" Lander put the pieces together. "The drugs explain my delusional state; the atrophy is related to my physical inactivity. He knew something extraordinary happened when people were around me. I must have frightened him. He used the drugs to subdue me, when all along I just needed to be clean to understand and use my talent."

Lander stood up, feeling the need for space. "But how will he justify that I've recovered? Well, sort of." For emphasis, Lander walked over and pointed to the last entry from just a few days prior. "Who's in my hospital bed? We're living parallel lives. Compare these notes to the week I'm having. My level of agitation has increased tenfold since I met you."

Cassandra frowned at him—she didn't appreciate the humor—before returning her attention to the computer screen. "There isn't much else. We'd better get packed up and out of here."

Lander locked the cabinet, pushed the keys into his pocket and put on the glasses. With their belongings gathered, they left the room. The administration area was isolated from the wards, and Lander looked wistfully down the corridor, contemplating going the wrong way so they could explore. He could feel the keys against his leg and wondered just how far they might get.

For the third time in two days, Lander faced the knowledge they had reported him as dead. And when he looked over at Cassandra, he realized that they both had issues fitting in. At least she was rooted in the land of the living. But there were more questions now.

At the end of the hallway, they paused, waiting to be

buzzed into the waiting room. But before they could open the door, it swung inward, and Dr. Aradice entered. Lander spun around and bent to the floor, hiding his face while he pretended to look for something in Cassandra's briefcase.

The doctor stopped blocking the doorway and looked at Cassandra. Lander wondered if he might recognize her from the hospital. He waited, hoping he would excuse himself and let them pass; instead, he addressed Cassandra.

"I'm Dr. Aradice, Director of Clinical Studies. You must be Cassandra Bowen. I've read your past research. You are very thorough. Did you find everything you needed?"

"Yes, it was a good start. A compliment on your recordkeeping. It's very organized and efficient for a printed archive." As they spoke, Cassandra stepped back, apparently hoping the doctor would follow and give Lander more room to escape. When he did not, she became more effusive in her praise, which had the desired effect. He puffed up like a prancing quail and circled her, drawing closer to the nurse's station where the audience would be larger.

As Lander passed behind him, he resisted the urge to slow down, lean in, and dig into the doctor's past. He knew there would be plenty of awful findings, and there might also be something helpful to their research.

"Your own published works have provided excellent arguments to support my position in earlier papers," Cassandra continued.

Smiling at the praise, he only glanced at Lander. "Will you be coming back?"

"Yes, I expect to. If not Monday, later in the week."

"And your friend at the hospital? How are they doing?"

He remembered her. Lander winced, but Cassandra stayed calm. "I think everything will work out. Thanks for asking."

There was an uncomfortable moment of silence, and

Lander worried he might ask more questions. Instead, he nodded and excused himself. "Please call if I can be of any assistance."

Chapter 39
Friday,
November 6, 2009 (10:35 a.m.)

A s he settled into his desk chair, Dr. Aradice pressed the power button on the office computer. A peculiar two days to reflect upon. First the incident at the hospital, then the scene at Lander's mother's house. The scrambled state of Lander's brain led him to wonder how any memory had arisen from it, let alone one that connected him with Rosalie. It seemed impossible that Lander would even know where to look. He'd underestimated Lander. So now, even in the name of science, his decision to manipulate the Wrimo records and continue his study now appeared reckless. Only one staff member, Monica, knew the entire story, while one other assigned to Lander never had access to his medical file. Dr. Aradice had forced her to retire when she started asking questions.

The implant he'd installed in Lander generated a curious array of vital statistics. Unfortunately, the technology could not track Lander's whereabouts with any accuracy. With the upgraded implants available today, only a few years later, that limitation wouldn't exist. What he could glean from the signal strength was that Lander remained in the metro Phoenix area.

He glanced with annoyance at the slow-starting computer before his gaze came to rest on his key ring—or at least his backup key ring. *If you report your keys stolen,* he'd told himself, *it'll be a hassle.* He didn't want to deal with that while the Lander situation unraveled.

The fluttering green light on the edge of the screen exhausted his tolerance to wait. Picking up his keys, he headed to the elevator.

One floor above, he stopped at the end of the hall and looked around suspiciously before inserting a key into the lock.

Lander's room was little more than a broom closet. The doctor flipped on the overhead fluorescent light and glanced at the bare walls. An unmade hospital bed dominated one side of the room. Along the opposite wall, two mobile carts drew his attention. He caught a rolling stool with his foot and pulled it under him. The machine on the left connected to a printer. The continuous-feed paper coiled into a box on the floor. He lifted the accordion of paper and reviewed the previous pages.

The readings showed a trend. He'd been recording the changes in his log. Over time, the peaks were becoming less jagged. The length and intensity of the heightened brain activity grew more subdued each day. He wondered if it was due to the return of Lander's memories or failing batteries in Lander's implants.

An idea refocused the doctor's attention, and he pulled more paper from the box onto his lap. He scrolled back, using the printout as a timeline. When he found the page he wanted, he tore along the perforated edge and separated it from the stack. It represented the time when Lander had been at his mother's house. The report showed anxiety, then physical exertion. After scribbling notes onto the chart, he rifled through the box again, looking for the pages that coincided with Lander's hospital ER stay. He found them. These pages began with a stretch of minimal brain activity consistent with a drug-induced sleep. Next, the jagged graph traced a heightened emotional state consistent with fear. The printout told the story of his escape from the hospital. He'd missed Lander by only minutes.

The visit to Rosalie was the first time since Lander had escaped that he could compare what Lander was experiencing with actual knowledge of his situation. Previously, interpreting the lines on the paper was akin to mapping a mountain range without knowing where in the world it was located.

The doctor wasn't one to believe in coincidences. The timing of Rosalie's appearance at the clinic after Lander went missing had been unsettling. He still didn't know what had prompted her inquiry.

The decision to place a spy in her house had immediately paid off. Based on Charles's reports, he knew with confidence that Lander had not been in contact with his mother until the night before.

The doctor pulled a small notebook from his breast pocket and lined up the graph with the timing in his notes. He shuffled the pages back to his conversation in the kitchen with Rosalie. She wouldn't admit she had just seen Lander and claimed her visitor had left through the carport door as they came up the front steps. The printout confirmed that she'd lied to him.

He dropped his finger onto a jagged peak on the graph. He had looked at his watch when he walked into the kitchen to confront Rosalie. The time stamp corresponded with a dramatic emotional surge. The doctor spun on the stool and shook his head. "He was still there. He saw me." This was unsettling, because it also meant that Lander had recognized him. Lander had regained that memory. But how many others?

A few minutes later, back in his office, Dr. Aradice typed in his password to open his personal files. A message popped up that brought him to his feet: *Access denied. To proceed, close connection: research library.*

Chapter 40
Friday,
November 6, 2009 (12:15 p.m.)

Cassandra took Lander for lunch at the hotel where he'd met up with Andrew Peller. This time, he didn't require any clandestine sneaking about but could walk in through the front door. He looked for the juggling cocktail server and was disappointed she was not working.

Over lunch, they agreed their research had hit a wall painted with giant question marks. They did know that Lander had triggered a trap and nearly got caught. Dr. Aradice was pursuing him. Two lingering questions challenged them both: if there were log entries in Lander's computer medical file from the previous day, who did the hospital have as an active patient? And how had Dr. Aradice hidden a patient without an identity for over a year?

"We need to see who's in your bed at the clinic."

Lander's head popped up at Cassandra's announcement. He knew she was right, but wasn't ready to commit. "Are you kidding?"

"Remember the drunk's goodie bag? The prescription pads and pills? I think they had a way in and out. The keys belonged to Dr. Aradice, and it doesn't appear that they've changed the locks. He's so arrogant. I bet he didn't tell them they were missing."

Lander let the topic slide, and they finished their lunch. Out on the sidewalk, he pointed up the block to a man that held his hand to his forehead like a visor as he peered down the alley. "Déjà vu."

"What are you talking about? Do you know him?"

"A little. I met him around this same spot on Monday morning. It was where my week of revelations began."

The man walked toward them, his gaze passing over them and showing no sign of recognition. After he walked past, Lander called out. "Andrew, how's the shoulder? And the face?"

Andrew spun, for a moment unable to reconcile the voice with the trim, well-dressed man who stood in front of him. Upon recognition, he became flushed and excited. "You won't believe what happened!" He stopped when he noticed Cassandra. "Oh, I'm sorry to interrupt. Lander, may I speak with you privately?"

"It's okay. She's involved as much, if not more, than you are."

Cassandra led them down the block and back to the Coffee Train. Lander's usual table was the most private, and they settled in to get caught up. Lander told Andrew about meeting Cassandra and helping decode her fear of water. In return, she'd cleaned him up. He avoided any mention of the intrigue with Dr. Aradice or finding his mother, and he embellished his story with a comment about a job offer from a building management company. This raised an eyebrow from Cassandra, since he hadn't told her.

Andrew fidgeted, impatient to speak.

"I told you I've been to Seattle. I did a little digging." Andrew paused for a moment and looked from Cassandra to

Lander, his finger waving back and forth between the two of them. "Does she know the background of this story?" he asked.

"No. I haven't told her anything about you. We've been—"

Andrew cut off Lander's narrative and backtracked to the night in the plaza. He told the story of the young man with a fear of dogs and their later attempt to find more information on the Internet.

"At the *Seattle PI* newspaper, I looked up events from that time. Do you remember mentioning that the Seahawks logo was blue and green? It changed around 2002, so I worked back from that date. I discovered a story of a missing young boy who had last been seen wearing a Seahawks jersey. I found enough information to track down an address. The backyard is just as you described. At the land title office, I pulled the deeds on both houses." Andrew's excitement almost had him almost crawling onto the table.

"The people with the dog still own the house. So I did another search. A few years later, the man was charged with assault—or at least his dog was, after it attacked a boy in the neighborhood. He paid a fine, and they put the animal down. But it gets better. The house is for sale. I booked an inspection and snapped a picture of the garage floor." Andrew stopped for a moment, took a gulp of water and dug into his pocket, handing Lander a four-by-six photo.

Cassandra leaned in as Lander lifted the wrinkled picture. Her proximity overwhelmed him. A sharp intake of Lander's breath accompanied the scrambling of his thoughts.

"Sorry," Cassandra mumbled, and scooted her chair a short distance away.

The picture showed a dusty, cracked, and poorly cured concrete floor with the unmistakable shadow of a stain. Lander passed the picture to Cassandra while Andrew continued.

"I knew you didn't want the tip to lead anyone back to you.

So I printed the two stories and went to a business center and typed up a note telling the police that the owner of the house had covered up the killing of the boy. If they did a DNA test of the concrete in the garage, they would find the boy's blood, and a search of the backyard would uncover the bones. That last bit was a guess."

Andrew looked between Cassandra and Lander and beamed. "Look what's in the morning's paper." He reached into his computer case and withdrew a folded section of newspaper. It was the lead story on the general interest page: *Man Bitten by Dead Dog*. The article went on to finish Andrew's account of events. Acting on a tip that tied in with some other evidence in a cold case, the police had obtained a search warrant. They confirmed the presence of blood. A forensic sweep of the backyard had uncovered the remains of the child.

Andrew slapped his hand down on the table. "Isn't that fantastic? You solved a crime from someone's past life."

Lander had to agree; the news felt good. Cassandra congratulated him, and they all leaned back in their chairs, smug in their accomplishment. Lander couldn't help but reflect on the strangeness of his situation. He looked back and forth between Cassandra and Andrew. The word *friends* still felt awkward on his lips, but he was grateful for their companionship.

The approach of Katherine interrupted his thoughts.

"I see Lander's entourage is growing." She handed him an envelope. "My neighbor dropped this off this morning for you. She's been looking for you in the park and asked me to give it to you."

At first, Lander didn't understand. Inside the envelope was a flyer and two tickets for a music recital that afternoon at a local high school. It was Andrew who reached over and curled the paper under so Lander could see the writing on the back.

Mr. Lander, I'm performing in this recital. It's all thanks to you. Please come and see me.
Alice

Lander sat back in the chair, a broad smile on his face. "I did a past-life reading for her. She was one of the first, in the park. I saw she'd been a talented piano player in a previous life and encouraged her. What time is the recital?"

Cassandra plucked the flyer from his hand. "We've got lots of time. Andrew, are you up for a concert?"

Andrew frowned and sighed. "I can't. I've a work event." He looked toward Cassandra, then back at Lander. He hesitated, then with a nervous stutter, asked, "How do I get in touch with either of you when I'm back in town?"

Phoenix wasn't a small town, and yet Lander and Andrew had crossed paths with no effort. Lander allowed himself a moment of self-importance. He had two people in his life that wanted to find him—and not cause him pain. Being in demand was an altogether unfamiliar experience.

"Give Andrew your new email address," Cassandra chimed in. She turned to Andrew. "He doesn't have a computer but has periodic access."

"I'll keep tracking the Seattle story, and then we can look for another case."

"I'm not sure if that will happen. This was a very unusual confluence of circumstances. I can't say I've seen this type of situation in anyone else."

"At least not yet," Andrew said, finishing Lander's thought.

As Lander looked at Andrew, another childhood memory arose. He found himself on the floor of a bookstore with middle-grade paperbacks fanned out around him: Encyclopedia Brown and Hardy Boys mysteries. They were books that featured children solving mysteries that perplexed adults.

Lander's awareness returned to the café, and he didn't think Andrew had noticed the lapse. The connection to the memory was obvious. Andrew seemed caught up in the fun but oblivious to the dark side of what they were digging into. They weren't children, and Andrew wasn't Frank or Joe Hardy. Lander tried to hold on to the memory, hoping it might reveal more about his past, but it dissolved as quickly as it had come.

Out on the street, Andrew hailed a taxi and Lander contemplated the next step in their plan. Cassandra had urged him to get some proof of identity. A driver's license would only be so useful, but a social security card seemed important. How would they react at the government office when a dead man appeared in front of them? And what might it mean for Dr. Aradice?

Cassandra drove him to the social security office. When he stepped out, she leaned out the car window. "I'll be back in sixty minutes. That should be enough time." She scanned the parking lot. "There aren't that many cars."

Lander took a number and sat on the plastic benches in the large waiting room. Each cluster of chairs faced a display counting down the numbers "now serving." The middle of the afternoon was a busy time and Lander watched the diverse crowd made up predominately of immigrants trying to prove they belonged. His own situation wasn't that much different. He had no reason to believe that he was not born American. But how could he prove he was still alive?

A middle-aged woman greeted him with a smile. A plastic name tag stuck to the side of her computer screen identified her as Susan.

Lander cut right to the point. "I've lost my social security card. I've also been institutionalized for about five years and have not filed tax returns or had a job." The woman rolled her chair back a few inches from the counter, her smile fading. Lander assumed that when she'd profiled him she'd hoped for an easy inquiry. What problems could a well-dressed, middle-aged Caucasian man have? Plenty, she was about to learn. He handed her the driver's license and showed her the top of his Wrimo file, pointing to his admission date.

She punched the information into the computer and gasped. "You were declared deceased. I'm sorry, but I have to report this to my boss. This is a common form of identity theft."

Lander desperately needed this woman's help. After making eye contact, he slid his hand within an inch of hers and shuffled through her past. He marveled at how much better he was getting at sifting through people's memories.

"You aren't a suspicious person by nature. Look at me; feel the trust that lies between us. If you were in a situation where your story seemed impossible to explain, and someone helped you, even just a little, imagine the goodness that would carry with you." He had her. Her fingers inched forward, and he clasped her hand in his.

He took her back a hundred years. She had been a domestic accused of stealing. All the evidence pointed to her. Lander could feel her body tense up as the fear washed over her. It had all the makings of a Victorian romance. She and the son of the family were in a relationship. It was a love affair that trapped the noble-born son. In the retelling, her lover stood off to the side. She was desperate for him to provide her with an alibi.

Sitting in her cubicle, Susan straddled both realities and sobbed. Lander had to end this quickly. He pushed ahead in the memory to the moment when the young man stepped forward and admitted that they had been together. As he called out his love for the girl, the woman in front of Lander, with ink stains on her hands and carpel tunnel syndrome in her wrists, beamed. She was awash in emotion. Lander gave her one more mental push of memories as he leaned over her keyboard and tapped the escape key three times.

Susan stared at the laminate desk, disoriented. She realized she was smiling, the lingering effect of a wonderful dream. Emotions tingled up and down her arms like the last flicker of a sparkler with the metal still burning hot. The office melded and re-formed. She glanced at her screen, surprised to see it back at the main menu. The empty seat in front of her prompted a vague memory that she'd just been talking to a man the computer listed as deceased. But he was gone. Her knee bumped against her purse under the counter, and a dog-eared paperback thumped to the floor. She leaned over and retrieved the book, considering for a moment the stylized cover of *Impossible Love,* a romance novel. She could write better than this, and she knew the perfect story.

"Susan." A sharp voice from her coworker brought her head around. "You've been idle too long—the supervisor is going to notice." Flustered for just a second, she hit the advance button, and the display above her desk blinked out a new number. The strange man with the story of not being dead was all but forgotten.

Chapter 41
Friday,
November 6, 2009 (3:45 p.m.)

A large shopping mall would be their next stop before the music recital. Just inside the entrance, Lander moved into the shelter of a planter with a towering art deco cactus that leaned dangerously toward a shop window. It was a good hiding place from which to observe the people coming and going—and in particular, to keep an eye out for Cassandra's return. She had needed to run an errand, and Lander already wished he had stayed in the car.

This mall hadn't been part of Lander's beat. He had been shuffled out of other stores and learned to stay away. His eyes scanned the well-swept simulated stone floors where the flakes of granite and marble were frozen, as if by the frigid air conditioning. The security guard's attitude toward homeless people was equally chilling.

Now able to relax unmolested because of his disguise, he watched the happy consumers who walked by. Lander reflected on their conspicuous consumption, so visible in the rope-handled bags swinging from their arms. He'd lived for two weeks with nothing.

The lady carrying two designer shoeboxes in a clear plastic

bag likely wasn't concerned about her next meal. Lander bore her no malice. He'd benefited from people just like her who supported the charities that had been feeding him. The holiday season was approaching, and their generosity would increase. Unfortunately, their attention would wane the day after Christmas. Some newspaper editor got to decide when it was appropriate to be compassionate—and when to remove the "family-of-the-day" feature as if there were no more need.

A movement, or more accurately a lack of movement, drew his attention. His senses pricked as he became aware that someone was watching him. Without turning, he tried to observe the details of the person reflected in a store window, but the image wasn't well enough defined. Resigned to a confrontation, Lander turned to find Natalie, the young girl from the Coffee Train. She stood about six feet away, looking up at him. A wider survey confirmed that her mother was nowhere to be seen. Lander sensed that this could be a problem —if not for the girl, then for him.

"Good afternoon,, Natalie."

"Hello, Jane's friend." Her polite demeanor was complimented by a tailored flower-print dress with a crisp white collar and scalloped lapels.

"My name is Lander. I don't remember a proper introduction. Where's your mother?"

The girl turned and angled her head toward a storefront three doors down. "She's getting a pedicure."

"Won't it worry her, you being out here alone?"

"She doesn't know I'm gone. She can't see the seating area from where she's getting her toes done."

"But what if she gets up?"

The young girl rolled her eyes. "Mr. Lander, you've obviously never had your toes done. You can't get up partway through. And it will take twenty-five minutes to have both feet done." She twisted her arm to read the bright pink plastic watch on her wrist. "I have eight more minutes before there's any chance."

Lander was struck again by the girl's self-assurance. "Where did you meet Jane?" *And more importantly*, he wondered, *are you aware that she's passed?*

"I spoke with her again this morning. Kind of. She seems a nice person. She's gone now. But you already knew that."

This gave Lander a shiver. "Gone? From the special place where you visit people? Dead people?" The last word hung between them. Lander didn't want to push his luck and freak her out, but he wanted her to know that he believed her.

"Yes. I went back this morning to tell her I'd seen you."

"Do some people stay for a while in your special place?"

"Only a few."

"Who are some of your other friends?"

"There's not many I call friends. They're mostly nice, but only because they want something from me. It's different from being here with Mom, where I have to ask for everything."

Natalie sensed his confusion and continued. "Once they realize that I'm able to be here and there, they all get this crazed look on their faces and want me to bring a message back. They forget I'm only seven years old. It's not as if I can jump in the car and drive across town to find Bob Jones and tell him his wife found out about his girlfriend. I can't even tell my mom about it or she'll send me back to the doctors."

Lander chuckled, and once again he adjusted his perception of this young girl with her apparent maturity. "Last words, so to speak—things people wish they'd said when they still could."

Natalie nodded. "For all the talking my mom does, I'm guessing she won't leave anything unsaid."

Instead of responding, Lander waited; he was testing the

little girl to see if she believed that. She scrunched the left side of her face in an attempt at a wink. "You're right. My mom may talk all the time, but she never really says anything. Maybe when I'm an adult, I'll understand. Why do people wait to say what's important?"

"We all believe we've got more time than we do. We're always putting things off. Why do you think some people don't leave your special place?"

"They don't understand they're dead. It's lucky that there are so few of them and they don't talk much among themselves. Dead people aren't very sociable. When people find out about me, word travels fast. If I visit over two or three times a day, they come pushing at me. It's scary. I'm so small."

"Where is it you go?"

"It's here." She raised her head and looked around to emphasize. "It's everywhere. I just stop and listen, and the pictures come. It's kind of like being inside a TV. Everything dissolves, and the place goes white, and then the process reverses and I'm there."

"A fade-in—or out," Lander said, and chuckled. "Can you go there now?" Lander had an idea.

Natalie nodded, and Lander directed her a few steps to his retreat at the side of the big cactus.

"Okay, can you try?"

He could see her take a long deep breath, a slow exhale, then a second breath. He leaned in and placed his hand on her wrist. The sensation caused his balance to waver, and he rocked slightly; the vision differed from what he was used to. He was disoriented, and he wasn't in control. He could see the fade-in she had described and the people milling about. One or two were chatting in small groups, but most wore a profound look of sadness as they stared off into nothing. It was like an absurd caricature of a cocktail party. An aged man approached Natalie, though he didn't walk like an old man.

"You're so young to be here," he said, looking down at Natalie.

"I'm not really here," she replied with tenderness. "I'm just visiting."

Lander took his eyes off the two for a moment to survey the scene in a wide frame. A teenage boy who had been watching Natalie vanished.

He snapped his focus back to Natalie and then to the man who was trying to understand Natalie's meaning.

"You mean you're in the real world?"

"Yes," said Natalie. "I'm actually at a shopping mall waiting for my mom to get her feet done."

The man's eyes widened, but before he could speak, Natalie turned to Lander. It was also the first time that the man acknowledged he could see Lander as well.

"Give him about thirty seconds," she whispered. "It's so predictable. He'll want me to take a message to someone."

Lander exhaled and nodded in agreement. These people were needy. At the same moment, the older man, now mid-sentence, dissolved. Gone.

Natalie switched her attention back to Lander and looked up at him with disapproval. "Why do you think you would be any different?"

Lander didn't understand.

"Last time when you were here, you also asked me to do something for you."

Lander blinked in confusion. "I was here?" In a state of growing confusion, he brought his hands to his hips and straightened. Natalie looked frightened by his more combative stance.

At that instant, the visualization they shared shimmered;

the fade-out had begun. Lander dropped to one knee to get closer. "What was the message?"

Natalie stuttered and began nodding, her composure flagging as her ponytail bounced out behind her.

"What was it?" Lander repeated.

Natalie scrunched up her face. It was the first time he had seen her exhibit a lack of self-confidence. She took a half step back, and he wondered if she was struggling to stay in the vision or simply couldn't remember. Lander grew increasingly flustered as the shopping mall came back into view. He wasn't finished in that place. His fingers wrapped around Natalie's slender arm and he pulled at her, rougher than he intended. His other hand reached for the other wrist. He only intended to reassure her, to encourage her to keep the "window" open, when a firm hand grabbed his shoulder and pulled him backward, throwing him off-balance and onto the floor.

From above, a deep male voice boomed, "Is this man bothering you, little girl?"

Natalie looked frightened as the uniformed security guard towered over them, but Lander believed the fear was more for his sake than hers.

Lander attempted to stand, but the guard pressed against his chest with his boot, pushing him back to the cold stone floor. There was a moment of tense silence.

Natalie still looked flustered and terrified. Tearing up, she sniffled and struggled to find her words.

By now, a small crowd had gathered, and Lander cowered under the scrutiny of a single-minded mob. Perception was everything, and the situation looked bad. There would be no innocent-before-proven-guilty reprieve.

"Where's your mom, little girl?"

"My name's Natalie, if you please. She's over there getting her feet done. She should be done."

On cue, a frightened woman's voice called, "Natalie!"

"Over here, Mom," Natalie called back, and in the same instant, Cassandra came pushing through the crowd from the other side. Lander cowered even further. Cassandra's aggressive demeanor suggested she held Lander responsible for the situation.

Lander projected his mind outward, trying to access his accusers and find a scenario to reverse the situation. He didn't need to worry about Natalie; she was already pleading his innocence. Her mother was like a deer in headlights. The security guard was juiced by the support of the crowd and being viewed as a hero.

The standoff had begun. Lander, now seated but still on the floor, felt the impotence of his negotiating position—one made more difficult by the guard's black boot poised again to restrain him. The imprint of the first time was still visible on his white shirt.

The two police officers that arrived were less ready to accept the situation without some investigation. They helped Lander to his feet and led him to one side. The second officer began by speaking with the security guard and then dismissed him to move on to the mother and Natalie.

Cassandra, who appeared eager to insert herself into the fray, was given the signal to wait and be quiet. Lander didn't imagine that would endear the officers to her.

Lander tried to catch Natalie's eye. Despite the precarious situation, he longed for her to reveal the message for his mother. A change in the body language of the security guard caught Lander's attention. He seemed to be getting a lecture from one of the police officers. The second officer approached Lander.

"I'm sorry that this situation got out of hand." He looked at the boot print on Lander's shirt and Lander wondered if he was considering making a joke that *something was afoot.*

The officer apparently thought better of it and continued in an official manner. "The girl and the mother both vouch that they know you from a nearby café and it was the young girl who approached you. Do you wish to file a complaint about the security guard? These militia types get too much encouragement to be heavy-handed from their local hero, 'Sheriff Joe.'"

This caught Lander off guard; he wasn't accustomed to being given the benefit of the doubt. "No, I can see how the situation might have appeared."

The officer nodded in agreement and stepped away. Both looked at the security guard, who shifted uncomfortably from boot to boot but seemed to know what was expected of him.

"Hey, man. I'm sorry. I was only concerned for the little girl."

Lander nodded. "It's okay." Lander felt strange being the one giving out forgiveness.

Cassandra came up behind and directed Lander toward the entrance by the elbow. He looked over his shoulder to see mother and daughter heading in the opposite direction.

He would have to wait to find out about the message for his mother.

Chapter 42
Friday,
November 6, 2009 (6:45 p.m.)

They were fifteen minutes early to the high school for the start of the recital. Lander stood in a buttress-like shadow created by the concrete building and let Cassandra walk on, unaware he'd stopped. With a spring in her step, she looked at the small crowd gathered in the colonnade of the large high school.

He placed his hand against the wall as if he needed steadying; he didn't, but his thoughts were already jumping ahead to cope with the impending throng of turbulent minds. The coarse painted surface was simple and reassuring to a man who couldn't touch those around him. In summer, the hairs on his arm would likely curl in submission from the intense heat that radiated from these walls.

Lander reflected on what he radiated when people were in his presence. Overhead, triangular strips of sheet metal converged like spokes at the center of the courtyard: a designer's attempt to shield the students from the sun.

His was a different type of heat—what protected everyone from him?

Cassandra's enthusiasm for the concert was surprising.

He'd told her the story of the woman and how he'd nudged her to awaken a latent brilliance as a piano player.

Lander smoothed out the crumpled envelope containing the tickets. He tried to estimate the strength he would need to suppress the onslaught that awaited inside the theater. The chairs would be so much closer together than in a restaurant, and on all sides. It seemed a waste of time to be here; he would have no concentration available to enjoy the music. At a minimum, they would have to sit at the back.

Still ahead of him, Cassandra rose on her the balls of her feet and completed a jaunty spin, her coattails flaring out, before she stopped and placed both hands on her hips. The tilt of her head and her raised brow commanded him to catch up.

He moved up alongside her, giving a wide berth to a group of people loitering at the bottom of a short staircase.

Phoenix high schools were huge, with upwards of six thousand kids apiece. Second only to their football stadiums, they all boasted large, well-equipped auditoriums, which they often rented to dance competitions or, in this case, a private music recital.

Lander and Cassandra looked up when a gray-haired woman stepped out of the theater foyer and played an eight-note tune on a handheld xylophone. The chimes invited everyone to take their seats.

Cassandra didn't resist when Lander held back in an attempt to be the last ones to enter. But he was no longer worried about getting an isolated seat—there weren't many people attending the recital. They settled at the back of the theater surrounded by empty, polished wooden seats that resembled grave markers.

Cassandra sat next to him, the swirling eddies of their energies mixing. She was now familiar enough that he spun the tendrils of her past lives like a thumb on a flywheel.

"What are you doing?" she asked, after they had settled.

He raised an eyebrow, not knowing what she meant.

"I've got this unusual sensation. It's as if someone's tickling my emotional gut in that spot where stress folds in on itself." She placed her hands on her sides as if to contain it. "Then, little electric shocks connect my fear with my sexuality. Imagine a current flowing between the sacral and root chakras."

She scrunched up her face, aware that she sounded ridiculous, and looked at Lander. "Do you know what yoga and meditation are? Or what a chakra is?"

"Let the kundalini rise. Access your Shakti," he said sarcastically.

Her eyes widened; he hoped his knowledge impressed her. He felt a flash of pride but also a sting. Even Cassandra succumbed to the stereotype that the homeless were uneducated. In his short time on the street, he had met some skilled and educated people.

"Before the accident with the wrong prescription pills," he explained, "Remember all the in-patient entries in my file? I was often a guest at Wrimo. For some of those stays, I have recovered memories of sharing a room with a former yoga instructor. He taught me a lot about meditation and controlling the mind."

Cassandra chuckled nervously. "I hope you don't take this the wrong way. What I'm experiencing has a carnal quality. It reminds me of our scene in the hotel room. You're doing something to my sacral chakra." Cassandra blushed and looked around. They were still alone in their section. "It's like a mental flicking of my clit. Too rough and it hurts for a second. It's not all bad. It makes me think of the classic concept of pleasure and pain. Sometimes the two need to be together." She stopped, expecting him to either react or to explain himself.

"I'm shuffling through all your memories. Imagine a spinning roulette wheel, but I'm not letting the ball settle. The black numbers are the good memories. The red, also whizzing by, are the bad memories. The ball skates and bounces, with momentary flashes of both."

They both lapsed into silence as the house lights dimmed and the woman who'd played the chime stepped up to the podium. After a brief welcome and introduction, the show began with a trio: bass and two violins. As the music drifted toward them, Cassandra reached down and intertwined her fingers with Lander's.

Lander drew a sharp breath and then slowly let it out; at least with Cassandra, even with physical contact, he could now manage the flow. He picked a series of memories where that roulette ball skittered past the red to grace the black slots. The action fell into a rhythm with the music. By expanding his reach, Lander included the people in the rows below them. There was a collective sigh and a deeper settling into the seats as Lander's gift gave them so much more than just a recital. He resisted the urge to turn and look at Cassandra. From the fuzzy periphery of his vision, he knew she was looking at him and smiling.

Lander's friend, the piano prodigy, came out last, a clear sign that she was something special. The gray-haired woman introduced her as a life almost lived without ever knowing the depth of talent it possessed.

Alice began her set with what Lander assumed was an interpretation of a modern song. While he didn't recognize it, the audience was enthralled. Her set shifted to a classical piece and then she was joined by two musicians to be accompanied by a double bass and violin for her finale. Lander experienced an immense warmth and pride at the gift that had helped open. It also raised a question of his responsibility: he could now manipulate his ability, but should he? A quote from Lawrence

Block poked into his psyche: "There are eight million stories in the naked city; this has been one of them."

At the end of the performance, as the audience filtered up the aisles toward the exits, the performers received flowers at the front of the stage. His protégée was the last to appear, and she kneeled at the edge of the stage to be greeted by well-wishers. Then he noticed a figure standing half in shadow against the opposite wall. Lander was sure that the man was staring at him. He dropped his head and feigned a stretch, and when he looked back, the man was gone.

"Are you okay?"

"I just had a creepy premonition I was being watched... Never mind." He was willing to dismiss it to allay Cassandra's fears, but a larger concern was growing. If others knew the potential of his power, would they be threatened by him—or want to control him?

A moment later, the man reappeared with a woman by his side, carrying a bucket of flowers.

Lander relaxed. The man had been watching him as a *vendor*, with no ill intent. Lander should have brought flowers.

Cassandra purchased a cellophane-wrapped red rose, and the two waited to congratulate Alice near the side of the stage.

Chapter 43
Saturday,
November 7, 2009 (9:45 a.m.)

The next morning, Lander found himself back at the Coffee Train. He had trouble finding a familiar face in the weekend crowd. Katherine acknowledged him with a raised eyebrow. He had some money, though he had lost track of where it had come from. Cassandra must have given it to him.

He trolled the café, gathering abandoned sections of the morning paper, and settled at a corner table inside. It was a cool day by Phoenix standards, and the wind found its way through his new clothes, leaving him chilled.

Lander wondered why his old rags had been warmer—perhaps dressing in mismatched layers had its advantages. The more likely explanation was that temperature-controlled rooms, a proper diet, and sleep had reactivated his nervous system. Stored somewhere in the evolutionary history of a person's genetics was the ability to survive the natural range of temperatures. His existence had seemed like that of a Neanderthal rather than a modern man; it was odd that the more "modern" his lifestyle became, the less he could cope with the environment.

These thoughts washed over Lander as he contemplated

the buttoned cuff of his new shirt and the steaming, five-dollar cup of chai. A lingering slick of bacon fat coated his lips from the sandwich he'd just consumed. A song from the house sound system mocked him with the lyric that on any given day, the world could change.

He flipped through the newspapers, only reading the first one-third of most articles before losing interest. In the second section of the local paper, under the heading "News in Brief," the word *Seattle* caught his eye. He leaned in and read a short piece on the solving of a cold case of a missing child. It recounted the details Andrew had shared.

The more he controlled his ability, the stranger his life became. But some good had come out of it: criminals caught, piano recitals performed, and—perhaps the most unusual of all —friendships made.

Lander looked up to find Andrew approaching. He wore a big smile, and Lander acknowledged him with a raised hand.

"I hoped you would be here." Andrew pointed with a questioning look at the empty seats.

"Cassandra's not here; we're meeting later."

"That's too bad. I was hoping to see her again—and you, of course."

A tincture of jealousy assailed Lander, and it must have been visible on his face.

"It's nothing like that. My romantic leanings are for the other team, and you're not my type."

Lander wondered when he'd become so transparent.

Andrew dropped his computer case on the second chair and slung his coat over the back. He pointed at Lander's cup. "Can I get you something?"

"A hot green tea with a honey packet would be great."

As Andrew wove through the tables toward the barista station, Lander exhaled a contented sigh. The inventory of changes in his life continued to expand—the laptop case that, only days earlier, Andrew had pulled close to himself like a shield now lay discarded with unspoken trust just a few feet away.

When Andrew finally settled in after two trips to retrieve his breakfast and the tea, Lander pointed at the article.

"Did you see this?"

Andrew leaned in, his lips moving as he read the news story. He sat back. "Last night's local television news mentioned it only toward the end, as a minor public interest piece. It would have been a much bigger story if they knew the source of the lead."

When Lander didn't react to his comment, Andrew took the cue, and they sat in companionable silence while he ate.

"How long are you in town?"

"I was supposed to leave this morning, but I changed my flight to this afternoon. I hoped to find you." He pushed his plate to the side as Katherine cycled past with a tray, clearing dishes.

"Gentlemen," was all the friendly greeting she offered.

Andrew waited until she moved out of range. "Don't take this the wrong way, but I think Cassandra and I have been a good influence on you."

"My life is certainly more complicated than a few days ago."

"At least now you're not so alone. Have you done any more..." He paused, as if seeking the right word. "Readings?"

"A few." He hesitated. "I enjoyed the recital. The woman's very talented."

Lander couldn't mention the social security office without revealing he was officially deceased, and he also didn't want to tell Andrew about the conspiracy unfolding around the doctor. He would keep that a secret until he knew how desperate Dr. Aradice was to make the Lander story go away.

With friendship comes the responsibility of keeping people safe. He was already considered dead. If he went missing, it's not as if there would be a drop in the census. A term he kept hearing in the news—*collateral damage*—was on his mind. Cassandra and Andrew needed to be shielded and protected from becoming a nominal mention in the narrow columns of a newspaper.

Andrew was prattling on, and Lander needed to refocus. He did not want to appear rude.

"That's a great thing you did. Why are you so reluctant to... 'connect' with people? Think of all the good you can do."

"You have a talent for putting a positive spin on things. I wish what you're saying was true, but in most cases, I cause suffering. The piano player was a rare instance where her talent was entwined with the sadness of her life and the conditions that led to her death. It wasn't a violent death. But look at your story."

On hearing these words, Andrew massaged his shoulder with one hand. The resurfaced memories were still powerful and real.

Lander wondered again if his interactions reduced the barrier between a person and their past lives. *Am I creating a new form of mental illness?*

Andrew dipped his teaspoon into his coffee mug and stirred, allowing Lander to continue. "There's a lot more to this story than I've shared with you. It runs much deeper than a parlor game. Cassandra knows everything. If something ever happens to me, she'll tell you."

Andrew slumped. "I want to help."

"And you will. I just need to get through some important next steps. There's a lot I don't understand about what I can do, or if something happened that made me this way. A big piece of this puzzle is about to fall into place. Can I use your computer to check my mailbox?"

Andrew shrugged and set to retrieving and starting his laptop.

"One thing you should know. I have only a few memories of anything prior to a few weeks ago, when I woke living on the street." He pointed at the screen. "It was Cassandra's idea to use the web for research."

Andrew swiveled the computer around to face Lander. The screen was open to a browser's welcome page. Lander hesitated and poked at the keys. "I don't really know what I'm doing."

As with Cassandra, it was growing easier to be close to Andrew without either of them being consumed by the connection. Andrew opened Lander's email, then his Facebook page. Andrew pointed at the login name. "Why the fake name?"

Lander offered only a regretful, close-lipped smile.

"More secrets." Andrew sighed. "At least now I have your email address. I lost the piece of paper you gave me." He tapped a plus sign to add Michael Emory to his contacts.

"I thought finding my father or brother might be helpful."

"You have two new messages." Andrew sat back, giving Lander some privacy.

One message was a link to a Facebook friend—someone he had never heard of. The second one was from Tim Gate. An involuntary gasp caused Andrew to look up. "It's nothing. I didn't really expect to find my brother so quickly. I'm not sure how I feel I about it when there are so many other questions in my life." Lander's finger quivered over the mouse as he hesitated before opening the message.

Take me off your list. I moved away. I wasn't at that school long enough for it to matter.

Lander felt it was a small victory. A green indicator in the margin showed the person was online. Lander leaned in to type a reply: *Thanks for the update. One more question. Did your brother graduate? If yes, do you have his email?* Lander hit send and leaned onto his elbows, pulling the computer closer to shift the screen beyond Andrew's view.

He was rewarded when the computer chimed and a new message appeared. *He died. Leave me alone.*

The abrupt reply didn't sit well with Lander, but at least he had found his brother. He stared at the blinking cursor that mimicked his rapid heartbeat. His brother's lack of interest hurt. He'd hoped for another ally. Until he knew more about his situation, there was nothing more to be said. Apparently, his brother wouldn't be his first Facebook friend.

Andrew was looking at him. "Did you learn anything?"

Lander closed the browser window. "No, it was a dead end."

Chapter 44
Saturday,
November 7, 2009 (5:45 p.m.)

Just after sunset, they parked within sight of Rosalie's front door. Once again, her car was visible at the side of the house and Charles's functioning motorcycle was parked in front of the spare tires.

Lander swiveled in his seat to face Cassandra. "Can you tell me more about what it's like when I activate these memories? At the recital, you described the sensations in the body. What about in your head?"

Cassandra considered this for a moment, her eyes going distant, as if replaying the experience. "It's impossible to separate the mind from the body. You're helpless. There's a flash of cognition that you might have been able to block it." She looked around the car as if seeking inspiration, before her hand came to rest on the louvered plastic air vent on the dashboard. "It's like the sour smell of skunk that sneaks into a car's ventilation system before you can close the damper." As if acting out her analogy, she turned the wheel to close the vent. "It's already behind you, but there is nothing to do but tolerate it as it builds to an overwhelming stench. With your touch, however, the intruding memory consumes the mind. It doesn't end there.

The drowning still pokes at me, flashes of panic in a lucid dream."

"Are there sounds?"

She considered this. "No, it's silent."

With a shake of her head to dispel the memory and change the subject, she reached into her purse and handed Lander a cell phone. "I prepaid for two hours of calls. There's no registration, so it's not traceable."

Lander rotated the small handset and flipped open the front. A bluish light lit up the darkness of the car.

"Call her." Cassandra held out a slip of paper and Lander punched in the number before raising the phone to his ear. "Nothing is happening."

"Give it to me." She grabbed the phone back. "You need to push the green button to start a call. Did you wake up from the dark ages?"

"I don't think I ever owned one... It's ringing."

"Be careful. They may have hacked into her phone line."

Lander doubted that this conspiracy merited those actions. Rosalie picked up after three rings.

"It's Lander. Please don't hang up."

"I wouldn't do that."

Lander experienced a small rush. *She believes me.*

"We need to talk. Dr. Aradice is looking for me, especially now, since I've tried to contact you."

"I don't understand why we're not celebrating that you're alive. All this running and hiding. What has he done?"

"I hope combining our stories will lead us to the answer." Lander lowered the phone and turned to Cassandra. "Do you know somewhere nearby that's public, but with private tables?"

"Yes. Give me the phone." Without introducing herself, Cassandra gave Rosalie the name of a restaurant. "Fifteen minutes." She flipped the phone shut and handed it back to Lander. "Should we go on ahead and find a table?"

"No. Let's wait and see if she actually goes."

Rosalie appeared almost immediately in the carport. They watched her pull out and proceed up the street. Cassandra, ready to follow, reached to switch on the car's lights, but then she stopped. The headlights of another car, pulling out three or four cars behind her, washed across them.

Cassandra and Lander looked at each other. Rosalie was being followed. The brown car passed, and, despite the tinted windows, they could see that the driver wasn't the hulking form of Charles.

They took a different route to the restaurant and began trolling the parking lot. They spotted Rosalie's car and the brown car. Both sat empty.

Lander let out a frustrated growl. "I can't go in, and you can't approach my mother without being caught up in this mess."

Cassandra removed her seat belt and opened the car door. "Let me at least see what's happening inside. You stay here! If you're seen..." She considered the options, wide-eyed. "At a minimum, it will increase the surveillance on your mother and make it much harder to connect with her."

As soon as Cassandra entered the restaurant, Lander slipped out the passenger side. Careful to avoid the light, he moved along the building. From the shadows at the end of the patio, he had a clear view through to the seating area.

His mother occupied an isolated table in the corner. The restaurant wasn't busy, and none of the other patrons seemed suspicious. There were two single men. One sat at the counter with an empty plate, so he must have been there for a while. The other read a book, facing the opposite direction from Rosalie, and hadn't looked up even once.

A woman emerged from the restroom and paused for more than a casual glance at his mother before sliding into a booth. During this time, Rosalie fiddled with her car keys, her head cast down. A plastic number on a stand signaled she had ordered something.

Lander jerked away from the window as Cassandra rounded the corner by the host stand and took a seat at the counter near the kitchen entrance. She pulled out a pencil and began writing a note. When a table steward stepped out from the kitchen carrying a tray, she gestured to him. Smart move, Lander acknowledged. Cassandra glanced at the number on the ticket and nodded. She handed him the note and some currency.

His mother looked up and smiled when her food arrived. The server picked up the metal stand with the order number and placed the slip of paper on the table beside her.

Before taking the first bite, Rosalie scanned the restaurant. She chewed a few mouthfuls before casting her eyes down on the note. Lander worried she might overreact, but she played her role beautifully. She continued to eat her sandwich while she read, before scrunching up the scrap of paper.

The woman whom Lander suspected was following Rosalie had ordered a coffee and at that moment was leaning on her elbow, watching a large screen monitor with a football replay.

Lander had lost track of time when Cassandra appeared beside him. "You freaked me out when you weren't in the car."

"I know. I had to watch. Any idea who owns the brown car?"

"I have my suspicions, but let's see who comes out."

"What did you write on the note?"

"*Being followed. He will come to you. Clean up the pantry.* I figured you can go back through the tunnel."

Lander nodded his agreement with the plan. There was no reason to suspect the doctor knew of the tunnel.

Rosalie finished her sandwich and sipped her iced tea. When she rose to leave, Cassandra and Lander moved to a discreet spot to observe the brown car. His mother walked past without looking in their direction, got in her car, and pulled away. The young woman Lander had suspected approached the brown car. Cassandra raised an eyebrow in surprise.

"What did you expect, a guy in a trench coat?" he whispered, not wanting to admit he'd imagined the same thing. For the briefest of moments, Lander wondered if her presence had just been a coincidence. Many people in the neighborhood probably ate at this restaurant. Then they overheard her on a cell call.

"... She ate on her own and just left. If I don't hurry, I might lose her... I agree, she's just heading home. Do you want me to stay with her?" The woman stood by her car, waiting for a response. It must have come abruptly, because she dropped the phone into her purse and climbed into her car without saying goodbye.

Back in his mother's neighborhood, Cassandra dropped Lander off. "I'm going to drive around and find the brown car."

Lander handed her the binoculars. "She'll be out front again. Be careful."

There were lights on in the house that shared the toolshed but thankfully no window on the carport side. This time he'd brought a flashlight. He wasn't sure if this was a blessing when it illuminated the condition of the tunnel. The choking dust twisted and spun past the narrow flashlight beam. Every tumbling crumb of soil became a scorpion, every tree root a snake. He summoned up the courage and began the crawling trek to the house.

His mother stood above the trapdoor in the pantry. He

waved away her offer of a hand and emerged from the hole. An awkward moment followed as Lander wondered if they should embrace—and, if they did, if he would be able to control his thoughts and influence. She decided for both of them by stepping away from the pantry. A single candle provided the only illumination in the small kitchen.

"Only the bedroom light is on. Charles is working on his bike in the carport. I'll walk past the window shade once in a while." She winced. "I'm not well trained for these secret meetings, but if Charles is spying on me, everything will seem normal. He knows I read in bed at night."

A kettle for a pot of tea whistled on the stove, and she shuffled to retrieve two mugs from an upper cupboard as Lander seated himself at the kitchen table.

"Charles rents the room your dad built at the end. It has its own entry and a solid brick common wall. He won't hear us, even if he goes into his room." As if to double-check their privacy, she moved to the window next to the kitchen table, ran her finger along the closed fabric shade, and pushed the doweling at the bottom into the sill.

After positioning the wooden trivet, Rosalie set the Brown Betty teapot in front of him. "Most people would describe me as a rational person. I'm not one to exaggerate or romanticize a situation. While the facts around your death seemed credible, my mother's instincts were never satisfied. The few people I spoke to said it was a natural reaction. I never got to see you, after..."

It pleased Lander that she spoke plainly about his death. The most important point was that she believed him.

Lander took over the conversation and described how he had found her. It was trickier to explain about the incorrect medication. He avoided mentioning his special skill, choosing to draw attention to the ongoing cover-up. "When I first woke up, I considered going to the police, but there were too many missing pieces. How would I explain myself? They'd lock me back up in a padded room." Lander looked up at his mother, hoping she didn't see this as an accusation. She sat impassive, attentive, but cast her eyes down at her teacup. "I've had a few memories resurface."

"You remember things about this house?" She nodded toward the pantry and the tunnel.

"That memory seemed to pop up during my fight-or-flight panic. But beyond that, nothing."

"Why did you wait over a week before you contacted me?"

"I woke up on the street a wreck, physically weak. Even now, while I am stronger, the slightest exertion tires me. I met someone who is helping me. She has been driving me around."

"The other voice on the phone. Why didn't she come in? Please tell me you didn't leave her waiting in the car."

"Mom, we're taking this seriously. Your gut told you it doesn't add up. Why would he report that I had died? Why is he trying to find me using such clandestine measures? I'm concerned that this has bigger implications than just the abuse of my personal rights. What else is Dr. Aradice capable of?" He paused, hoping to add gravity to his words. "Right now, there is nothing to connect us to my friend. I don't want to put her in any danger." His mother frowned, and he wasn't convinced she believed him. "I need you to fill some gaps in my memory to piece all of this together."

He paused until she nodded. "Let's start at the beginning. What was I like growing up?"

"You were a prolific reader and constantly riding your bike. I half expected you to figure out how to do both at the same time. You raced everywhere. I don't know how you weren't killed." The death reference abruptly silenced her.

Lander coaxed her to continue.

"You were bored at school. It was too easy. My father, your grandfather, was the genius of past generations. I wondered if those genes might ever resurface." She stopped to stir her tea and lifted the cup to take a small sip.

"You spent most of your time foraging in the library. When I could lure you into a conversation, I was in awe of the amount of information you absorbed. You didn't fit in anywhere. And you hated to be touched. You avoided people, and in high school became even more introverted. A loner. Your brother was no help." She looked toward the living room and Lander imagined she was seeing the picture on the mantel of the two of them. "The two of you were strangers. He told me you embarrassed him."

He considered telling her about his brother's abrupt message from a few hours earlier, but she was mid-thought and didn't want to interrupt.

"Your father also rejected you. It wasn't until later that I realized he had a crippling lack of self-confidence that he hid from everyone. You being different made him fearful that others would see the same quality in him. I imagine he saw his flawed genetics being paraded for all to see. He and your brother allied against you. I was collateral damage. They both left when you turned sixteen. I paid someone to find him and serve divorce papers. We never spoke again."

"Did you get any help?"

"Only after your suicide attempt." Rosalie's eyes tracked Lander's fingers as he unconsciously traced a scar on the inside of his right arm.

"You haven't forgotten everything."

Lander looked at the shadow of scar tissue and felt the slight variation in the skin texture.

"I couldn't handle it anymore, so I went looking for help. I didn't have any money. When Dr. Aradice accepted your case as part of a social services package, I believed our dreams had been answered."

Lander felt he needed to speak. The silence that followed weighed heavily. "You did what you had to do. But there's more to this story, isn't there?"

"The doctor was charming. I was lonely; he gave me a sense of protection. We started having a relationship. An affair. I was considered a patient, at least that's what he said, and he told me it had to be kept a secret." It was clear to Lander that his mother did not like admitting this. "I was flattered that he would be interested in me, and I tricked myself into thinking that I was doing it for you. I believed he had your best interests at heart."

She tapped two fingers on the wooden table, *pa-tah*, then again, a rhythm like a heartbeat. "The affair ended, but his control over me didn't. He pushed me to sign you up for a new drug study and a neural implant to monitor your progress."

Rosalie reached over and poured herself a second cup of tea. "Then, less than a year ago, you collapsed. They told me you had stolen some pills and it would be ruled a suicide. You'd done it before."

Lander tried to assemble the timeline in his mind. "What year was I first admitted?"

"What year? I can tell you the day. It's not like I'm going to forget October 25, 1989. It was a Wednesday."

Lander started counting on his fingers. "So 1989 to 2008, then deceased... I was his patient on and off for nineteen years—and then his guinea pig starting last November—and you suspected nothing?" He didn't intend it to sound like an accusation, but his mother's jaw tensed.

"You were in and out. And from your late twenties, more in than out. There were long stretches where you were unresponsive. The 'expert' suggested your brain was rewiring itself with the help of the protocol. Then you were dead. I have a death certificate."

Lander redirected the conversation. "When did Charles show up?"

"Just a few days ago, to rent the guest room. I listed it a while back." Exasperation flooded Rosalie's face. "It didn't occur to me he was spying on me."

"You couldn't have known."

"But I should have been suspicious. Especially after what happened in the days prior. I was in the park downtown. I watched a man telling stories or trying to read people's minds. I was too far away, and didn't stay long enough to figure out what the show was about, but there was something about him that unsettled me. That night I had dreams about you." Rosalie looked at him and a smile of awareness rose in her face. "It was you, wasn't it?"

Lander nodded. "I did it to rustle up a few dollars."

"You seemed good at it."

Rosalie pushed her empty mug to the center of the table and pointed at his own empty cup. Lander shook his head as she leaned back in her chair and stretched her legs. Lander flinched and slunk deeper into his own chair to increase the distance, but only by inches. If Rosalie noticed, she didn't let on.

"The dreams rattled me enough that I had new questions about your death. I went to Wrimo the next day and asked to see Dr. Aradice or to get access to your file. They said no on both counts. The woman claimed the file had been destroyed during a routine purge of closed cases. On Monday I inquired at the medical examiner's office to see if I could read an autopsy report." Rosalie shook her head. "A very bored civil servant spent a long time punching buttons on their computer just to tell me they couldn't help. If I were a television detective, I wouldn't have backed down. It didn't feel right. I don't think they could even find you in their system, but admitting that to me would have created a lot of work for someone."

Rosalie sat back, lost in her thoughts for a moment. "Charles replied to my listing the next day. He offered to fix things around the house for lower rent. I didn't know that included the mess he created with the motorcycle. When he was supposed to be painting or fixing something, I'd find him hovering when I was on the phone. I thought he had grown fond of me as a mother figure. When did I become so naïve?"

She got up and opened a drawer next to the sink. "This morning I found this in his garbage."

Her weathered hands smoothed a scrunched piece of paper on the table in front of Lander. It was a familiar-looking page from a prescription pad, with *Dr. Aradice* printed across the bottom. A phone number had been written on it.

"Did you call the number?"

"No."

"May I have it?"

She moved her hand away, and the paper partially recoiled into a ball. Lander picked it up, folded it, and placed it in the breast pocket of his shirt.

He now knew more than ever that he had to get into Wrimo and find the patient linked to the active medical file. Whoever was sleeping in his bed might corroborate his story. He still believed he couldn't tell his mother everything. She now understood that Dr. Aradice had masterminded a cover-up and withheld information about testing a powerful drug. Had it done this to him? Lander needed to know more. The side effect could even be the purpose of the doctor's research. Or had the drug awakened something unique in his biochemistry? "I'm going into Wrimo to find some evidence that I can use to expose Dr. Aradice. I somehow doubt that I am his only victim."

"Isn't the fact you are alive enough?"

"It doesn't feel like enough to go up against such an admired institution and a celebrated doctor. I have some help, and a plan is coming together. The less you know, the better." His mind flashed to the keys, Charles, the woman in the brown car, and then to his end game: a triumphant public revelation of a scandal.

His mother's confidence and poise seemed to dissolve. "I'm out of practice being a mother—someone who worries. I can't imagine losing you again." She reached across the table, and Lander triggered the bouncing ball to scramble his influence, but there was nothing there. He took her hand and gently directed her to stand before stepping around the table to give her a hug. He braced himself for the full contact, expecting a searing melding of their thoughts. But as before, there was nothing but her warmth and the physicality of her slight frame. He was stunned, and pulled her tighter into the embrace.

Lander let himself out through the tunnel, pausing to look at the carcass of his old bicycle where it leaned against the back wall, confined by the detritus of the garden shed. The tires were nothing more than dried strips of rubber, and years of grime and dried mud covered the once-shiny surfaces. Three rusted springs were all that remained of the seat, the leather chewed away by the smaller inhabitants of the garden. He wondered if it could ever be ridden again. It wasn't meant to sit still.

He called Cassandra to pick him up and asked her to circle the block. When they spied the brown car again, they parked where they could observe the occupant watching the house.

Lander recounted the exchange with his mother, pausing with obvious excitement before the big reveal.

"What?" Cassandra held up her hands in a gesture of openness in the narrow space.

In a breathy exhale, he blurted, "I can't read her. I have no effect on her. We've hugged twice, and there was nothing but my own thoughts."

Cassandra looked confused for a moment before smiling weakly. With little conviction, she replied, "That's lovely for the two of you."

Lander was about to reprimand her for a lack of enthusiasm when she shifted away, leaning into the car door. She was jealous. Cassandra and he couldn't share such a simple pleasure. Lander slumped back in his seat, and the two sat in silence.

Cassandra tapped the steering wheel with the knuckle of her right index finger, the rhythm of a private tune playing inside her head. She interrupted the song to turn to Lander. "You saw the woman at the restaurant. She doesn't look the part of a henchman or spy."

"Burly biker-dude Charles has that look cinched. I wonder..."

"How do you think she is connected to all of this?"

Lander retrieved the piece of paper Rosalie had given him and dialed the number. When it began to ring, Cassandra nudged Lander in the shoulder and pointed. Across the street, the woman in the brown car had just lifted a phone to her ear.

A female voice on his phone answered. "Hello?"

"Sorry, I must have the wrong number." Lander flipped the phone shut. "If there was any doubt before, that just settled it. They're all connected to each other, and to me—but how, and for what purpose?"

They sat again in silence, and Lander detected a new tension in Cassandra. Her playful sense of adventure had been replaced by the quiet grinding of her teeth and fidgety hands. The song in her head was over.

Shortly after eleven, the brown car pulled away. They followed her into Old Town Scottsdale to a block of expensive condominiums and lost the trail when a building parking gate closed behind her.

As Cassandra maneuvered the car to make a U-turn and leave, Lander exhaled a triumphant, "Aha!" Dr. Aradice approached the front door of her building. Lander grabbed the binoculars and focused on the building's intercom panel just as the doctor punched in a code: 1277.

"Write that down. We might need it."

Chapter 45
Sunday,
November 8, 2009 (8:15 a.m.)

At breakfast the next morning, Cassandra looked tired. She barely touched her meal and, as in the car the night before, she fidgeted.

After leafing through the local morning paper, she pointed to an article. "Dr. Aradice will be speaking at event Monday night." She carefully tore around the notice and passed it to Lander. "This might be helpful."

"What's bothering you?" Lander asked.

"How am I supposed to explain what I'm feeling? You're oblivious to what 'we' have become." She held up her hand to stop Lander from speaking. "Let me finish. Why can't you look forward? Just this once," she blurted out. "What's in our future? You have this incredible gift. I want you to take my hand and show me my past lives. Let me learn from my mistakes. I want to watch you help people. Let's move north to Sedona. There is a lot of strangeness attributed to the vortex lines that converge in the mountains. You'll fit right in. Why does all this cloak-and-dagger and sneaking around have to come into it?"

Lander tried to take her hand, but she snatched it off the table and glared at him.

"I didn't mean to literally to take my hand." She leaned back and shifted away from him on the bench seat. Lander could feel the connection weakening as the distance increased.

"At first, meeting you was exciting. At Wrimo, I was in my comfort zone, digging for answers. But last night it just seemed dangerous. I haven't told you, but after I dropped you off, I saw Charles. He was outside my building. I drove past and parked a block away. I waited about half an hour, then took a taxi back. From the front entrance, I couldn't see him, but he must have connected me to you. I'm frightened."

They both looked around the restaurant, now suspicious of everyone in the room.

"I am afraid for both of us. Maybe I've seen too many movies that make the pharma companies out to be the bad guys. You know the plot: big money willing to do anything to hide their secret." She dropped her face into her palms, shaking her head back and forth. In a muffled voice, she continued. "I realized last night that I live in a cloud of philosophical investigation. I love to dig and debate topics—but concepts, not cold, hard reality. Between Charles having the girl's cell number, Dr. Aradice showing up at her condo for a late-night visit, and Charles scoping out my building, it's all too organized. I can't do this anymore."

Her gaze bored into Lander. "I need you to make a choice. Come with me somewhere else and we'll learn how to harness your skill. Or leave now and take on the bad guys by yourself."

Lander wanted to consider her offer. He was asking a lot of her and had misjudged her commitment to finding the truth. A week earlier, he'd woken up each day in his coal dungeon in blissful ignorance, hovering on the edge of society, on the edge of reality, unable to even be Lander Gate. But now his life was intertwined with hers. The vacuum of his missing thoughts would never give him peace. And, if there was someone else caught up in the conspiracy, he could spare them the suffering and loss.

He reached forward and this time Cassandra let him take her hands. He was careful to block the signals before they peaked. When he squeezed her palms, she raised her head. Her eyes were glassy and, even when pursed, her lips quivered.

"Thank you for getting me this far. I'll leave now and you can forget about me. In a few weeks, this will seem like a strange sort of fairy tale. Tell a few people, and an urban myth will be born. You may even bump into Andrew Peller and swap stories of the strange man you once met. But in time, it will no longer seem real."

Lander released Cassandra's hand and swallowed hard. "I share your interest in discovering more about my skill. It could be a gift, and I will explore that. But not while this situation with Dr. Aradice hangs over me. I did a reading of a lady on a bus. Her story was a sad one—lifetimes of missed connections with her soulmate. It's a theme straight out of a Shakespearean tragedy. I imagine it happens more often than anyone truly believes." Lander swept an arm in an inclusive gesture to the others in the restaurant. "I wonder, with all the billions of souls in the world, if I'll ever bring two people together who otherwise wouldn't have met. Or is it a mistake to mess with the karmic stream of people's lives? There is no heaven in my world —only a cycle of death and rebirth. Do you realize how this could invalidate a person's faith?"

"You don't know that. What if a person ascends to some other plane of existence that you can't see? Your view is limited to one level of rebirth. Maybe heaven and hell are premium channels you don't subscribe to."

Lander paused to appreciate this little seed that was both

wisdom and her attempt to comfort him. It brought to mind the Buddhist cosmology. At the bottom, hungry ghosts inhabited a hell realm; at the top, enlightened beings carried out, albeit temporarily, a heavenly existence. The concept of being a god and mortal at the same time was not a new idea to eastern religions, but for Christians, it could dampen enthusiasm for a pious life. "I see experiences that manifest in all realms, like a 'day from hell,' but you're on to something when you say my view is limited. I'm not good enough, when I shuffle the cards of a person's past lives, to see if there are gaps in the timeline."

This time, she took his hand and watched him expectantly.

Lander drained his teacup and cleared his throat before continuing. "I have a lot to learn. But before I can pursue that, I have a responsibility. I can't walk away from how this happened or who is responsible. Others may be trapped like I was. Thank you for all you've done. It's no longer enough for me to live in ignorance."

Lander looked out the window. He saw her watching him in the reflection. She released his hand and brushed a tear off her cheek.

Without turning to look at her, Lander sighed. "Goodbye, Cassandra."

Pulling his sweater off the chair, he walked toward the door, as close to tears as he could ever remember being, and he hoped she would call out. A few yards from the door, he glanced back.

She was coming toward him, holding up a paper bag. "You'll be needing this." It was the leftovers from breakfast, and quite a lot of food. Cassandra had seemed undecided when they ordered. It only then occurred to Lander that she had been purposely stocking him up with provisions.

There was an awkward moment as he reached for the bag

and they both held it. Then Cassandra dropped her hand and maneuvered past him out the door.

She rounded the corner to the parking lot without looking back. Her suggestion to move to Sedona played on a loop in Lander's head. If she asked again, he might just as easily have said yes, and run away with her.

Back at the apartment, he used the super's computer to check his email. He had a few replies—spam, they were called. With the search for his brother ended, he wondered only briefly about looking for his father. In time, he would ask his mother for more details, but the search for his father and brother felt like a project to tackle another day. His desire to be part of a family had been satisfied by the growing connection with his mother. Any interest he had in his father and brother was transforming into anger. If he ever found either of them, it would be on his terms.

With a sense of finality about what he was about to do, he finished the payment system training manual. While he had no direct plan, he believed he wouldn't be coming back. There was not much to collect from his coal chute, and it was soon tidied and organized.

His next step required more information about the Wrimo building. There was little to be accomplished on a Sunday afternoon, so he enjoyed the safety and solitude of the apartment. There were reminders of Cassandra in everything around him. It tugged at his emotions and stirred a sense of doubt in the path he had chosen. Because a larger question loomed. Where would he be at the end of his quest: dead, back on the street, or forever institutionalized? The expression *happily ever after* was conspicuously absent from his storytelling repertoire.

Chapter 46
Monday,
November 9, 2009 (9:40 a.m.)

T he previous day's leftovers easily sustained him, and a good nights' sleep nurtured an uncharacteristic energy to get up and get going. Lander packed a few items, including the binoculars, into a nylon messenger bag he'd found on one of his dumpster foraging trips.

He walked to Wrimo and circled the block as an idea formed.

The county records office needed to be his next stop. He spent the following hour studying the architectural permits and drawings for the Wrimo Center. His ability to memorize information helped him retain the layout of the building. From his experiences in the pie-shaped rooms, he narrowed it down four places he may have been sequestered. He thought it odd they weren't listed as patient areas on the diagrams. He knew from their exposure to the sun that they had to be on both the east and west sides of the building. Updated drawings showed a more stylized renovation on the sixth and seventh floors, where curved walls had been cut out of the otherwise flat building. The angle of the walls explained the pie-shaped layout.

These floors housed labs and offices—a strange place to

319

have hospital rooms, he thought to himself. The floor plan labeled one room as "Records Storage," but that didn't feel right. He'd been in the records room, and it was a different place.

Lander traced with his finger from the loading dock along the back corridor to estimate how the Dunk Tank Drunks might have snuck in. The pharmacy was on the basement level next to the main service elevators. It would have its own security. Lander identified staff locker rooms on the opposite side of the service hallway. The lockers seemed more in line with their thieving expertise. It was unlikely, though, that they'd stolen the prescription pad and the keys from that location. The above-ground parking area drew his eye to the edge of the chart. *They probably found the doctor's car unlocked.*

Lander felt he could get to the service elevator without being challenged. But he would need help to get further.

From the records office it was a short distance back to Wrimo, Lander retraced his steps by walking the blocks in front of and behind the center. He needed a location that would allow him to peek into the windows.

The building across the street on the east side was a commercial building with a large *Office Space for Lease* sign in the window. From down the block, Lander observed that the windows facing Wrimo on the seventh through ninth floors were bare. It was a long shot, but worth a try.

Lander approached the security guard. "Good afternoon. I wonder if you could point me toward the leasing office. I have an appointment with a Mr. Danforth." Lander had seen the name on a sign for the company that represented the building.

"I'm sorry, sir. Their offices aren't here on property. Are you sure you weren't supposed to meet with them somewhere else?"

Lander let out an exasperated sigh. "This isn't what I need

to have happen now. I'm supposed to tour the vacant office on the eighth floor, west side. Let me call them." Lander pulled out his cell phone and walked away from the security desk, pretending to make a call.

He mimicked a one-way conversation, letting the guard hear just enough to gather there had been a misunderstanding. Then he played his deception. "I don't know if he has access. Let me ask him." Lander turned back to the guard. "Can you open the elevator and let me onto the eighth floor?" Before the guard replied, Lander spoke again into the phone. "I'll pass the phone to him. You can arrange it."

As he reached to pass the phone, the guard held up his hand. "No problem. I can let you in."

Lander wrapped up the fictional phone call and followed the guard into the elevator. On the eighth floor, the guard unlocked a glass door and led him into a deserted reception area.

"There you go. Dial 3 on the service phone if you want to view anything else. There are lots of choices. More than half of this building is empty. Just let me know when you're done."

The office had been vacant for a while. A lack of air conditioning left a musty smell. Wires hung loose from wall sockets. Bits of paper littered the floor. While they had scraped the name of the company off the window, many of the offices still had personal nameplates. It reminded Lander of when he looked into people's memories. This had once been a vibrant and busy office. Now it was little more than a skeleton, but Lander sensed the stories the walls might tell.

He walked through the deserted cubicles, heading toward the west-facing wall. His first vantage point was too far south. As he walked up the hallway, the offices became larger and the decor changed from padded dividers to old-fashioned wood paneling. Indentations in the carpet showed where a board-room table had once sat.

Kneeling by the window in a large corner office, Lander raised the binoculars to his eyes. It was the perfect vantage point. The pie-shaped room was visible. In fact, one of them had the blinds open. It was as he remembered. Next to the room was a large open lab that stretched across a dozen windows. The staff were all dressed in white lab coats. Many of the technicians were set up in front of scientific glassware, like a high-school chemistry set on steroids. Others worked at large machines with attached computer monitors. To the immediate left, despite the blacked-out windows, a sliver of an opening revealed a row of cages. As Lander trained the binoculars on the gap, he was rewarded with flickers of movement; rabbits, rats, and a ferret paced in an enclosure. This explained the need for the masked windows. Wrimo wouldn't want the public to know about their testing. Lander wished PETA were also taking in the view.

The floor below appeared to house offices, a waiting room, and another pair of pie-shaped rooms, both with the blinds closed. Instead of a lab, there was a boardroom and a conference room. A small group sat watching something on a screen. The angle of the building and the level of daylight made it difficult to see more than a few feet beyond the windows.

A movement in the periphery of his vision brought his gaze to an office at the corner of the building. Lander squinted, and the binoculars bumped against the glass. Across from him, Dr. Aradice was pacing up and down in front of the window. He gesticulated as he spoke, facing an invisible person who sat in a high-backed chair set in front of the window. At that moment, a man in a lab coat entered and Dr. Aradice turned to speak with him. Purely based on the man's body language, Lander's distaste for Dr. Paul Aradice grew. The man cowered and appeared diffident, like he was accustomed to being browbeaten.

After his subordinate left the room, Dr. Aradice walked over and resumed speaking with the person in the high-backed chair. When the person rose and turned to face the window, Lander rocked back on his heels. It was the woman from the brown car. Lander could see she was trying to maintain her composure. Whatever the doctor was telling her, it made her angry.

A few moments later, passing through the building lobby, Lander called out to the security officer. "Thanks anyway. I saw enough, and the view is terrible. It's unthinkable what is going on across the street—those poor animals." Lander had sensed that the man had been an advocate for animal rights in a past life. It wasn't too much of a stretch to conclude that he still carried those beliefs. Lander was confident that he'd invite others and if they watched long enough, they might witness something to report—and maybe bring Wrimo even more trouble than he was about to stir up.

Chapter 47
Monday,
November 9, 2009 (6:10 p.m.)

L ander placed himself outside the apartment of Dr.
Aradice's accomplice a few minutes after six. The notice
about the doctor as a keynote speaker that evening suggested a
plan. He was counting on the woman from the brown car to
join him. And, having seen him at her door late at night, he
expected him to pick her up.

He pushed his hand up against the glass to block the lens of
the building's intercom camera as he punched in 1277.

Almost immediately, an electronic ring vibrated from the
metal grill, three, four rings before a woman's voice rose from
the static. "Hello? Who is it? The camera's not working."

He used his hand to muffle his voice and, with a slight
Canadian-British lilt, said, "It's about time you answered." The
word *about* came out as *aboot*. Lander continued more softly.
"It's Dr. Aradice. I don't have time to come up. Meet me in the
garage. We're taking your car—we've got to go."

"But you're early. I'm not dressed."

"Damn it, woman. Then hurry." Lander worried he had
overdone it with the last comment. Paul Aradice was a
charmer, but also bossy and impatient. Lander guessed that

once he got his hooks in a woman, his self-importance took over and subtle mental abuse began. The door lock buzzed and Lander smiled.

He figured he had at least fifteen minutes as the panicked woman primped and preened herself for the good doctor and a public appearance. Two-thirds of the way down the second row, he found her car. A thick concrete pillar and a bright spotlight provided excellent cover. He waited.

As the time exceeded ten minutes, he imagined the girl getting more frantic. At last, he heard the chime of the elevator, and she entered the garage.

"Paul?"

He stepped out from behind the pillar in silhouette and, in a muffled voice, replied, "I'm on the phone."

The brown car beeped, and the headlights flashed, which startled Lander as she approached. Lander pushed himself up against the concrete pillar and slid around to get behind her. This would be his most complicated act of mind control. The scenarios involving Cassandra at the motel and the woman at the social security office had been straightforward. He needed this woman to get him into Wrimo and guide him deep into the facility. This task required a sustained and carefully curated set of memories. He was ready to replay the role of patient, and she needed to be his compliant nurse.

As she walked into his trap, he stepped out, placing one hand over her mouth and the other on her neck.

The ferocity of the images that flooded Lander's brain overwhelmed him. He had let his judgment of her as the simple secretary put him off his guard. The woman had a contradictory history. Memories of terrible suffering bookended other moments of pure evil. Her past included many violent deaths; each death fought Lander for top honors. Lander latched onto a memory of a drugged, pre-overdose stupor. He pulled the image to the forefront, and she slumped back against him.

He struggled to drag her the short distance to the car. The joint physical and mental effort to maintain the connection left him gasping. He leaned her against the passenger door only for her to slide with a slight bump and a little squeal of, "Ooh," as she hit the ground.

Lander regretted doing this on his own. He slipped his fingers into her clenched palm for her keys but came up empty. It was only then he scanned the floor and saw the trail of debris. Her keys and a single shoe were at the edge of the pillar. Of greater concern was her purse, just out of reach.

Fear gripped him when he heard voices coming out of the elevator lobby. Lander squatted, placing both hands on her arm. He didn't know how soon she would recover after he broke contact. As it was, she was already emitting brief murmurs and incoherent mumblings. He had to risk it. For anyone driving past, the sequin purse would shine like a beacon. With a final push of memories, he let go of her wrist and scrambled out to grab the purse. The instant she called out for help, the rhythmic banging of the opening garage door masked her plaintive wail. Someone else was pulling in.

Back at her side, Lander hunkered down in the shadows. The departing vehicle suppressed any other revealing sounds. In a few minutes, the garage was empty again. Methodically, he accessed her imprinted memories at five- and then ten-second intervals, like doses of a tranquilizer. He opened the car and positioned her in the passenger seat before sprinting around the car to the driver's seat. It relieved him to see that the car didn't have a stick shift. Despite having a driver's license, he didn't recall ever driving. *This will be a very short trip if I mess up.*

Lander sat with her in the darkness, a calmness returning, but he was aware of the drain in his energy as he maintained the link with her. In the last week, a regular diet and proper sleep had made him more focused and improved his stamina. He didn't know the full extent of his ability, but he understood how living malnourished on the street, or drugged and sedated at Wrimo, had diluted his power.

He opened her purse and removed a driver's license, looking for her name. The picture was from her late teens, years earlier, and identified her as Monica Stewart.

She was a pretty girl, and it wasn't the first time Lander reflected on how physical beauty manifested in a person's life. This young lady had gone through many unsavory incarnations in which she'd wielded its power on others—mainly men.

Lander's attention returned to the present when she moaned and twisted in the seat. They needed to get going. With a deep exhale, he grounded himself to focus on their mission to Wrimo.

But first, he needed to remember how to drive. With the key inserted into the ignition, the blue LED clock on the radio lit up. Half an hour had elapsed since he'd first arrived at her building. What if the doctor were to show up?

Monica's lab coat was draped across the back seat of the car. Her name tag and lanyard with her security pass poked out of the breast pocket. This was a relief, though their absence wouldn't have stymied his plan. Nervous about his driving skills, he pulled around to the auto exit and waited while the chain-link gate clanged open. His foot pushed a too hard, and the car sped up the ramp before screeching to a stop on the steep grade, almost clipping a pedestrian. An approaching taxi signaled and pulled toward the curb. Lander nudged the car forward until it was level with the street and dutifully looked both ways before turning. On the sidewalk, a man in a long black coat paid a cab driver and then turned in his direction—Paul Aradice.

Lander panicked and slammed on the gas. The car lurched forward, and as he over-corrected the turn, Monica toppled from her seat onto his lap. A screech of brakes and the wail of a horn made his head spin. The driver whom Lander had cut off was leaning out the window, screaming at him. He wasn't about to wait around and apologize. In the rearview mirror, he caught a flash of the wide-eyed doctor staring after Monica's car.

His plan all along had required the doctor to believe there had been a misunderstanding. In this scenario, the doctor would arrive and, when he discovered Monica was not at home, believe that they were to meet at the venue. Seeing the car wouldn't change that. From the sidewalk, he could not have seen it was Lander who was driving. He would still have to attend his speaking event and therefore couldn't surprise them at Wrimo.

Lander chose a route that kept him away from highways. When he got closer to downtown, he maneuvered along the one-way streets he walked without the constraints of traffic rules.

A block from Wrimo, while he waited at a stoplight, a rap on the window startled him. It was Dave, his collection of cardboard signs tucked under his arm. Lander lowered the power window and Dave leaned in, eyeing the disheveled, supine figure of Monica before breaking into a gap-toothed smile. Lander checked that the light was still red and rummaged through Monica's purse.

"Wow, man, you've become a player."

He passed Dave a twenty-dollar bill. "This one's had too much to drink."

Dave laughed. "I wish we were all so lucky."

Chapter 48
Monday,
November 9, 2009 (6:30 p.m.)

At Wrimo, a responder clipped to the sunshade triggered the gate for the small surface parking lot, and Lander parked. A single camera pointed at the laneway. Monica's car wouldn't draw attention. All was quiet—no sign of a security guard or other staff.

He fumbled to get Monica into her lab coat and adjusted her blouse and skirt. Kneeling by the passenger door, Lander shuffled through her past-lives. He searched for an ordinary day-in-the-life situation where she would be conscious but controllable. Unfortunately, the mundane from people's past lives was buried or not available. He settled on a scene from a time when she was eight or nine years old. An older woman, a nanny, was demanding compliance and he knew it would not end well. He would avoid the end of that story.

This would be his most difficult manipulation. He had to arouse a sense of adventure that would appeal to an eight-year-old. But she also needed access to her current knowledge, specifically what she knew of Wrimo and his internment.

"Where am I? Who are you?" His influence pitched Monica's voice a little higher, childlike, as Lander let the memories ebb and flow.

"Monica, look at me. You should recognize me."

She squinted and her head bobbled. "You're a patient. We've been looking for you?"

"I need you to take me back to my room. Dr. Aradice asked you to make sure I got home safely."

A look of disgust drifted across her face. "I'm done cleaning up his messes."

Lander could use that. He pushed into her mind, seeking control.

"Let's go." He helped her to her feet, and they walked toward the entry door.

A second security camera near the rear door recalled the conversation in the archives. He shifted Monica's weight so that she stood upright. "Do you know if that camera works?" Her head bobbed both up and down and back and forth. She wasn't listening.

A few more awkward steps and they were at the door. Then Monica surprised Lander. She stood upright and, with the indignation of a child that pontificates rules, said, "I'm not allowed to enter this door after hours. My pass card won't work."

Lander had an alternate plan. He pulled from his pocket the set of keys Cassandra had recovered and lifted the plastic card to the reader. The light blinked from red to yellow, causing Lander to catch his breath, then a second later to green. A click in the locking mechanism signaled success.

"Monica, listen. There's a supply closet on this level. We need to get a wheelchair and some patient clothing. Can you show me where it is?"

"Are we playing dress-up?"

They reached the closet without incident. Lander changed

into patient garb and settled into the wheelchair. He took her right hand and placed it under the flimsy cotton against his left shoulder. His right arm reached across to clamp it down.

"Now, Monica, we're going to play a game. You're the doctor and I'm the patient. I need you to take me back to my room. Do you understand?"

"Okay," she trilled.

Monday evenings at Wrimo were thankfully quiet. Monica rolled Lander down the corridor toward the main elevators. She used Dr. Aradice's card again to gain access. Inside the carriage, on the main panel, the card produced another green light, allowing them to select the seventh floor. Other than a childlike bounce to Monica's step, nothing seemed out of order. They were accepted by the staff as they traveled deeper into the facility.

Lander noted the sixth-floor light on the panel as they rode up, passing Dr. Aradice's office. As they exited the elevator on the seventh, Lander grew eager to see the pie-shaped room and a patient with a chart labeled *Lander Gate*. It would be the proof he needed to expose the conspiracy.

He was struggling to maintain control of Monica. The prolonged exposure, coupled with flashes of his own memories as hew grew familiar with the area, exhausted him. He was having more difficulty keeping his current memories separated from the flashbacks, diluting the illusion that propelled Monica.

They drew closer, but Monica pushed him right past the pie-shaped rooms and came to a stop in front of a storage closet on the opposite side of the hall.

A male voice from behind them broke the concentration.

"Monica, what is a patient doing near the lab?"

She stopped pushing the wheelchair and her head lolled around to face the voice. Lander slumped over and peered under her arm to see a man in a lab coat. Lander switched his gaze to the door where they had stopped. The architectural drawings had labeled it a storeroom. He played the one ace he had been holding back and harnessed an occasion of compassion in this girl's past lives. He spoke to her in the spot where the currents of their minds coalesced. "Do the right thing. Tell him you're getting supplies before returning me to my room."

Monica straightened, and obediently spoke to the man, exuding uncharacteristic confidence as she told him, in a tone that would have made Dr. Aradice proud, to get lost.

The man stood for a moment in stunned silence, and then retreated to the laboratory.

Lander straightened up in the chair and fumbled for the keys. Unlike the other locks, this required a mechanical key, and Lander prayed it would open. The door popped with the sound of a breaking seal. Monica took the cue and pushed him with a slight bump over the threshold into the dimly lit room.

Along the right-hand wall, he stared at the unmade, empty hospital bed. He was having difficulty thinking but still registered a deep disappointment that the bed wasn't occupied. Was it the wrong room? Lander shook his head. It was familiar. After weeks of knowing nothing, the memory of this room was concrete and visceral. He remembered being tangled in those sheets, the chafe of nylon wrist cuffs, and the tug of electrodes mounted on his skull and body. In the weeks since he left, the doctor had kept the room looking as if its occupant had just stepped out. Or, Lander thought ruefully, *would be right back.*

An intense pressure built in his brain, the same sensation as when a word is on the tip of your tongue. But this was a tsunami of words threatening to crash in on him. Monica slipped from his grip and slumped to the floor. Lander pushed himself out of the chair and fell sideways until he was propped against the wall. He pulled the door closed.

He shuffled around Monica to lean on the rounded footboard. A single gooseneck bedside lamp splayed a crescent of light across the top third of the bed. Lander shook his head to dispel the urge to crawl under the sheets, to defeat the overwhelming sensation that he belonged there, and that everything else he had experienced was wrong. This wasn't home, but, to his exhausted mind, it would be so easy. A sense of peace washed over him, knowing his mother and Cassandra were safe.

Behind him, Monica murmured, and Lander could hear the rustling of her lab coat as she tried to rise. The bed frame steadied him before he took one awkward step and dropped to his knee. She squeaked in surprise as he pulled her to a sitting position.

"Why is the bed empty? Where is the patient the doctor writes about in his file?"

Half rising, she rocked unsteadily before slumping onto the rolling stool. It skittered with her across the floor and, with a metal-on-metal clang, collided with the bed. Only then did she point at Lander and then at a bank of equipment along the wall. "It's always just been you."

Lander returned his attention to the bed. He focused on his last memory. Two weeks before, he had risen from that bed and torn away the electrodes before escaping. *Electrodes?* Then he noticed a repetitive ping that only a second earlier had blended into the white noise of the room. The sound was coming from the equipment. The ping matched the pulse that pounded in his temples, though as an echo a millisecond behind. An old-style printer chattered on the end of the table, trying to keep up.

When he held his breath, the pings from the equipment seemed to speed up. On a shelf above, an antenna poked up from a long rectangular box and a thick coaxial cable ran the length of the exterior wall, exiting the room through a hole. *A transmitter. The implant.* He had been Dr. Aradice's patient all this time.

Overwhelmed by exhaustion, Lander lay on the bed. The indentation on the mattress from his months of lying inert embraced him like a familiar pair of gloves.

Then the wave broke, and there was no stopping the flood of images. His consciousness became awash in memories of the room—and everything that came before. He reached for his own wrist in the hopes that he could shuffle his own cards to pick a time and place of tranquility. That didn't work, leaving him to stare at a single hand of cards that represented his life.

Included in the fan of cards were memories of his last night at Wrimo. He remembered tearing the electrodes from his head and body then, without looking back, stumbling into the corridor. In a sleepwalking daze, he ended up in a laundry room. Patient clothing was lined up on a shelf. With difficulty, he got dressed in an oversized long-sleeved shirt and baggy pants with an elastic waist. Forgoing socks, he found a pair of shoes. Returning to the corridor, a voice rose behind him. "Come on. Your stay here is over. Hold out your right arm and show me your wrist." Lander did as he was told, pulling back the loose sleeve. The man produced scissors from his pocket, and in a deft move, slit the medical bracelet. Lander didn't even feel the cold metal against his skin.

The man with the scissors then called to someone further ahead. "Tony, lead this group out the back."

Lander fell into step behind three other men and, a moment later, stood at the edge of an alley. The other men dispersed, and Lander slinked fearfully into the shadows.

Lander returned to the here and now. Monica was now leaning on the end of the bed like the visitor of a dying friend. She watched him with empathy in her eyes.

He let childhood memories arise: his mother and his youthful days skulking on the street. His father and brother's departure, which imbued him with guilt. A wider cast of his childhood showed that, even back then, he experienced a confusing medley of emotions when he was close to people, which set him off as a loner.

Aware that his left hand was clenched in a fist, he relaxed his palm so it settled on the curve of the mattress. As a teenager, he had sought knowledge from books on meditation and Buddhism. Even at that young age, he understood the need to calm his mind, and he took naturally to the teachings. The writings on karma—or, in its simplest definition, action—made him consider the trajectories of everyone around him. He thought a lot about the choices people made in their lives. These early lessons served him well when later, as a patient, he had been mentored.

Lander could see the ripening of karmic seeds, a convergence of actions from any lifetime, all around him. His mother being assigned to Dr. Aradice was a one-in-a-million pairing that gave Lander the opportunity to access the unique puzzle of his brain. He reasoned that the drugs from the very first experiments weakened the electro-chemical barrier that typically blocks access to a library of experiences stored in our DNA. He'd been born with an ability to connect with a submerged level of consciousness. Dr. Aradice's meddling, including the charged tracking chip near his nervous system, had opened a gate in his mind. The synergy manifested in an ability to see the interconnected web of past lives buried in everyone around him.

Lander took three deep, calming breaths, and a smile creased his lips. His meditation instruction had served him well in his opposition to Dr. Aradice, acting as a passive but effective resistance. While less extreme than Buddhist monks who blocked tanks or lit themselves on fire, it was a subtle and daring opposition to a man who sought to study his brain.

He now remembered the hours and days that he spent lying on the bed, struggling to focus his mind, to keep some grip on the world around him. He counted ceiling tiles, breaths, and even differentiated sounds within sound, like isolating a single violin in an orchestral performance. In a way, these activities were a form of mental yoga, a meditation, that connected himself to his mind.

His meditation regime fooled the machines that monitored his brain activity. To Dr. Aradice, he appeared unresponsive. From the beginning, he'd frustrated the doctor. In so many ways, he was the wrong test patient for Dr. Aradice.

A strange sensation assailed him as he pushed further into his own memories. Weightlessness took over. He lost his perception of being in the hospital room. Was he dying again? He didn't believe that. While it felt as if time passed slowly, it was only a matter of minutes before he felt a sense of completion, an ordering of the cards. Like a finished game of solitaire, every image in his mind lined up both in number and suit, and the four kings stared back at him.

He lifted his hand and with an index finger traced the slight scar on the back of his neck. Somewhere beneath the layer of flesh, an electrode and a battery had both saved his life and betrayed him.

Lander twisted his head to look around the room, taking in the chaos and pain and fear that it represented. *All of this will be for nothing if I don't get out of here and expose Dr. Aradice. I may not have been his first victim, but I will make sure I am his last.*

Chapter 49
Monday,
November 9, 2009 (6:30 p.m.)

Cassandra was despondent about her separation from Lander. The analytical side of her brain affirmed that she had made the correct decision, but her concern for his well-being sapped her of any motivation to work or do anything but worry about him.

A trip to the Coffee Train ended up with takeout. She would have liked to speak to Katherine, but the owner had the day off. If Lander had shown up, he likely would have respected her wishes and left.

It was midafternoon, and she was deleting spam from her email when a message from Wrimo caught her eye. She had joined their mailing list. The message was a reminder that Dr. Aradice was speaking about his book that evening and offering a signing.

Without actually deciding to go to the event, Cassandra showered, then selected from her closet a navy wrap dress, knee length with a deep V neckline that distracted from her face. She pulled up her sleeves so the material bunched below her elbows. Cassandra exuded purpose and intent when she headed out the door.

The Moroccan decor of the Resort was tasteful and Cassandra wandered the gardens next to the ballroom where the talk would be staged. She had arrived early, but now the crowd in the foyer spilled out onto the patio as the numbers grew. Worried about getting a good seat, she began to navigate through the attendees.

Cassandra moved effortlessly through the crowd. She was too new to Scottsdale for anyone to recognize her, and the guests who packed into the foyer did not represent her circle of friends. She thought of Lander sitting across from her at the diner, and felt empty.

Even though the function room doors weren't open yet, she fell in behind a reporter and a cameraman who were being ushered past the stanchions that blocked the doors. The reporter eyed her curiously when she stood with them next to the seats reserved for media.

When their guide, a hotel staff member, had departed, Cassandra felt she owed the man an explanation.

"Thanks. I'm a researcher, not media, but I don't fit in with the *Real Housewives of Scottsdale* crowd that are bumping fists in the lobby."

The man laughed and offered her a generous smile. "Hardly fists. Maybe other body parts that have been artificially enhanced."

He turned to speak with his cameraman, and Cassandra assumed their conversation was over. She had just stepped over to a chair and lowered her bag on the seat when he addressed her again.

"Research. Are you a fan of this author?"

"No. You and I share a skepticism." His look of surprise prompted her to continue. "I'm an excellent researcher, and I watch the news. I know who you are, and your incomplete interview with the doctor is one of the few pieces that suggests all is not what it seems."

Cassandra introduced herself, and he unnecessarily repeated his name, Roberto Flores, as they shook hands. He was about to say something more when his associate signaled, and he moved to join him at the stage. This left Cassandra to drift down the aisle toward the back of the room.

A door opened, and the clamor of voices from the foyer was suddenly much louder. Dr. Aradice had entered, but he stopped and was looking straight ahead at the men up at the podium; with a scowl, he tracked Roberto Flores, who was now returning to the back of the room. Then his gaze then fell on Cassandra, who stood a few yards away. To his credit, his public relations persona kicked in as his eyes flitted over her outfit.

A practiced smile preceded his greeting. "Ms. Bowen. I'm surprised to see you here. This is a bit beneath your education level."

She smiled sweetly, and then, choking on her false sincerity, replied, "Any opportunity to see you in action is a worthy endeavor."

Thankfully, the doctor's phone chimed at that instant, and he turned away to take the call.

Even though he lowered his voice to a whisper, the acoustics in the room made it easy to follow the conversation.

"No. Monica's not here. I don't know where she went. We were supposed to come together. She has my updated speech." There was a pause as he listened to a reply. "I've got a copy of an older version in my email... No, someone else was driving. She was in the passenger seat. Find her."

Cassandra had drifted back to the media area where Roberto stood.

"Do you two know each other?"

"We met a few times when my research took me into Wrimo."

"You have access to Wrimo." His energy level perked up.

"Yes, I do." Her voice fell off as her thoughts raced ahead. *Monica, not driving. Lander, breaking into Wrimo. She would be his ticket in.* She looked up at Roberto. "I have a much better story for you if you're willing to blow off this PR stunt."

Dr. Aradice stood off to the side at the front of the room. He palmed his phone, looking at it, willing it to ring. The evening wasn't going the way he hoped. Monica's sudden disappearance, the loss of his speech, the fact that his publisher hadn't organized a green room for him to hide in, and now the nuisance reporter. *Why is he here?* The doctor would have to be ready for some off-topic questions.

He looked to the back of the room and observed Cassandra and Roberto having a spirited conversation. More shocking, though, was when Roberto said something to his cameraman that prompted the man to pack up his gear. The tech even sprinted toward the front of the room to retrieve the microphone he had placed there just minutes earlier.

Dr. Aradice came up beside him as he disconnected a cable. "Big news story?"

The man looked a little confused, as if wondering why he was being spoken to. "Huh? I guess. The boss just got a lead on something more important." The cameraman stopped what he was doing and chewed his lip for a second. "Sorry, you're the speaker. These things happen all the time. Don't take it personally." With that, he walked away, holding the microphone and transmitter, a piece of gaffer tape stuck to the back of his hand.

Dr. Aradice glowered at the man's retreating back and resumed pacing.

His sense that something was wrong increased a few minutes later when Cassandra departed in the reporter's company. He punched a number into his phone.

The receptionist at Wrimo put him through to the security office. When there was no answer, and with growing agitation, he made a second call to the lab.

"This is Dr. Aradice. Have you seen Monica Stewart, the hospital administrator, this evening?"

"Yes sir. I saw her a while ago with a patient."

"Where were they?"

"Just outside the door of the lab. She said she was getting supplies."

Dr. Aradice punched the phone to end the call and grabbed his coat from a chair by the podium.

At that moment, his publisher's representative came through the door. Her smile quickly vanished when the doctor stormed up to her.

"There's been a medical emergency. I can't stay. Tell them we will reschedule."

The woman watched, wide-eyed, as the doctor hustled from the room.

Chapter 50
Monday,
November 9, 2009 (7:20 p.m.)

Awake and disoriented, Lander panicked. Suddenly, the bed didn't fit so well. With his right arm, he pushed himself up to a sitting position. The other flailed, tearing at imaginary electrodes and cables.

Monica watched him from the doorway. Finally released from the prolonged exposure to Lander's influence, she rubbed her eyes and looked confused.

Lander wanted to thank her. He now understood and Natalie had confirmed it, when she saw him in her special place. Dr. Aradice had killed him twice, the first time with the overdose, the second time with his shock therapy. In the latter instance, his implant had been slow to shut off, maintaining an electric current to his fractured brain. For a few seconds, he had inhabited both death and life. His brain was pre-wired to be different. The synergy created a continuity of being that existed in two dimensions.

An image of Natalie in her special place flashed through his mind. He would see her again. There was still so much to figure out. *But not here, not now.*

Monica said, in a hushed voice, "Why did you come back?"

Kevin S. Moul

"I need to know my story, connect with my past. Will you help me?"

Her face remained neutral; her eyes showed exhaustion. Lander knew she was seeking a voice that just minutes earlier had guided and anchored her. Unless he touched her again, it wouldn't be there.

Before he could lean in and connect, her eyes widened, and she nodded. "Yes. I'll help you. I'm tired of being the fool, and being an accomplice to so much pain." She looked at him with inquiring eyes. "I haven't always been this way. You somehow showed that to me."

"The choice is yours. You can change." As he rose, she took his arm to guide him back into the wheelchair. Feeling the pressure of her fingers, Lander exhaled. He used his escaping breath like a pressure valve, his power shutting down.

He fumbled in the bag that hung from the handle and passed her the cell phone. "In the history, dial the number for Cassandra. Tell her to come and pick me up. Please."

After making the call, Monica flipped the phone closed. "She's already downstairs. She said she has someone she wants you to meet."

Monica pushed Lander back to the elevator. The tech that had spoken to them earlier spied them through the glass from the far end of the lab. Rising from his chair, confusion etched in his features, he summoned them to stop.

"Too late," she called out as she backed Lander into the elevator.

Monica pressed the button for the main floor, but before the elevator doors closed, Lander reached out and pressed six.

"Can you get me into the doctor's office?"

Monica's eyes flashed with fear, but, in a gesture reminiscent of her recent compliance, she held up the ring with the fob. "Yes."

346

"Is there anything in there that might help prove his guilt?"

"There's the internal report on your death—the one that wasn't made public."

The elevator bumped to a stop, and Monica wheeled Lander down the corridor.

Her hands trembled as she placed the fob against the sensor and the light flashed green.

Lander had only seen the room from across the street, but sensed the doctor's power play with the enormous desk facing the doorway. A grouping of chairs suggested a missing table off to one side.

While Monica rummaged in the filing drawer of the desk, Lander rolled the wheelchair over to a bookcase on the side wall. After a brief scan, he plucked a book from the shelves.

"I knew I'd seen this somewhere."

"What's that?" Monica asked from across the room.

"A gift for a friend." He held up Warner Lampkin's book on mental illness.

A moment later, Monica exclaimed, "Got it!" In triumph.

Monica handed Lander a legal-sized folder. He opened it to see a two-page document, dense with text, with the Wrimo logo at the top. Lander rose from the wheelchair, and Monica put her hand on his shoulder. "No. You're less conspicuous in the chair."

Lander stuffed the file folder and the book under his seat and then fumbled to roll the wheelchair forward.

"I got it." Monica turned him around and pushed.

The door then opened, and there stood Dr. Aradice, blocking their retreat.

A flood of fear impaled Lander, and he slumped over in the chair. To an observer, it might have appeared to be the result of inertia when Monica stopped the wheelchair to avoid a collision.

To Dr. Aradice, it would have been a familiar sight: Lander, semiconscious.

Monica spoke first. "I was just going to call you. He forced me to bring him here. Then, as if the memories were too strong, he passed out. I tried to put him back in his room, but a lab tech saw me. I thought we would be safer in here."

With his head lolling to one side, Lander couldn't see the doctor's reaction, but he saw him shuffle his feet.

"Bring him back inside." When Dr. Aradice reached to push on the armrest, Lander grabbed him around the wrist. He squeezed, hoping that would enhance the connection.

The result was immediate. Lander shuffled through the imaginary cards to assemble a winning hand. He thrust two visceral death moments into the doctor, who collapsed, almost landing in his lap.

With his other hand, Lander pushed him away. The doctor bumped against the doorframe before sliding to the ground. Lander jumped out of the chair, careful not to lose his grip and break the connection. Together, they dragged the doctor further into the office.

"What have you done to him?"

"I can be very persuasive. Let's go. He won't be out long."

Before Lander let go, he plucked the doctor's lanyard with his security fob.

Lander returned to the wheelchair and, with a squeak of rubber and a slight bounce, Monica directed them toward the elevators.

Lander had a sinking feeling in his stomach that he had played the wrong hand. He'd shown his cards to Dr. Aradice. The scientist's inquiring mind would be consumed with questions about what had happened.

On the ground floor, Monica pushed Lander toward the sliding security doors that opened into the main reception area.

She waved her access card, and the doors slid open. As they crossed the threshold, they both heard a wild howl. From the opposite side of the security perimeter, Dr. Aradice emerged from the other elevator and screamed for somebody to stop them. Without his pass, the door wouldn't open. Monica pushed faster, gaining speed on the ramp that led to the outer doors.

A blast of fresh air assaulted them, followed by a bright light and the murmur of voices. Lander looked up to see Cassandra flanked by a two-person TV news crew and a few passersby. With a pulse of flashing light, an ambulance pulled up to the sidewalk.

Lander pointed, and Monica brought the wheelchair to Cassandra, who kneeled in front of him then caressed his face, pushing the wiry hair black hair off his forehead before turning to the camera. "His life can begin." For emphasis, she waited an extra beat. "Begin again."

A medic reached to take his pulse, and the reporter rested a comforting hand on his shoulder and spoke to the camera, though his words were not audible to Lander. Cassandra squeezed his hand and leaned against him. These people were touching him, but the only images that clouded his mind were his own. All the past lives were parked. He visualized the deck of cards still in the box—a white box with the word *Bicycle* across the top in red lettering. *I'd like to ride a bike again.*

Cassandra leaned in and whispered. "Remember that urban legend you prophesied? Where someone, who knows someone else, might have known the man that could read minds? This is where the urban legend and Lander Gate get to go different directions. You and I go that way." She pointed her index finger down the street.

For the first time, Lander had a choice. His touch was his touch alone.

A few miles away, Lander's mother flipped through TV channels.

"This is Roberto Flores reporting live from outside the Wrimo Hospital, where a moment ago there was a rebirth. A man that the institute reported last year as dead has just emerged onto the street." The camera shifted to a wider angle of two men in uniform walking a third man out the institute's front door. "Being taken for questioning by police is the facility's director and well-known author, Dr. Paul Aradice. He's answering to allegations of falsifying records, illegal confinement, and ethical violations related to human test subjects. Unrelated to this evening's revelation, our newsroom also knows of a suit filed by PETA for alleged cruelty to animals."

The camera panned to a woman wrapped in a blanket, sitting on a landscape bench. She was speaking to a police officer and pointing, presumably, at Dr. Aradice.

The commentary continued. "The whistleblower, Monica Stewart, an administrator at the Wrimo Hospital, has told police she only just discovered the truth of what the doctor had been doing. She has also stated that she would no longer be silent about the suffering caused by the doctor's methods."

The broadcast dissolved to a close-up of Lander, now sitting on an ambulance gurney. His eyes seemed unfocused but were bright, catching the light from the video camera. Had it not been for the tiny shift of his hair on the evening breeze, it could have been a still photograph. Rosalie walked over to the bookshelf. Her picture of Lander and his brother had fallen over when Lander had hastily set it down a few nights earlier. She picked it up and repositioned it on the small stand. It had been taken the night before her husband and son left. She looked at the dark circles that were Lander's eyes. He looked back at her, one eyebrow slightly raised, as if they shared a secret. In contrast, his brother looked down, bored and detached. He was already gone. She shifted the frame to create a space. "I'll need a new picture."

Cassandra stood off camera. She appeared to be studying Lander without making eye contact. He took comfort in being the subject of her attention. His slack arms rested on his lap; his hands were loose, palms open, and for the first time in weeks they were just hands, albeit deeply etched, as if he was an old soul that had weathered many lives.

When he lifted his head, their eyes met and she smiled. This shared moment was the most important way they could touch each other.

Lander let his index finger drop onto an imaginary map resting in his lap. Beneath his finger, he pictured a city name: Sedona. The map transitioned into an image of the two of them together. It was a refreshing change, for the experience that filled his mind was a simple daydream, a hopeful vision of the future, and nobody was dying.

Thank you for reading Lander's Gate.
Please consider leaving a review.
Your feedback helps other readers discover the book—and
supports authors like me in sharing more stories.

Connect with the Author

https://www.kevinsmoul.com

Please join the author's online community for curated updates
on new titles and bonus material.

About the Author

Kevin S. Moul writes speculative fiction exploring the liminal space between perception and the unknown. His paranormal and urban fantasy narratives examine the boundaries of human experience, weaving in Buddhist themes of karma, reincarnation, and consciousness.

More than forty years in the hospitality business provided a front-row seat to people at their best and worst, creating a reservoir of stories where 'you couldn't make this stuff up' rings true.

Before turning to novel writing, Moul was a widely published professional photographer, approaching prose with the same reverence for discovery.

Born and raised in Vancouver, British Columbia, today, he splits his time between Southern Arizona, where he finds inspiration in the stark beauty of the desert landscape, and Vancouver, where the rhythm of the ocean grounds him and informs his creative sensibilities.

Essays by the author, influenced by Buddhism and meditation, available on Medium.com, @kevinsmoul

My gratitude to the authors, editors, and writing communities that empowered me.

The Creative Academy for Writers
The Quillians
Stephanie Candiago
Eileen Cook
Natalie Goldberg
Ann Sager Kinsman
Jenny (Graman) Lang
Joseph Nassise
Tony Ollivier
Sherry Ramsey
Gillian L. Roberts
Michael A. Stackpole
Richard Summersgill
Robert A. Vardeman
Leslie Wibberley

Please support organizations that help people in a state of homelessness or food insecurity.
The Author supports, along with other organizations:
Why Hunger
https://www.whyhunger.org

www.ingramcontent.com/pod-product-compliance
Lightning Source LLC
Chambersburg PA
CBHW020549120726
47903CB00001B/199